P9-BYS-986

THE FIRE HORSE GIRL

KAY HONEYMAN

ARTHUR A. LEVINE BOOKS
An Imprint of Scholastic Inc.

Text copyright © 2013 by Kay Honeyman

All rights reserved. Published by Arthur A. Levine Books, an imprint of Scholastic Inc.,
Publishers since 1920. SCHOLASTIC and the LANTERN LOGO are trademarks and/or registered
trademarks of Scholastic Inc.

No part of this publication may be reproduced, stored in a retrieval system, or transmitted in
any form or by any means, electronic, mechanical, photocopying, recording, or otherwise,
without written permission of the publisher. For information regarding permission, write to
Scholastic Inc., Attention: Permissions Department, 557 Broadway, New York, NY 10012.

Library of Congress Cataloging-in-Publication Data

Honeyman, Kay.
The Fire Horse girl / Kay Honeyman. — 1st ed.
p. cm.
Summary: When Jade Moon, born in the unlucky year of the Fire Horse, and her father
immigrate to America in 1923 and are detained at Angel Island Immigration Station, Jade
Moon is determined to find a way through and prove that she is not cursed.
ISBN 978-0-545-40310-8 (alk. paper) — ISBN 978-0-545-40311-5 (pbk.) 1. Chinese
Americans — Juvenile fiction. [1. Chinese Americans — Fiction. 2. Immigrants — Fiction.
3. Astrology, Chinese — Fiction. 4. Angel Island Immigration Station (Calif.) — Fiction 5. San
Francisco (Calif.) — History — Fiction.] I. Title.
PZ7.H7473Fi 2013
[Fic] — dc23
2012018015

10 9 8 7 6 5 4 3 2 1   13 14 15 16 17

Printed in the U. S. A.   23
First edition, January 2013

The *tibishi* poems beginning "There are tens," "In the quiet," "My parents," and "It was on the
day" were found in *Island: Poetry and History of Chinese Immigrants on Angel Island, 1910–40,* by
Him Mark Lai, Genny Lim, and Judy Yung (reprinted by University of Washington Press,
1991). Reprinted by permission of the University of Washington Press.

To the birth parents of my two children, Jack and Lily. I don't know their stories, only the greatness of their love.

THERE ONCE WAS
A GIRL, A FIRE HORSE GIRL.

IN CHINESE ASTROLOGY, the Year of the Fire Horse is a bad year for Horses. All of their worst traits — their tempers, their stubbornness, their selfishness — burn with increased strength. Girls should *never* be born in the year of the Fire Horse; they are especially dangerous, bringing tragedy to their families.

But desperation flowed fast and thick through my mother's veins. Children did not come easily to her. After four born only to be buried, she ignored the warnings of the zodiac and bore a Fire Horse girl, who was too stubborn to die like the others.

Bringing forth something as vicious and powerful as a Fire Horse destroyed my mother. Her last breath mingled with my first. Stories are like that too — deep breaths, one ending so another can begin. One sacrificed so another can survive. We often dwell on the endings of stories, forgetting how they were born, but you must inhale to exhale.

Storytellers know this, for they choose their first words with care. If I began this story with the words "Out of the mist of time comes the story of Jade Moon, the Fire Horse girl," you would expect it to throb with adventure and end with heroics. If I began it with "It is said" or "There is an old saying," you would search the story for wisdom. But this is not a story of heroics or wisdom; it is my story.

There once was a girl, a Fire Horse girl.

CHAPTER 1

THE BOWL CRASHED on the tile floor and split into clattering shards at my feet.

"Clumsy girl! That was your grandmother's," Nushi said. "And one of the last fine pieces."

"The table is full," I pleaded, sweeping my hand over its collection of porcelain bowls. "It would not fit."

"So you decided to break it apart!"

"Nushi, I *am* sorry."

"As sorry as you were when you dropped the plucked chicken in the dirt this morning? Or maybe when you spilled syrup on my slippers?" She shook her head and bent to pick up the larger pieces from the floor.

"I'm cursed. I can't help it," I said.

Nushi snorted. "*You* are dangerous. It is the rest of us who are cursed." She swept the remaining fragments into a pile by the door, then returned the broom to the cabinet and began to cut the chicken. "Where are the flowers you picked yesterday?" she asked me without looking up.

"The flowers?"

"Yes, the flowers, the flowers! The ones I asked you to get from the Wus' garden. You left for two hours!"

I stared at her. I *was* supposed to get flowers yesterday. And I had gone out intending to get them. Instead, I had walked to the flat rock, half-buried in the earth, that marked the farthest distance from home I had ever traveled.

I wanted to go past that rock. Then past the place where the road disappeared behind a hill. And, if it was possible, past the reach of marriages nursed by fears and desperation. The rock was a place for dreaming about what was beyond the hill, not for gathering flowers.

"Can't you send someone to get them now?"

"I sent *you*." Nushi gripped my arm, marched me to the door, opened it with one hand, and shoved me outside with the other. She was our servant, but also the closest thing to a mother I had.

"Nushi, no . . . I can't go to the Wus' house."

"Don't be gone longer than an hour. We have much more to do."

"But . . ."

The door slammed in my face.

The homes in the small village of Jinjiu were strung like pearls along the river. Our land began the string, followed by the Wus', then a thick cluster of smaller homes. From the outside, the structures that housed the Wu clan were much like ours — long brick buildings surrounding a courtyard, and enclosed by a gate. Both families owned vast expanses of terraces built over generations. In lucky years, the workers filled and fertilized their fields three times to produce the rice that fed us. Between the lines of rice we grew cabbage, spring onion, and corn. What we did not need, the men

4

traded or sold down the river, beyond the flat rock and past the bend in the road.

But behind the latticework windows and the tall double doors of our compounds, the differences between our family and the Wus' emerged. Their inner hall clamored with mouths and feet, as mothers had sons, and sons brought wives carrying gold and gifts, and those wives had more sons. Women embroidered caps with small tigers to protect the babies in their bellies, and children cried until one of their many aunties held them on her lap.

Our courtyard was quiet, with only me, my father, my grandfather, our servant Nushi, and bags of rice stored in empty rooms. No one bore children. No one brought wives or husbands. Since my birth, nothing had survived our walls — the curse of a Fire Horse.

When I reached the road that lay across from the Wu home, I took a deep breath and turned into the Wus' garden. Auntie Wu took a special pride in two of her accomplishments — the sons she bore and the flowers she grew. They were equally useless, but the flowers smelled better.

I wanted to get the flowers and fly from the yard without having to speak with anyone, so I slipped along the far edge of the garden, behind the corner of the house, and bent to yank some of the flowers growing at my feet.

One of the young Wu girls peered around the corner. It was Mei Mei. I had seen her the day before, trying to climb a tree, until her aunt dragged her down and sent her into the house. She looked up at me, her eyes big and dark like new moons. I turned back to the flowers, but I could still feel her watching me.

"Do you have something to say, Little Sister?" I said, jerking a fistful of stems.

She shook her head.

I stood. "Are you in trouble again?"

She nodded.

"Me too. I forgot to pick the flowers for the New Year's Eve meal," I said.

"I forgot to pull the weeds like Grandmother told me to," she said in a small voice.

"Then what are you doing here?" I asked.

"Watching you pull the weeds."

I stared at the collection of stems I had gathered. "These are weeds?" Mei Mei nodded. I dropped the bundle to the ground and tried to smile at her. "Well, now that we are done with that chore, maybe you can show me where the flowers are."

Her face lit up. "There are some pretty ones by the door. They just bloomed yesterday." She skipped around the corner. I wiped my hands on my tunic and followed her.

When she stopped next to a bed of flowers, their tight white clusters just starting to open, I bent next to her. After I had snapped a few off, the girl asked, "Is it true you cursed Second Wife's embroidery last winter?"

"What?"

"Grandmother said she was getting careless, and Second Wife said she couldn't make a decent stitch since she crossed paths with you one morning."

"I have no power over embroidery. If I did, Nushi would not describe mine as the entrails of an ox."

She giggled. "I was going to ask you to curse First Brother. He's been tattling on me to Grandmother. I was thinking boils on his face. Or can you make one leg stop growing?"

The sound of a throat clearing interrupted us. I turned. Auntie Wu stood in the garden, a parasol tipped behind her shoulder. The roundness of the parasol mirrored the roundness of her figure, balanced on her tiny, useless bound feet. She looked at me, displeasure rolling off her. I quickly shifted my gaze to a point in the air just in front of her forehead. This was a technique I used often. It blurred people's faces and kept me from seeing the disdain in their eyes.

"Jade Moon, your betrothed was just here," she said sweetly.

"I don't have a betrothed." I stared at the ground, hiding my hot face.

"Maybe not yet, but soon. I hear your father is arranging a marriage with the brickmaker, Fourth Brother Gou." My heart froze. "At least you will not have to worry over him reading all night like my poor husband. And he does not have all the land to care for that my sons have."

Every word she said was an insult to my family. I knew that my father had hoped to match me with a wealthy farmer or scholar, not a brickmaker. But I was a Fire Horse, and I was going to be seventeen soon — too old for even Fourth Brother Gou.

"Nushi sent me to get flowers," I said, swallowing my anger.

"You are welcome to anything from my poor excuse for a garden," Auntie Wu said. "It is nothing compared to the garden your grandmother kept. When she was alive, I could open my window and smell the perfume of her roses, but so much is not as it used to be."

I nodded and picked a handful of the yellow-centered narcissus.

Auntie Wu's face kept its scowl. "Jade Moon. Please be careful. Those aren't weeds."

I bit my lips. "Thank you, Auntie," I said.

Mei Mei whispered to me, "She is just in a foul mood after another wart sprouted on her chin this morning."

Auntie Wu flicked her fan over her chin and fixed her gaze on the girl. "Get back inside the house."

Mei Mei moved to go. I grabbed her. "*We* know that I can't do any harm, but if your brother causes you any more trouble, tell him I taught you how to shrink his eyes to peas so they'll fall right out of his head."

I winked, and her face brightened.

After making my good-byes to Auntie Wu, I fled back to the river where I could hide. I dropped into the curve of a tree where it sent its roots into the river and brushed my fingers through the water. Tiny waves followed them on their trip across its gray surface as the trees stretched their branches in a canopy above me.

I was not ignorant of how ridiculous I seemed to people. My feet wandered the village with little purpose other than my own pleasure, my mind constructed ideas that no one seemed to understand, and my heart held hopes that were far beyond my reach. But I could not help my thoughts or my dreams. I watched the wind lead the leaves in a dance, and I wondered if any of them ever wished that they could find their own steps.

I sat there, trying to erase Auntie Wu's scorn from my head, imagining I was past the half-buried rock, until I heard voices from above. I realized that I had lost track of time, and I needed to return home before Nushi set out to find me. Tucking my legs underneath me, I prepared to stand. Then I recognized the high, sharp voice of Auntie Wu.

"Down this road. You will see their compound," she said.

Did Auntie Wu mean our house?

"Thank you," a strange voice said. A *man's* voice. Peering around the curve of the trunk, I found I could see them through a curtain of leaves. We didn't get many visitors in our village. Since we didn't have a market where merchants could sell their goods, and the road that led to the village ended at the river, there was no reason for people to travel here. Until now. The man was younger than Fourth Brother Gou, and he stood taller than Auntie Wu, maybe Father's height.

"Are you family? Visiting for the New Year?" Auntie Wu asked.

"I am here for the New Year," he said.

"Perhaps some good fortune for the Chans." She leaned toward the stranger. "Yes?"

The stranger folded his hands in front of him. "I think visitors always hope to bring fortune to the home they visit."

"I am sure they do," Auntie Wu said, leaning forward even more. But he only smiled politely. His clothes were not new, but crisp and clean, free of dirt and worn patches.

"Perhaps you bring wealth," she tried. "That is always welcome, although not as welcome as a son-in-law would be in that house."

The stranger only nodded. My heart started to pound, filling the hollow spot in my chest with its rhythm. I had spent years sneaking into my father's study to read letters from his faraway friends — the poetry of new scholars, the hopes of young officials, the dreams of men who wanted change. Lately, the letters were full of worry over the dragon that was China, the difficulties of waking her, and once woken, the impossibility of controlling her. If this man was the son of one of those friends, someone who might take

9

me to see important things happening in faraway places, I would never complain about going to the Wu house again.

"Well, if this poor self could be bold and offer some advice," Auntie Wu continued. "While the Chans have always raised rice carefully, they are careless with their children, especially the daughter there now."

"It is a dangerous thing to be careless with a daughter," the stranger said.

Anger bit at my skin. I tried to pull myself up to tell Auntie Wu to hold her tongue, but I had sunk deeper into the mud beside the river, and my knees and feet were stuck.

"Ah, true. You are like me, keeping to the old ways. These days girls stomp around on their giant, flat feet and children think they can marry whomever they wish. My sons were all matched the traditional way, but Elder Chan allowed his son to marry a girl he loved. Love matches always end in tragedy."

Had my father loved my mother? He never spoke of her. I always imagined a traditional marriage between them — one built with the strong bones of respect but stripped of the soft skin of love.

"I heard Younger Chan studied to be an official."

"That is true, but it seems to have brought him nothing but dissatisfaction and pride. He would have been better off staying at home."

"There are men who have much learning, but little wisdom," the stranger said. So, perhaps not the son of one of Father's friends. "Not that I know anything about it," he added quickly. "And the daughter?"

He wanted to hear more about me. I prayed it was a good sign.

If only he had asked someone else — maybe the mute man who lived at the edge of the village.

"Oh, yes." Auntie Wu's voice warmed to her favorite subject — my shortcomings. "She is the disgrace of the neighborhood, wild and headstrong. She runs alone through the village and the countryside. She was just here, tearing up my garden. Not that my garden is much," she said with feigned modesty.

"Your garden is as fine as any in Hong Kong," the stranger said.

Auntie Wu giggled, pleased with the compliment. "She has the red cheeks of a peasant farmer and the tongue of an old servant. Even if her skin was as pale as a lily, she would still be cursed."

"She is unmarried, then?" the stranger asked.

"Yes, and almost seventeen. Her father is desperate to match her." She paused to give this news weight. "Perhaps you were considering a match with her, sir?"

I prayed that he would say yes; it would cause Auntie Wu to lose face and save me from a lifetime of conversations about bricks. But I had barely begun to plead with the ancestors when he replied, "Me? No, I would never marry such a girl. I have business with the men of the house."

My heart began to boil. Auntie Wu paused to see if he would reveal more. "During your stay, I invite you to visit my poor house and worthless sons. You may grow weary of the Chan house."

"Thank you." He bowed. "I hope I have the honor of visiting soon."

I wanted to shout to Auntie Wu to mind her own business, and to the young stranger to return the way he came, but I knew that Nushi would not approve, and Father would be furious. And, perhaps, coming from someone stuck in a bank by the side of the river, it would not have the effect I wanted.

When I heard their footsteps fade, I decided it was time to pull myself out. I tugged against the root of the tree, but I could not move my legs. Dirt and bark collected under my fingernails as I pushed and pulled. Finally, the ground released my stuck leg with a slurp and sent me flying forward. But as soon as I put my weight on the bank, my foot slipped. I grasped at a few branches, the limbs sliding through my mud-covered fingers, but I struggled and fought only to fall backward and tumble into the river.

When I stood up again, I found myself chest-deep in the water. And right as I thought that all my bad luck had been used up in creating this calamity, I heard the same smooth voice that had just said he would never marry me.

"Do you need help?"

CHAPTER 2

HE STOOD AT THE EDGE of the bank and looked down at me, not with the hard eyes of my father or Auntie Wu, just observant. His face was gentle — even skin, with lips that turned up at their corners, holding a ready smile. It was an easy face to look at. Too bad it was attached to such an impossible person.

"Can I help you?" he said again, taking an unsteady step onto the slick bank.

"No, stay where you are," I answered, looking for something to pull myself up with. My voice shook with the chill.

"I can get someone. Your husband? Brother? Father?"

"No, just leave me alone. This happens all the time." *This happens all the time?* Nushi was right — I should think before I speak.

His face tightened. He was trying not to laugh. "How did you fall in?" he asked.

"The shock of your rudeness sent me flying into the river," I mumbled to the water, wrenching one leg, then the other, from the muck.

"Did you say something?" he called down.

"No," I called up.

"I would like to help you," he said, peering over the edge.

"*I* would like to be left alone." My feet had sunk into new holes and were starting to go numb with cold. When I tried to pull them up, I slipped and fell in the water again with a loud splash.

The stranger let one loud "Ha" escape before beginning a coughing fit to cover his laughter. "Perhaps I can fetch the woman from the Wu home. I was just talking to her."

"No!" I sputtered, managing to stand and yank my feet free from the mud all at once. I stumbled out of the river to a flat spot on the bank. "See, I am fine. You can go about your business."

He opened his mouth to say something, but decided against it and turned back to the road. His shoulders shook with laughter as he shrank into the distance.

When he disappeared behind the curve, I struggled up the side of the bank. Tears of frustration and embarrassment threatened to fall down the islands of heat on my cheeks. I wrung a stream of muddy water from my slippers, then slid them back on my feet. Plucking a few of the flowers I had promised Nushi from the mud, I slipped back home along the edge of the river, cursing the stranger for my situation.

When I entered the kitchen, Nushi's eyes widened, and she gasped.

"I fell into the river," I announced.

"What were you doing by the river?"

I held out the flowers. She stared at the limp tangle of torn petals, bent stems, and mud. When she did not take them, I flung them on the table.

Nushi touched the strands of hair plastered to my face — the same hair she had carefully cut that morning for the New Year. "It will take until tomorrow to get you clean. Think of the bad luck! You could not use the road?" She pushed me outside.

"Where are we going?"

"We will have to clean you up at the well. You can't walk through the house like this."

Nushi was brutal, pouring bucket after bucket of cold water onto my head. Every time I opened my mouth to speak, she shut it again with another wave of water. When she had squeezed out as much of the dirt as she could, she marched me to my room, yanked my rough tunic over my head, and handed me a bowl of water.

"Again?" I protested.

She gathered my clothes, pointed to the washbasin as her answer, and left. After she returned with two more jars of water, she snatched the towel away from me and scrubbed my skin, making it sting and itch. Basin after basin of muddy water pooled on the ground outside my window. As soon as my blood warmed my skin, Nushi would pour cold water over me again.

"It wasn't my fault."

She continued to scrub.

"There was a stranger asking where our house was. Auntie Wu told him all of this horrible gossip about our family. I had to hide down by the river to hear."

"You were spying on them."

"Yes . . . No . . . Nushi, it was cruel what she said."

She stood up, her jaw tight. "Did she mention the disobedient daughter who covers herself in mud and listens to other people's gossip?"

"Yes, but she added it was no wonder she is so wild, since their servant tortures her with cleaning all the time." I tried to smile, but it faded as I remembered something else Auntie Wu had brought up. "She said there might be a match in the future of this tortured, disobedient daughter. With the brickmaker — Fourth Brother Gou."

Nushi's voice softened. "Nothing is decided for certain, Jade Moon. And they did not start with the brickmaker. They started with the sons of wealthy farmers and your father's friends, but it is difficult when . . ."

Her voice trailed off, but I knew the rest. It was difficult when you had a father and grandfather doing what a mother should do. It was difficult when we were trapped in this remote village. It was difficult when the most appropriate matches for me were Auntie Wu's sons and she saw daily reminders of the kind of daughter-in-law I would be. It was difficult when you must find a match for a Fire Horse.

"Why did no one tell *me*?" I asked. But I knew that too. I was the daughter of the house, far beneath Nushi in importance. I had no right to demand even a single grain of rice, but somehow I forgot that two or even three times a day.

"Bricks are useful," Nushi tried.

"For knocking people senseless who talk of bricks too much," I muttered. "Maybe I won't marry."

"Not marry!" I winced. "What a stupid thing to say!" she hissed, moving her face close to mine. "Jade Moon, the Chan name is not what it used to be. If they do not find you a husband, the family will die out and you will all become hungry ghosts, wandering the spirit world with no ancestors to care for you. You should pray that

Fourth Brother Gou will agree to marry you. If he doesn't, then your grandfather and father will start to get desperate."

"And if they become desperate?" I asked.

"Desperate people are more dangerous than Fire Horses. They will break something beautiful to see what they can gain from it, forgetting what they lose as it crashes around them." Nushi bent down to wring the cloth out into the bowl, then reached for me again.

"I am clean," I said. "Cleaner than I was when I left."

"And you need to be," she said, attacking the dirt under my nails. "Your father has a guest."

My face hardened. "A tall guest with a smooth voice and a fondness for gossip?"

"A guest who has heard horrible things about the daughter who lives here. Who will now see either that she is as wild and willful as everyone claims, or that Auntie Wu should mind her own business."

I nodded. "I will try to be good."

My father narrowed his eyes when I stepped through the doorway, neatly dressed, clean, and silent. He and my grandfather stood with the stranger by one of the silk paintings my father had done, the guest decorating it with compliments as thick as the brush strokes. When he saw me, a small, amused smile tugged at the corners of his mouth. Bitter saliva stung the inside of my cheeks.

Our guest's feet were planted firmly again, his back straight and his long arms resting at his sides. He wore his ease like a second skin, and I could barely swallow my resentment toward it. Many people mistake confidence for comfort. Confidence was something I could provide for myself. Comfort was not. People around me offered or withheld it.

"This is my daughter, Jade Moon," Father said, gesturing vaguely in my direction. "Daughter, our guest, Sterling Promise."

I cupped one hand inside the other and bowed.

"It is an honor to meet your daughter. She is as full of grace and beauty as I would expect from the Chan family," this Sterling Promise said. He bowed to my father with a formality he had not shown by the river. I thought with a grain of satisfaction how his words would grate against Father's ear. He would prefer to ignore that he had a daughter. Unfortunately, I was difficult to ignore.

But as everyone's attention shifted back to our guest, I realized that my father would not insist that I leave. He had dismissed me from his world, and this made it unnecessary for him to dismiss me from the room.

Father sat in a chair behind the desk, inviting Sterling Promise to a chair across from him. Grandfather rested in the lone remaining chair against the wall. I shuffled my feet for a second and then backed into the corner.

"I have brought a gift for your family. To repay a debt," Sterling Promise said to Grandfather. "It is from your son."

"My son," Grandfather said.

"I am his son," my father said.

Sterling Promise tapped his fingers on the side of his leg. "Yes, of course. But did you once have a brother?" Father turned away. Sterling Promise looked at Grandfather. "Sir, did you have an younger son?"

Grandfather straightened, his head lifting slightly. "I do."

"I have an uncle?" I said.

Father whirled around. The anger he could not show Grandfather or our guest landed on me. "Silence," he hissed. "You *had* an uncle until he abandoned his family." He turned back to Sterling Promise. "We don't want anything from you or my disobedient brother."

Sterling Promise shifted his feet, looking less comfortable.

Grandfather spoke softly. "I will listen."

"But —" my father began.

Grandfather held up his hand and shook his head. "I am old, and my family shrinks with each generation." He glanced at me, and even the brush of his look stung. "It was irresponsible to ignore what little family I had."

"Your son often spoke of your wisdom," Sterling Promise said. "I have been sent with this letter from him."

"Give it to him to read." Grandfather nodded toward Father. "He is the scholar."

Father opened the letter and read silently, his lips pressed together as if he was tasting one of Nushi's sour teas.

"He died two months ago," Sterling Promise said softly.

The harshness on my father's face dissolved for a moment. Grandfather rubbed his hand along the lines of gray on his head. "More bad luck," he moaned.

"I hope not, sir. All the funeral rites were done properly. The body was prepared and buried, and you can bring it to your family's burial plot if you like." He turned to Father. "Sir, he knew the mistake he made leaving his family. The shame haunted him, and he asked me to repay his debt to you before the New Year. He spoke of you with respect."

Father looked up from the letter. "This Sterling Promise is his son."

Sterling Promise nodded. "His adopted son. He looked out for me after my own parents died."

Grandfather lifted his head. "An adopted grandson." His eyes looked past all of us. "Yes, I would like to hear about this gift you bring."

CHAPTER 3

STERLING PROMISE STRAIGHTENED his back. "I bring papers to enter Gold Mountain."

"Gold Mountain." I breathed out the words.

"Why would we want these papers?" Grandfather said.

"Your son could use them to get into America." He pulled some yellowed papers from his waistband. "There is great prosperity, great opportunity there. People leave from Hong Kong every week. They send back such wealth. And the Americans who live in Hong Kong have everything." He slid the papers across the desk. They were covered with foreign words and a picture of a man that looked like Father. "Sir, your brother went to America for the first time seven years ago. He wanted you to have this chance at fortune, to repay your sacrifices for the family." Sterling Promise's words dripped off his tongue, like oil meant to soften thick skin.

"A world of white ghosts," Father said. "Cheaters and thieves."

"So my son went to America," Grandfather said. "He was always bold."

Father studied the papers, then lifted his eyes to Sterling Promise. "What do you gain from this?"

"Since the papers have your brother's picture on them, only you can use them." Sterling Promise looked at his hands in his lap. "I would like to go as your son."

Father threw the papers down on the desk. "I will not pretend to be my brother."

"It would not be —" Sterling Promise began.

"We can talk this over later tonight," Grandfather said, rising from his chair.

Sterling Promise stood. Grandfather walked to him, patted him on the shoulder, and shuffled out the door. Father followed.

What a day of news! Auntie Wu would give five of her ten remaining teeth and one of her daughters-in-law to know what was said today. I did not know of any sacrifices that my father had made. Of course, I also did not know of any uncle—much less an uncle who went past the half-buried rock and all the way to America. It was a good thing that we were a small family; we had no room for children with all of the secrets we stored.

Sterling Promise slumped back into his chair. He rubbed his eyes and sighed.

"My father won't change his mind," I said, settling onto the wide wooden chair my grandfather had left.

His forehead wrinkled for a second before his easy smile resurfaced. "We'll see. I know many in Hong Kong who would give a fortune for a chance to go to Gold Mountain."

"You should ask *them* to join you."

His smile tightened. "It is no concern of yours. *You* will not be going to America."

It sounded like a fact I should have known, so I tried to hide my disappointment. I spent more time in Father's study than anyone realized, and I had traced the outlines of places I would never see on his maps. Only one showed the whole world, with America at its edge, almost falling off the unrolled linen paper. I had heard Father talk about the Americans — their new land, their readiness to change — with the mix of awe and fear that vast differences inspire. "Why can't I go to America?"

Sterling Promise shrugged. "You can't start a business like I will. You can't make money to send home like your father can. You would be useless there."

"You don't know that," I said, lifting my chin.

"A person does not have to be in the village long to hear about the Fire Horse living in the Chan home." The slow rumble of boiling anger began in my chest. "But it isn't just you, Little Sister. Any woman would be a waste. The opportunities there are for men."

The spikes that Nushi said covered my tongue emerged.

"Perhaps, but without women like Auntie Wu, who would feed you the gossip you listen to so faithfully?" I watched with satisfaction as Sterling Promise's face reddened. "I don't think my father would want to help you if he knew what little wisdom you thought he had."

"That wasn't your conversation to hear." He gripped the arms of the chair. "You were spying."

"I was stuck!" I cried, standing.

Sterling Promise stood as well. "You are everything their gossip promised," he said. "Wild, with a quick temper. Thoughtless. Dangerous."

My heart throbbed with indignation. People should not let the truth through their teeth so easily. "You should not talk of things you know nothing about."

"You should not give people so many opportunities to talk about you."

"Perhaps you should behave less like an old woman."

"And you should behave more like a young lady."

Disgust flowed thick between us. His presence pricked at my skin like Nushi's scrubbing from earlier. Grandfather had smiled at him. He had a seat during talks. He knew secrets about my family that I didn't know. He was the son that I could never be. What stung most: He had traveled far down the road, past the rock, and he would go past it again when he had gotten what he wanted. And I would still be here.

My jaw tightened and my hands formed fists as I marched out of the room. Nushi appeared and blocked my way down the hall. "You know better than to insult our guest," she hissed.

"But —"

"Little One, you said you would try."

But it is hard when you are a Fire Horse.

On the way to my room, I approached Grandfather's doorway. His voice spilled into the hallway, so I softened my footsteps.

"We don't know anything about him. He may bring disgrace," Father argued. I could hear him pacing back and forth. "Remember, he is the son of my brother."

"I don't want to see my family wither away like a useless branch on a tree. If he brings disgrace, we will have to swallow it." My father's steps stopped, and my grandfather continued, "We don't have any more options. Let's hope he will do anything to get to America."

A chair creaked and scratched against the floor.

"You will go with Sterling Promise if he agrees," Grandfather said.

"And what will *I* do in America?"

"You will ensure that this family survives."

"Father . . ."

"You must. You accuse your brother of selfishness. Would you be guilty of the same?"

"I have always put this family first," my father said, defeat threaded through the word.

"I think your brother has saved us."

Father was silent.

"I will tell him that you will go," Grandfather said. "And explain our terms."

"And Jade Moon?"

"Should know nothing."

Tears burned in my eyes. Father was going to America, and, just like when Sterling Promise found me in the river, I was stuck.

CHAPTER 4

I HAD A SEAT at dinner, but only because we had many extra chairs at the table, left from the time when the family was larger.

Nushi bustled in and out of the kitchen carrying plate after plate of food. I helped until I tipped a pile of tangerines into a bowl of rice. Then she pushed me into a chair, thumped my shoulders to remind me to sit up properly, and left me at the table with the men.

It is surprising how distant three people who live in the same house can be. Father, Grandfather, and I saw one another little; we talked even less, haunting one another more than living together. Normally, dinner meant we would scoop food into our mouths in the shifting light of candles, pushing back from the table as we swallowed the last noodle. Father and Grandfather had nothing to say to me. I had much to say but nothing that would please them.

Sterling Promise ignored our tradition of determined silence.

"I have never seen a table so heavy with food," he said, smiling.

Grandfather returned his smile. "I am glad you are pleased with our humble meal."

"Your son always said that it was the best-run estate in China."

"I have not seen every estate in China," Grandfather replied.

Father made a small coughing noise in the back of his throat, then lifted his tea when Grandfather looked at him.

This only caused Sterling Promise to turn his attention to Father. "Your good sense could make you very rich in America," he said.

Father did not look up from his cup of tea. "A man should be happy with the wealth he has when it is enough."

"America has opportunity," Sterling Promise continued.

Grandfather nodded.

"What kind of opportunity?" I asked.

"People make their fortunes there and send back trunks of money and treasure to their families," Sterling Promise said, keeping his focus on Father.

Father sent him a chilly look. "Yes, you mentioned that."

"An American fortune can make the next generation even richer and more successful."

"The next generation." Father spat the words like they stung his throat.

Grandfather slurped his soup. Sterling Promise continued with only a thread of nervousness in his voice, "Americans own vast pieces of land, the size of whole villages. 'As far as the eye can see' — that is what they say."

"Hmm," Grandfather said.

"Yes, I see that we are inferior to the great landowners of America," Father said.

"No, I just . . ."

I grinned into my bowl. Sterling Promise shoveled rice into his mouth.

The crickets started their evening songs.

"We hear little news here. What is happening in Hong Kong?" Grandfather asked.

"Things are changing fast. The foreigners bring much trade. People pour in from all over the world."

"When will they let China be?" Father said.

"What are they doing to China?" I asked.

"They bring wealth," Sterling Promise said to Father.

"The bribes of spies and thieves," said Father. "China is sliced up and served to the barbarians."

You would think I would get used to being ignored, like I grew accustomed to an ant bite on the inside of my foot or the collar of a tunic that is just a little too tight. But I never had.

"But if you saw . . . ," Sterling Promise began.

"You are too young to know how change should occur," Father said, waving Sterling Promise's words away. "I can change the outline of a rock quickly by carving it, but the edges will be sharp. If I set it in a river, it will be carved slowly over one or two generations, and those changes can happen without harming anyone."

"I fell in the river today," I tried.

"China does not have time to wait for change," Sterling Promise said. "The world is carving us now. If we wait for the river to shape us, we will be left behind."

"Perhaps that would be best," Father said.

"You do not think that China needs to modernize?"

"So we can have deadlier armies? So our governments can take land that does not belong to them? So we can force people to worship as we do? The things done in the name of modernization seem backward to me."

"How are they backward?" I asked.

"China needs to honor what is here," Father continued.

I shook my head and blew breath on my fingers to make sure I was not a ghost.

"That is enough talk about politics." Grandfather leaned back in his seat. "I hope you will have a chance to look around the village."

"Yes, I would like that very much," Sterling Promise said.

And then it bubbled up in me, the irresistible urge to knock the veneer from Sterling Promise. "He has already met some of our neighbors," I said. "He was listening to Auntie Wu tell stories about us this afternoon."

Father's face darkened.

Tiny beads of sweat gathered on Sterling Promise's forehead. "I did ask for directions from your kind neighbor."

"She was helpful, I'm sure," said Grandfather.

"Certainly, she helped answer all of his questions about us," I said.

Grandfather rested his chopsticks next to his bowl and fixed me with an icy stare. "Whatever their conversation, it is none of our concern."

"He —"

"Granddaughter." Grandfather raised his voice. "Go help Nushi."

I slammed my chopsticks down. I was too filled with fury to squeeze in another bite anyway.

When I appeared in the kitchen, Nushi shook her head and shooed me outside. I pushed open the gate and stomped down the path in front of our house to a bench in the far corner of our yard.

Why were my words always silenced? Why was I always sent from the room? After a few minutes, Nushi came to sit beside me.

A round of fireworks for the New Year spiraled from the Wus' house. After the lights surrendered to the night sky, I asked, "Do we have enough luck to survive the year?"

Nushi smiled. "You don't need luck. You are a Fire Horse. The luck is for those of us who have to live with you."

I managed a small smile. "What do you think of our guest?"

Her smile faded. "I think he will need the most luck."

We watched the sky in silence. Before each firework, you could hear the whirl of its flight and the pop that announced its arrival.

"I wish we had some fireworks," I said.

"Why? We have never shot off our own. We have always watched the Wus'."

"I know, but this year, we have a monster to scare off, like in the New Year's stories you used to tell."

Nushi snorted a small laugh. "If the sight of you covered in mud didn't scare him, a few fireworks won't."

"If I tell you something, will you promise not to mock me?"

"You found *more* trouble today?"

"Why do you assume it is trouble?" Nushi frowned. I took a deep breath and rubbed my hands along the coarse fabric of my long skirt. "When I saw Sterling Promise talking to Auntie Wu, I thought he was coming to arrange a marriage with me."

"Oh, I see."

"I know. I am even more foolish than people say."

Nushi remained silent. She was good at silence.

After two more firecrackers pierced the sky, I said, "Did you know Uncle?"

"I did."

"Why didn't you ever tell me about him?"

She brushed some dust from between us on the bench. "You know that your grandfather would want nothing said about him."

"Why can't we ever talk about important things?"

"We don't have to dig up everything that gets buried, Little Sister."

"Then how do you understand it?"

"You watch and listen. And if you still don't understand, you choose courtesy over curiosity."

"What was his name? What was he like?"

"You are hopeless." Nushi smiled. "His name was Chan Jan Keung. He ran away when he was your age. At his best, he was strong, intelligent, and determined. At his worst, he was thoughtless and selfish."

I let loose a sharp laugh. "That sounds like me."

"Maybe he would have understood your wildness a little better than the rest of us. But truthfully, you are like all of the men in the family. You are clever like your father, driven like your grandfather, and willing to take risks like your uncle."

"What about my mother? Am I like my mother?" I had to force out the question, pushing my desire to hear yes through my fears of hearing no.

"The ghost of your mother haunts your every feature," she said. "Everyone can see it, especially your father."

The sky quieted and the darkness deepened. I heard steps behind me. A halo of lantern light guided Father, Grandfather, and Sterling Promise across the grass.

"Sterling Promise wanted to show us another gift he brought," Grandfather said, a rare grin on his face.

Sterling Promise trotted to the far end of the open area in front of our house, toward the river, carrying a large basket.

"I hope you enjoy my small gift from Hong Kong," he said as he passed us.

"Where is he going?" I asked Nushi.

"Be patient," she said.

"Do you know what he is doing?"

"I do. And if you watch, you might enjoy it."

We squinted through the darkness. I could just see Sterling Promise's outline bent low to the ground. After a flash at his feet, his figure retreated.

Then a pop broke the silence, and trails of light rained down from the sky. A second pop followed, then a whirling, and more light — red and green, white and purple, umbrellas of color and streaks of fire. Firecrackers spun into the night, exploded, and trickled into darkness. The sky over our house was brightened by the chaotic rainbow. I had never been so close to fireworks before. They were tiny promises that blossomed into tremendous things, like seeds that grew into trees, a drop of ink that birthed a poem, a dream nurtured into a life.

Nushi's and Grandfather's faces tipped toward the sky. Even Father's face softened. The display continued long past the Wus', and I knew Auntie Wu would tell her husband to increase their order of fireworks next year.

Eventually, the sky darkened again, and the sharp odor of burning pots hung in the air. I kept my face lifted, watching the stars appear from behind thin clouds of smoke. Sterling Promise strode over to his audience.

"Wonderful," Grandfather said.

"An impressive show," Father admitted.

"Jade Moon was wishing earlier that we had fireworks, weren't you?" Nushi said, amusement in her voice.

"I am glad my poor skills pleased you," Sterling Promise said.

I walked toward the shadows where dark cylinders littered the ground. Father and Grandfather followed me. "How did you get them to explode so quickly — one after another?" I asked.

"They are built that way. The fuse goes through many different containers of powder," Sterling Promise explained in a superior voice. "It is very difficult. You would not understand."

I snorted my disgust and bent to examine one of the containers. As I studied it, there was a popping sound. Before I could react, a weight knocked me backward.

The back of my head hit the ground. I looked up to see an explosion of light framing Sterling Promise's face. I could feel his breath on my cheeks. His eyes searched mine, hair falling over his forehead. With the weight of him pressed against me, I lost the rhythm of my heart.

He scrambled to his knees. "Are you hurt?"

"The firework. You pushed me out of the way." I sat up and looked at Sterling Promise. For a moment, he didn't look like a monster, but like a scared little boy.

CHAPTER 5

"WHAT HAPPENED?" my father barked.

A curtain fell back over Sterling Promise's eyes. He rose and addressed himself to my grandfather, who was staring at the scene. "I apologize a thousand times, sir. I should have been more careful."

"You could have killed us!" Father yelled.

Sterling Promise hung his head.

Grandfather put a hand on Father's arm. "I think we should go inside." Sterling Promise stood still, head bent, until Grandfather turned back to him. "We need to talk about your offer."

He nodded and followed them.

Nushi helped me up off the ground. My head was still spinning as I settled next to her on the bench. So far today, I had fallen in a river, learned I was practically engaged to the town brickmaker, and discovered a disowned uncle, and now, a firework had almost exploded in my face. "I need to hear the story," I said to Nushi.

"'Cowherd and Weaver Girl?'" She pressed her lips together. "Your father doesn't like me filling your head with love stories."

"Think of the bad luck we will have if I am in a sour mood all day tomorrow."

"You know every word. You should tell it," she said.

"No, Nushi. You tell it much better than I could." I slid to the damp grass, folded my legs under me, and faced her.

She spread her hands in front of her as she always did when she began a story. They would carve the air into mountains and streams, heroes and barbarians.

"In a small village tucked between two hills, there once was a boy who herded cattle. No one paid much attention to him. Everyone just called the boy Cowherd."

"He was poor, remember?" I said.

"Yes, the holes in his coat grew bigger every winter. Straw escaped the weaving of his hat. Despite his poverty, Cowherd was happy with his life. Every morning, he whistled as he rode a beautiful golden ox out to the field to drive the animals toward fresh tufts of grass."

"And he slept in the barn with the ox," I said.

"Would you like to tell the story?" she snapped.

I shook my head.

"Cowherd told the most wonderful tales, and he would talk with the ox late into the night. The ox was happy to share his stall and straw with him, and Cowherd was glad to have the ox as a friend, for he was a clever ox."

"I think a clever ox would be very helpful," I said.

"If you would listen to him," Nushi said. "One day, the golden ox said to Cowherd, 'Today, the daughters of the Jade Emperor of the Sky come to swim in the lake.'

" 'That must be a wonderful sight,' Cowherd sighed, imagining the beauty of the Jade Emperor's nine daughters reflected in the glittering waters.

" 'I can take you there if you like,' the ox said.

"Cowherd grinned, and off they went, deep into the forest. It was spring, and bright green leaves trimmed the banyan trees that edged their path, cutting the light into latticework. When they got close to the lake, they could hear the sweet voices and gentle laughter of maidens, ringing like bells in the wind. The golden ox followed their sweet song until he reached a crystal lake where the nine girls bathed.

"Cowherd admired the sight for a moment from behind the trunk of a thick tree."

"And that is when he fell in love," I said.

"First, the ox had to push him a little. 'You could marry one of them, young master,' the ox said.

"Cowherd shook his head. 'A poor cowherd like me? This beauty belongs in the Jade Emperor's palace.'

"But the ox thought his friend deserved a beautiful, gentle wife, so he continued to prod. 'Why shouldn't you have happiness?' the ox asked. He did not understand the barriers to love."

"Maybe love should not be so difficult," I said.

Nushi frowned. "Do you want to hear the story, or do you want to share your ignorant opinions on love?" I squeezed my lips together. "The ox made a suggestion. 'Steal one maiden's clothes and refuse to give them back until she agrees to marry you.'

"Cowherd hesitated, but when the maidens' gentle laughter brushed against his ears a second time, he decided that he would like nothing more than a small house with tamped earth walls where he could hear that laughter in every room. He slipped down from the ox and crept to where the maidens' robes were draped over a branch in a silky rainbow.

"'Take the red robe,' the golden ox whispered. 'It belongs to the seventh daughter — Weaver Girl. She weaves the blues of a clear day and the grays of a rainy morning, the reds, oranges, and yellows of a sunrise, and the pinks and purples of a sunset.'

"Cowherd peeked between the leaves of the willow trees. He spotted the seventh daughter, and his heart left him. What could he do but slip her robe under his tattered coat? When the nine daughters came out of the water, they picked up their robes. But Weaver Girl could not find hers.

"Cowherd stepped out from his hiding place and cleared his throat, his words hanging in his chest as he stood in awe of Weaver Girl's beauty. Her sisters surrounded her and tried to persuade Cowherd to give her clothes back.

"'I will gladly return your clothes to you,' he said gently, 'if you promise to be my wife.'

"Weaver Girl blushed at being approached by this stranger.

"'You don't want Weaver Girl for a wife. She works at her loom all day,' declared one sister.

"'She will never remember to bring you tea,' announced a second.

"'She laughs the loudest,' said a third. 'It will give you headaches.'

"But Cowherd had already given his heart to Weaver Girl. And Weaver Girl, who saw his kindness and love, agreed to marry him.

"They loved each other more every day. But where Weaver Girl used to work at her loom hour after hour, weaving the silk that

37

would drape the skies, now she preferred to talk with Cowherd. She sat next to him and told him stories of her sisters or described her father's palace. Cowherd entertained her with stories of the animals he cared for. The golden ox was glad to see his friend so happy.

"But it wasn't long before the Emperor of the Sky noticed the disorder of colors in the heavens — purple streaks in the middle of the day, yellow horizons at night, rain clouds in the dry season and none in the wet season. No one knew when to wake up and begin work in the rice fields. The women would put the laundry out to dry just before rain fell from a clear sky. Cowherd and Weaver Girl were too blissful to notice the chaos their love had caused.

"The Emperor of the Sky decided that the two lovers must part. While they lay sleeping, he plucked a silver pin from Weaver Girl's hair and drew a line across the black sky. A canyon of bright stars yawned open between the couple. When they woke, Cowherd tried to cross the starry sky to reach Weaver Girl, but he could not. Weaver Girl reached out to Cowherd, but she could not span the divide either. Realizing that she would be separated from her Cowherd forever, she started to sob. Buckets of tears rained down from the sky."

"Fathers can be so cruel," I said.

"Jade Moon, you know he did not want to make his daughter sad. If the world is to live in harmony, everyone must fulfill his role," Nushi said. "You tell the ending, since you are determined to open your mouth and let absurdity spill from it."

"Nushi . . ."

She rested one hand over the other in her lap and stared at me, waiting. The wind made strands of gray hair brush across her still face. I thought for a moment, and then continued the story.

"The Emperor was sorry to see his daughter so sad," I said, pursing my lips. "He told Weaver Girl, 'I cannot have chaos in the skies throughout the year, but you and your love can meet once every year, on the Seventh Night of the Seventh Month.' He kept his promise. On that night, the Emperor orders every bird who roams the skies to line up wing to wing and make a bridge for the lovers."

"What happens the day after they meet?" Nushi asked.

"It rains — the tears of Cowherd and Weaver Girl when they must part."

Nushi always said that it was no surprise that I loved this story; after all, I had all the wisdom one could expect from youth. I *did* have trouble understanding love. I had studied and studied the handful of love stories that Nushi told me, but every story said something different — the meaning of love shrinking and growing in a moment. Most of them spoke of the duty of love. I knew plenty about that, but I had a feeling there was more. Was it built on a sturdy, strong friendship? Was it woven together with a thousand kindnesses? Was it born with a breath, a look? How would I ever know? It was frightening to want something that I didn't understand.

"I wish I knew what love was made of," I said, moving to sit next to her on the bench.

Nushi's eyes met mine. They were worried eyes, with the beginning of tears in them. "It is made of the same stuff as life — tears, joy, hurt, healing . . . betrayal."

"Do people give it to you? Do you stumble on it? Do you trade something of yourself for it?"

"I suppose the best love is grown inside you." She wiped the tears away before they could fall. But new pools formed.

"What is wrong?" It frightened me to see her crying.

She gazed at the river, where the moon sent drops of light over its surface. "It's nothing. It is just a strange beginning to the New Year."

CHAPTER 6

EARLY THE NEXT MORNING, I put on the new linen jacket and loose skirt Nushi had sewn for me and walked toward the rice terraces, hoping to avoid the string of people who would visit the house this morning for the New Year. Auntie Wu would come to make sure her sweets were better than ours. Villagers would come to meet Sterling Promise and bask in his charms. Even Fourth Brother Gou might come to measure the worth of the house and land against the risk of marrying a Fire Horse girl.

I preferred the terraces. For centuries, generations of men in our family had stacked the terraces into the side of the hills. Stones packed one on top of another, old hands replaced by young hands, again and again until the steps wound to the sky. The terraces would be empty today, as the villagers who worked them were home with their families for the New Year.

The rice fields had taught my grandfather his brutal, practical version of love. In his younger days, he had worked tirelessly to buy enough land and hire enough laborers to secure a comfortable life for the family.

Father was supposed to be a scholar. Grandfather had even found him tutors, anticipating great wealth and respect. But in our family, good luck comes only if chased by bad luck. The civil service exams were abolished before Father could take them and earn a valuable government position. Instead he gained another sad story of disappointed dreams for the Chan family.

I slipped through the wisps of fog that had wandered into our yard from the river, my footprints making a bright path in the dew-covered grass. My head swam with the events of yesterday — Sterling Promise's arrival, his and Father's trip to America, his infuriating presence in general. Between those thoughts kept intruding the closeness of his breath on my face when the firework exploded, and the gentle touch on the back of my head.

As the outline of the sun tipped over the horizon, Sterling Promise appeared. Only a moment of surprise washed over his face before he veiled it with the calm, pleasant mask he always wore.

I forced my tongue into the traditional greeting. "Congratulations. Blessings and happiness in the New Year," I said.

His brow relaxed with the relief of finding familiar social footing. "Congratulations and prosperity." We stood face-to-face for another second before he turned to the field. Some of the fog had dissolved, uncovering the pools of watery sky held inside the terraces. His mouth softened in appreciation. "Your grandfather said I should come see the rice fields. They are beautiful," he whispered.

"You have never seen a rice farm?" I asked.

"I saw some along the riverbanks outside of Hong Kong, but nothing like this. I had never left Hong Kong until now."

"You act like you have seen a lot of the world." The words were sour on my tongue.

"The world is a big place." He scanned the fields. "Your grandfather owns all of this?"

"Yes."

"And then your father will inherit it?"

"I suppose." Sterling Promise could probably have it if he wanted it. He could have anything.

As if he saw my thoughts, he said, "I would be proud to own something like this."

"Yes, but it is also a burden," I added, trying to disrupt the easy flow of his good fortune. "Father will be here early tomorrow to oversee the workers. If the rice isn't grown properly, my grandfather can't keep his land and the workers can't feed their families."

"Having something of your own gives you value in the world. People treat you with respect."

"I am more likely to be the property than the owner," I said, acid in every word.

His gaze rested on me again. "As you say, there is great burden in ownership." Was there a sting in his words too?

"Is that why you will go to America? To own something?" I asked.

His eyes stared past the field in front of us. "Partly," he said. "The Americans in Hong Kong, they move with this freedom, like they have shrugged off any burdens from the past, like the world will mold itself around them." Pulling himself back into the moment, he turned to me. "You would not understand."

The knowledge that I would never see such a place tore at me. "You think I understand very little."

"I think you *try* to understand very little. Like the fields." He looked out over the pattern of mounds and water spotted with green. "It would be ungrateful of anyone not to want to spend the rest of their lives here."

"You don't want to, and you don't think Father should. Why am *I* ungrateful?"

His jaw tightened. "This is what you can do. Your father and I can do more. Going to America is a duty, a responsibility, much like the fields."

"So I should be content to stay behind?" My chest felt tight, like a string pulled to its breaking point.

"The sun does not try to water the fields. The moon does not try to light the day. You belong in China. *That* is your duty." His voice rose to a satisfying near-shout. A man from the village stared at us as he walked by. Sterling Promise bowed to the man and waited while he passed. "Why do you do that?"

"What?"

"You push and poke. You bring out the worst in people."

"It isn't my fault you lost your temper," I said. There was something hard in his eyes, in the hollow center of their pleasantness, something that wasn't there yesterday.

"You're doing it again," he said. "You force people to bicker and fight with you. You will bring nothing but misery to the man you marry."

I turned my face away only to see Fourth Brother Gou walking toward us from the house. His short legs carried his round body with quick, rhythmic steps. He stopped in front of us, his breath coming out in puffs, red patches on his forehead and cheeks.

"Congratulations and happy New Year, Jade Moon. I was at the Wu house, and they mentioned your guest from Hong Kong." His speech was like his steps — steady, rhythmic, flat. Sterling Promise began to reply, but Fourth Brother Gou was already moving on to his favorite subject. "I hear Hong Kong is a wonderful place for brickmaking. Have you seen the new homes and businesses being built? Many men have gone to the city. They say there is much work there."

"We do have a lot of buildings," Sterling Promise said.

"Are they using bricks of quality? I wonder, with the speed of construction, if they are inspecting the bricks properly." He tapped a finger against his puffy lips. "Bad bricks can bring down an entire city."

"Yes, that would be terrible," Sterling Promise managed to reply. He brought his two fingers to his chin.

"You should look at the buildings when you return," Fourth Brother Gou said. "Especially new buildings. If I were going into a structure in Hong Kong, I would walk around first to see the quality of the bricks. Do you know what to look for? I will tell you." He gave Sterling Promise a detailed lecture about what a quality brick looked like — its texture, weight, coloring, shape. He counted off the warning signs of unstable brickwork on his thick fingers. Sterling Promise nodded along.

Maybe Nushi was right about bricks being useful. I could think of several uses for one right now. The longer Fourth Brother Gou spoke, the more they left me out of the conversation, the angrier I became. The muscles in my legs started to twitch, aching to escape, to run. Next to me, Sterling Promise stood still and calm.

"You are welcome to visit my poor home while you are here," Fourth Brother Gou concluded. "I have not yet told you how to check the mortar. We can save that for your visit."

Sterling Promise thanked him, and they exchanged good-byes.

As Fourth Brother Gou disappeared over the hill, Sterling Promise turned toward the house.

I took a few quick steps and spun to face him. He came to an abrupt halt, his face inches from mine. I could see the gold outline around the dark brown of his eyes, and I had to concentrate to steady myself.

"*That* is what I have here," I said. "A marriage to him. A *lifetime* with him. That is why I cannot stay in China."

"You would be lucky to be matched with him. He is the only person I've met here who makes you seem sensible," he said, his words fast and unmeasured.

"Did my ancestors send you to torture me?" I growled.

"They sent me to bring your father to America." The hard core of anger in his eyes spread. "It is very simple. It is a chance for him to escape the curse of a Fire Horse."

"There's no curse!" I yelled. It was getting harder to breathe.

"I think your mother would disagree."

Before I knew what I was doing, I pushed him with both hands, knocking him off balance. He tipped over into the terrace, breaking the smooth glass of the water with a satisfying splash. I spun around and stomped toward the house. When I got to the door, it swung open.

"Father!"

"Daughter." He stood in the doorway, feet planted, his arms crossed. "Where have you been?"

A rhythmic squishing came from behind me. I watched Father's eyes shift from mine and narrow as Sterling Promise walked toward us. Muddy water dripped from his sleeves and down his fingers. More mud dotted his neck and cheeks.

"What has happened?" Father said, his glare bouncing from me to Sterling Promise and back.

I would be beaten for what I had done to our guest. Beaten, then locked in my room. Beaten, locked in my room, then married to a brickmaker. "Father . . . ," I began.

"I apologize," Sterling Promise said. "I grew up in the city. I am not skilled at walking along the terrace walls." I turned and stared at him. He bent his face toward the ground. "I am ashamed that you must see my ignorance, but I fell in."

The familiar disgust settled into Father's features. I tried to catch Sterling Promise's eye. He looked at me for a moment, then shifted his glance over my shoulder.

"Daughter, it has been decided. You are going to America with me." Father turned his back and started into the house. "It is where you will finally be useful."

My mouth dropped open, then slammed shut. I would get to see the place where people shrugged off their pasts. A place that would mold around me instead of closing in on me.

"Thank our guest, not me." He looked over his shoulder at Sterling Promise, whose face lifted for a second before dropping again. Father sniffed and turned back to me. "Guard your joy. Your happiness only proves what a fool you are."

I barely heard him over the singing in my heart.

CHAPTER 7

GRANDFATHER CONSULTED FORTUNE-TELLERS to find an appropriate day for our departure. Once a lucky day for travel was found during the second moon, he whistled as he made lists of supplies and went with his purse to seek out the merchants in the market town up the road. His high spirits were a strange contrast to Father's low ones. Father confined himself to his study. He was distant at dinner and unsociable with Sterling Promise, avoiding him when it was possible and ignoring him when it was not.

Sterling Promise spent his time cultivating his popularity in the village. He brought news to the men and compliments to the women. Auntie Wu declared through her brightly painted lips that he "must have been sent by the Chan ancestors to save them."

I let Father, Grandfather, and Sterling Promise ignore me, not wanting to remind them of the burden my presence could be. I busied myself dreaming of the freedom I would have once I'd left the tight expectations, suffocating rules, and disapproving looks behind me.

Nushi prepared the trunk that Father and I would take to America — one trunk for both of us, our two lives in one box. On her path through a room, she would pick up a bowl or a book or a cake of ink, look at it, and stomp out with it, her straw sandals smacking against the floor. Any interference was met with deaf ears and angry stares. But what did I know about packing for America anyway, when I had never left our village?

The day before our departure, I found Nushi in the kitchen, slicing thin circles from the pepper in front of her, the wrinkles gathering on her forehead. I stood in front of her, but she did not look up or stop cutting. "Can I hide here with you?"

"Why are you hiding?"

"I think Father wants to send me on an errand to Auntie Wu's."

"So go."

I widened my eyes, pleading.

"Fine, stay here. But I have too much to do to have you bothering me."

"What is left? You packed the trunk, although I can't imagine with what."

"Don't worry about what I'm packing. You'll have exactly what you need when you leave."

Sterling Promise walked through the doorway. "I was sent for more tea," he said, holding up the pot.

"Leave it. I will bring it up."

"I can take it, Nushi," he said.

"I said leave it," she barked at him.

He straightened. "I apologize if I have offended —"

"I don't have time for your apologies. Go!"

49

Sterling Promise set the pot gently on the table and left. Nushi turned her back on it, so I picked it up, scooped the old leaves out, and dropped new ones inside before passing it to Nushi to be filled with hot water.

"Father said Sterling Promise is the reason I am going to America." I had been thinking about this, puzzling over it, since his announcement.

"And you think that is something to thank him for?"

"Haven't you heard him talk about it? So open . . . so free . . . so full of everything. This is a good chance for me. To find my place."

"You are leaving your home, your family. It is irresponsible."

"What do I have here? A family who thinks I am a burden. A village that thinks I am a curse. Oh . . . and if I am very lucky, a lifetime of conversations about bricks."

"You have a good life here."

"If only I could fit myself within the boundaries of it," I said, stepping closer to her. "Oh, Nushi, you know I will miss you terribly."

"You will not. You will be happy in the new country, America. You will forget me. You *should* forget me."

"I could never forget you," I said. "Father says we will come back in a year or two. To visit."

She tightened her lips and went back to chopping. "No, you're right. It is a new start. Don't come back."

A tense feeling grew in my throat. She attacked an onion with the knife, then stopped and glared at me. "Get out! Get out!" she said with the same sudden venom she'd unleashed on Sterling Promise.

I stared at her, frozen.

"Get out!"

I left the kitchen with tears stinging my eyes.

That night, the house was quiet except for the singing of the night birds and the low voices of Father, Grandfather, and Sterling Promise going over the last details of our trip. I lay on my bed, staring into the dark. When Nushi slipped through the door, I pretended to sleep.

"You know I can always tell when you are pretending to sleep."

I shifted to face the wall. I would not speak. My heart was still sore. I heard the stool scrape across the floor.

"I am sorry about this afternoon," she said. "I should not have scolded you." Nushi reached into the pocket on her apron. "I have a present for you, not that you deserve it." The light of the moon showed a tiny red pouch tied with a long silk string in the palm of her hand.

I took it from her and peeked inside. In the corner of the pouch was a fragment of uncut, unpolished jade, smaller than my smallest fingernail.

"It is beautiful!"

"It will bring you good fortune and ward off evil spirits," she said, her voice unsteady. "And you don't have to tell me I'm being superstitious," she added quickly. "You are going to need all the good luck you can get."

"Thank you." I closed my eyes, trapping the tears burning inside them.

"It will also remind you of who you are. Jade is sharp, but not cutting. It is beautiful even though you can see its flaws."

"Nushi . . ."

"You need to sleep," she said, getting up.

"Nushi." I stood and took her hands. "How will I survive without you?" It had seemed so easy to go before that moment.

She looked at me and shook her head slowly. "I don't know anything about this country, America. I asked the peddlers who had been to Hong Kong about the foreigners there. They said that Americans would rather break their skin making a new path than follow an old one."

"That sounds like me."

"I thought so too. I like the old path, but if you don't mind breaking apart what you have, I suppose a new path can get you there," she said. "I don't have any stories to help you."

"You've given me enough stories. I will take all of them."

"I hope you will find your own story. Remember, if America is everything you hope it is, you should stay there. Forget China. If you want a new life, you have to turn your back on the old one. Good-bye, worthless girl," she cried out, trying to convince any evil spirits that I was beneath their notice. Then she leaned close and whispered, "Good-bye, daughter of my heart."

"Good-bye, Nushi."

I breathed in the smells that had hovered around me my entire life. The smell of hair being brushed and tears being dried. The smell of mornings in the kitchen and evenings in the garden. And with that, Nushi slipped away.

The next day, I stood outside the door, shielding my eyes against the sun. I bowed a respectful good-bye to Grandfather under

Father's supervision. "Don't dishonor your family," Grandfather said as I settled onto a cushion of hay and quilts in the back of the cart packed with our trunk and bags. Sterling Promise and Father sat up front with the driver.

The cart bumped along the path until I could not see Grandfather. It rolled past where I could see the house, the terraces. In a moment, a breath, we passed the rock in the road that until that moment had served as the border of my life.

CHAPTER 8

WE MOVED FROM THE CART to a small steamboat that twisted down country rivers. The landscape was dotted with workers I had never met, farming fields I had never seen, and women who had never scowled at me on the shores washing their laundry. Father did not appreciate my enthusiasm for each scene as we passed it, but I could not help myself. I leaned over the side of the boat, taking in every detail.

We traded the small steamboat for a larger one, thin ribbons of steam for thick puffs. Large trees lined the banks of the wide river, and I was left to imagine what lay beyond. The river emptied into the bay at Hong Kong, and that is when everything changed.

Hong Kong was a giant of a city. We left our trunks at the docks in the care of the steamship company, took up the bundles of clothes and essentials that we would use for the journey, and followed Sterling Promise through the streets. Buildings piled to dizzying heights. Banners waved from the windows, with black, red, and gold letters shouting from their surfaces. Lines weighted with scraps of clothing crisscrossed the sky — a sky that had shrunk to a thick line of blue between the rooftops. Everything was tightly packed and in motion. Wide veins of humanity coursed through the streets. People tucked their hands into their sleeves and folded themselves into the city.

Dust flew up from beneath the parade of wheels and feet flowing along the road. Men harnessed to their carts and wheelbarrows stared at their feet as they twisted paths around one another. The stalls and shops were stuffed with crates of vegetables, fish, fabric, shining trinkets hanging beside red and gold lanterns, and woks piled halfway to the ceiling. Beneath canopies of faded red, people tossed numbers back and forth, hurling them at each other until they met in the middle; goods traded hands; lips spread in easy smiles, and the day moved forward. It only took a moment. In the village, these exchanges would have dragged through hours or even days, with thoughts tucked between words. Here, a frantic scrambling of merchants, shoppers, even beggars drove the energy of the city. It was exciting, breathtaking, the way a story should begin.

A cart rushed by me. I jumped to the side to avoid it and tumbled into another man, this one pale with a square face and wide eyes that flashed with anger. I stared. His tunic ended at the top of his legs, two hands shorter than the one Father wore.

A beggar lifted his broken body from a doorway. "A coin or two, sir. For a bowl of rice," he said, his head bent toward the ground. The foreigner tossed two coins into the filthy palms stretched out to him while his nose wrinkled with disgust. Sterling Promise dropped back to press me forward.

"They call it a suit."

"What?" I said, looking back at the beggar.

Sterling Promise followed my gaze. "No, the foreigner. His clothes. All the foreigners wear them. Your uncle brought one back from America. I will wear it when I am there," he said proudly. Then his face became serious. "Stay close. If you fall behind, you'll be lost."

But it was difficult not to fall behind when there was so much to see. Sterling Promise's pace had the purpose of someone who had soaked in these surroundings long ago. He slipped in and out of my sight. When I passed by a stand with crates of fruits and vegetables, a man held out an oval fruit the size of his palm with a swirl of green and yellow skin.

"Try it. It is a mango from Siam — very special, very rare." His smile spread across the bottom half of his face, pressing layers of wrinkles onto his cheeks.

I tasted the fruit. It was soft and dense. The sticky juice left a sweet coating on my teeth and tongue. I slurped the syrup from my lips. "Delicious," I said, smiling back.

The man nodded. "You want four or five — take them home to your husband. They bring love to a household." He raised his eyebrow higher on his forehead. "Guaranteed to please even the most demanding mother-in-law."

I shook my head. "No, thank you," I said, stepping back into the street.

"What about the one you ate? You must pay," the man called. His smile had disappeared.

"I only took one bite. You gave it to me!"

"I can't feed my family by giving fruit to spoiled empresses! You must pay for what you eat."

"You should have told me instead of trying to cheat me."

I started to walk away, but the man grabbed my arm. I jerked it back, but his small wrinkled hand held fast. "You are not going to steal from me!"

A crowd gathered, a sea of people. I had never had to blur so many faces before. My cheeks grew hot. "I am not a thief. I don't need to steal your bruised fruit. Better fruit grows in the garden behind our kitchen."

"Now you insult my fruit? I sell the best fruit in Hong Kong. I don't need insults from a thief. Police! Someone get the police!"

A few mouths shouted for the police, but no one moved. Then I saw a ripple at the crowd's edge. I straightened my back, preparing to explain to the policeman the trick that the man had played on me. But instead, Sterling Promise stepped up beside me. He made a small bow and asked, "Sir, is something wrong?"

The man's face lit up with recognition, and he returned the bow. "Ah, my friend, you are back from the countryside! I am sorry that you have caught me completing an unfortunate task. I was just waiting for the police to arrest this thief."

"I did not steal anything," I said through my teeth. "This man tried to cheat me."

Sterling Promise gave me a look I had seen before. It said, "Keep your mouth shut." He turned to the grocer, mirrored the man's smile, and said, "She is my guest. Perhaps there was a misunderstanding."

"A misunderstanding?" I shouted. Sterling Promise stiffened next to me, but kept smiling at the grocer. "He tried to trick me," I said. "He offered me the fruit as a gift, and then he tried to get me to pay for it."

"Ah, I see," Sterling Promise said, nodding, his voice smooth and calm. "My young cousin arrived in Hong Kong today. She is unfamiliar with some of the customs of the city."

"I did not know that one of the customs was to cheat people!"

Sterling Promise glared at me. "Quiet," he hissed. He turned back to the grocer and softened his voice. "I appreciate you telling her about your delicious fruits. They are truly one of the wonders of the city. Perhaps you would allow me to purchase three, along with the one my cousin ate. Now that she has tasted one, she will want another tomorrow."

"I will never put anything from this stall in my mouth again," I said.

"It is understandable that someone who comes from the country is ignorant of the rules of the city." The grocer frowned at me, but when he turned to Sterling Promise, his lips parted in his biggest smile, revealing another row of yellow teeth. "And who could expect her to appreciate the exotic fruits I sell?"

"Exactly," Sterling Promise agreed.

The crowd, robbed of further entertainment, bled back into the city. By the time Sterling Promise paid the grocer, only I saw their friendly good-byes.

When Sterling Promise and I stepped back onto the street, I stared forward, avoiding his glare. We walked in silence. As we paused to let a stream of carts pass in front of us, he said, "Your father is waiting at the corner of the next street." He bit his lip for a moment. "You cannot wander off in Hong Kong. It is dangerous."

His concern cooled my anger a few degrees. I shook my head. "That man would not hurt me. He was just a sneaky grocer trying to trick me."

"I don't mean dangerous for you. It is dangerous for me and my reputation. I can't have you angering my friends and neighbors, which seems to be your particular gift."

"You can't blame me for that! Just because I don't smile and say whatever someone wants to hear."

The stones in his eyes met the fire in mine. "We need to get rid of this fruit." Sterling Promise started walking again. I scrambled to follow a few paces behind him.

"I thought it was special."

"You can't trust everyone around here."

"But you defended him."

"You can't fight everyone either," he said.

Sterling Promise veered into a stall. The owner, almost buried in piles of paper lanterns, popped up from his stool and scurried over to greet him. "My friend, I have not seen you since before the New Year."

Sterling Promise softened his expression and bowed. "It is good to see you again. I was just in Mr. Lu's fruit stall, and he has a crate of the most delicious mangoes."

"Ah, how fortunate for you. My wife loves mangoes."

"Please, take one for yourself and your wife with my compliments."

"Oh, no. I could not."

"You must. My gift to you." They traded a few more pleas before a smile broke across the shopkeeper's face.

"Well, if you insist. Thank you."

"Once you have enjoyed those, you can get more at Mr. Lu's stand."

"Oh, yes, I will."

"Tell him I sent you," Sterling Promise said before we slipped out of the stall.

It was strange watching the give and take of the business world. "Is everything in your life an exchange?" I said. "This for that?"

"You never know when someone might be able to do you a favor."

"I don't need anyone to do me any favors."

"Ha! How many times have I had to rescue you? And I have known you for only two moons."

Father waited at the next corner, his arms folded. But then Sterling Promise handed him a mango. "Your daughter was just looking at the fruit and vegetable vendor's stall. She said you might like to taste this."

Father looked up at me. There was confusion on his face, but eventually his lips relaxed, and he peeled off a piece and bit into the fruit's yellow flesh. "I had forgotten about mangoes," he said. "I have not had one in so long." He sucked more of the fruit from the skin.

I looked at Sterling Promise. The corners of his eyes crinkled in a smile. He made it look so simple.

CHAPTER 9

STERLING PROMISE MANEUVERED us through the crowds until the streets narrowed and the shadows deepened. When we came to a shop at one of the countless corners where one street joined another, he stopped. The shop's windows were dark, covered in a thick layer of black dust followed by a layer of paper. It had no sign, and trash had gathered at the bottom corners of the door.

"We will go around back," he said. We followed him into an alley. He knocked on a door along the back wall. After a few moments, invisible hands opened the door. Sterling Promise disappeared inside, and Father and I followed.

Inside, the air was sharp. It stung my throat. The room was dark and crammed with bodies. Children knelt on bamboo mats, surrounded by wooden bowls filled with black powder, pearl-sized balls, string, and bits of paper. Their hands flew from one bowl to another — assembling lines and containers of fireworks, I realized, like those Sterling Promise had brought.

A large man stomped impatiently down the rows, leaning over the children's shoulders. His face and hands had a grimy tint to them, and half-moons of shadowy skin hung under his eyes. A fragile-looking woman stood silently against the wall. The man was raising a hand over a cowering boy when Sterling Promise stepped toward him and cleared his throat.

The man dropped his hand. "Ah, you are back," he said. "And you have been successful, I assume."

Sterling Promise bowed. "I want to present Chan Jan Wai and his daughter." He turned to us, a thick mask over his features. "I present my teacher and business partner, Master Yue."

Master Yue bowed his head. "You resemble your brother. That's good."

Father frowned.

The children at our feet continued working, their heads bent over the hollow shells in front of them. One raised his face to peer up at us, but Master Yue smacked him on the back of the head. The pop echoed off the empty walls. "Get back to work!"

"You didn't have to hit him!" I said.

"Daughter," my father hissed. "We are guests."

Wrinkles formed on Sterling Promise's brow. I lifted my chin, my anger burning under my skin. The boy wiped his eyes with the cuff of a black-stained sleeve. I put a hand on his shoulder to comfort him.

"This one, my wife spoiled when he was sick." Master Yue glared at the small woman leaning into a corner. She lowered her head. "Now he is completely worthless." He smiled at Sterling Promise. "He is even more trouble than you were when you first arrived."

Sterling Promise was once one of these children? I tried to picture him, kneeling on a dingy mat. I couldn't see his clear eyes, the ones that took in every detail, on these blank, sad faces. But, as the boy jerked his shoulder from under my hand and returned to work, I noticed Sterling Promise kept his gaze above the children's heads.

"We will get you settled in your rooms now," Master Yue continued. We followed him to the stairs at the back of the room. On the way up, I saw Sterling Promise slip the last mango into the tiny, wrinkled hand of Yue's wife. She gave him a sad smile and tucked it under her apron.

When I looked closely, the Yue home told a story of fortunes won and lost. Fine vases sat on plain tables. A beautiful screen was folded in the corner because one of the panels was cut out and, maybe, sold. Enameled boxes had their handles of ivory or gold removed. After placing our bags in our rooms, we sat down at a table in the dining room while Yue's wife and a servant bustled in and out of the kitchen with plates of food. Master Yue took up most of the small room with his long, heavy limbs and his loud voice. The rest of us fit in around him. Master Yue and Sterling Promise discussed business — or, at least, a vague sort of business.

"The man I spoke of is expecting you," Yue said. "You will to see to my affairs."

Sterling Promise nodded.

"I lose more money every month, and Lo does nothing but make excuses. You will write to me with what you discover there. Then I will give you further instructions, and you will carry them out. That is what Chan did. You understand?"

"Yes, of course," Sterling Promise replied, looking at the table.

"My uncle worked for you?" I said.

"Yes, he came to me when he was a young man, fresh from the country. He worked for me for . . . let's see . . ."

"Almost twenty years," Father said.

"That's right. How did you know?"

"That is how long I have been home, running the fields."

"What did he do?" I asked.

"He watched over my investments in America," Master Yue said. "He found new markets for my fireworks. He was a very clever businessman. He could fight like a tiger when necessary."

"That's enough questions about your uncle, Daughter," Father said.

Sterling Promise coughed. Master Yue's wife brought out another tray of vegetables. I looked at it and remembered a question I had that was not about Uncle.

"When do the children eat?" I asked.

Master Yue stared at me like I was a fly stuck on his rice.

"Where do they sleep? Do they ever go outside?"

"Daughter, you must remember your place," Father said.

Master Yue waved away my father's concerns, but his face hardened. "It is very kind of you to be concerned for the children, but I assure you, they are taken care of. You would not wish to accuse me of mistreating them?"

"I did not mean to accuse you of anything," I said.

"Of course you didn't. What would you know of business?" His eyes were as black as the powder I saw downstairs. "They are making the finest fireworks in Hong Kong."

"Like Sterling Promise used to?"

"Yes, exactly like Sterling Promise used to. And look how well I cared for him." He leaned back in his chair.

I had not meant to insult Sterling Promise, but the tightness of his lips told me that I had. I sat silently through the rest of dinner, wondering how he had come from this place to be my adopted cousin — the young man with so much ambition to spend in America.

The next day, I woke up in the corner of the room I had shared with Master Yue's wife and started down the stairs. Halfway down, I heard voices.

"It is a difficult business. You will have to be very clever," Master Yue said.

"Yes," Sterling Promise said.

"It is a bargain, five hundred dollars. A paper son would have cost three times that. And you may not even have to use it. But if you do, I expect to be paid back."

I peered around the corner and saw them sitting across from each other at a small table, a stack of paper money between them. Yue reached for a sticky bun and jammed it in his mouth. "Just remember, you have nothing if you cannot get into America. Nothing! You will rot in the gutters I pulled you from for the rest of your life." He leaned back in his chair. "You were clever to get the brother to replace Chan, but the daughter, she is trouble."

"She is not as difficult as she seems," Sterling Promise said, tapping his finger against his leg.

It was only a splinter of a compliment, but it kept my tongue still when I heard Master Yue's curses rain down on the children in the workroom that afternoon. It helped me to turn away when Master Yue stared at me a little too long, though I wished to meet his dark gaze with one of my own. It stilled my questions at the Yues' dinner table for two weeks while Father and Sterling Promise went back and forth to the steamship offices to make the final arrangements.

I discovered Master Yue's wife knew her husband's comings and goings well enough to avoid him. I followed her out of our room late at night to help her wrap the children's tender hands and wash out eyes, red from the powder. I scooped cups of water from a bucket that she brought down and put it to their lips.

One night Sterling Promise caught me going down the stairs with strips of cloth for bandages. He grabbed my arm. "Don't get involved. You're not doing them any good. He will only beat them more if he finds out."

I lifted my chin. "It's a little water and a few bandages."

"It's not your place."

"You were one of those children. You should understand."

"I do understand. I understand that Master Yue is the only thing keeping them and maybe their families from starvation."

I shook my head. "I wish I knew how you got from here to the door of our home in Jinjiu. Why do you come back to this man's house when he was as cruel to you as he is to them?"

Sterling Promise walked past me. "Why should I tell you? So you can make me look bad to your father?" He stomped up the stairs.

CHAPTER 10

AFTER TWO WEEKS AT THE YUES', it was time to board the ship that would take us to America. Hong Kong spilled crowds of people onto the docks. The docks poured them onto ships and boats, and those vessels fanned out into the bay, leaving the city in a thousand directions. Small boats, their sails unfurled, orbited the large steamers like flies around giant oxen. I watched passengers file over the wooden platform and onto our ship. Pale faces broke from the herd and paraded up another platform to a higher deck.

"Daughter," Father called, snapping me back to where he stood with a man and a woman. I walked over to join them. "This is my daughter, Jade Moon." I bowed. "Daughter, these are the Yings."

A broad smile that showed all her teeth spread across Mrs. Ying's small, round face. Her warm eyes were framed by short hair in loose curls. She wore a heavy dress of faded black fabric with a full skirt and fitted waist. I had never seen so much material used for one piece of clothing. I fiddled with the sleeves of my own tunic, soft from wear, the pants tied at my waist with a string.

Father explained that Mrs. Ying had agreed to look after me. I would bunk with her and the handful of other women travelers.

"She is stubborn and strong willed," my father announced.

"Then I think we will be good company for each other," Mrs. Ying said.

My father wrinkled his nose. But I liked Mrs. Ying. I liked the way she stood taller than Father and Sterling Promise. I liked that she took up space without apology, her head raised and her arms swinging freely from her sides. I like the way she smiled, teeth showing, no hand over her mouth. It was so different from Auntie Wu and her daughters-in-law, who giggled behind their fans. My heart grew surer that I would find the freedom I needed in America.

I followed Mrs. Ying to steerage — the belly of the ship — down a narrow aisle to the far end of a large room. It was dark, and the air was heavy. The hum of the waiting engine vibrated through the walls. People crammed into every corner, and the air already smelled of sweat and skin.

Mrs. Ying found the women's section tucked behind the stairway, separated from the larger room with a burlap curtain. It was a plain room with only six cots, brown blankets folded on top. There was not a speck of color or a single window to release the stale air. An older woman was already settled in her cot; a younger woman buzzed around her, tucking in blankets and settling sewing into her hands.

"Don't worry." Mrs. Ying nodded toward two of the cots. "It is a dreary voyage, but in four weeks, we will be home."

"You live in America?" I asked, settling onto one of the beds.

"Yes, we were visiting my husband's family here. It is the first time we have been back for many years. It was a hard thing to return to China. It is like asking a snake to get back in the skin it shed."

I nodded. She removed a series of tiny hairpins and brushed out her dark hair before re-pinning the stray pieces blown loose by the wind on the deck. Her hands moved with speed and confidence. Two other women trickled in and began to build their beds with the small pillows and worn sheets and blankets folded on top of the thin mattresses.

"Your father promised me a girl who talked too much," Mrs. Ying said, unfolding her own sheets and tucking them into the corners of her cot with energy.

"He did not mention how irritating I can be?"

"Yes, he did."

I looked down at my feet. Of course he did.

Mrs. Ying laughed. It was a loud laugh. The two other women stopped and stared at her, but she did not notice. "But what irritates your father may not bother me," she said, sitting on the bed next to mine.

"Questions irritate him," I said, hugging the blanket to my chest.

"Silence irritates me."

The other women smoothed their beds, checked that their luggage was locked, and left whispering.

"How long have you lived in America?" I asked, tucking the edges of the sheets under the mattress.

"All my life. My father came to work on the Central Pacific Railroad."

"Then you were born in America? You are an American."

"Yes. And no," she sighed. She unpacked a round sewing basket and several small bottles from her bag.

"Do you speak English?"

"Yes. I'll teach you some if you like."

"I would," I said eagerly. "What is it like, America?"

"Most countries are like their land. And America has good land — open and varied — but it is still a little wild."

"Americans? They are wild too?"

"My mother always said they are like children," Mrs. Ying said. "They have the best intentions, but sometimes they behave badly despite that. They are full of joy and anger, laughter and bitter tears. They let one emotion wash over them and then another. China is older and wiser, but there is a magic in the eyes of childhood, an ability to find the simple truths in life. These truths are appealing even if they are only fragments of what is real. Americans do no harm . . . most of the time." She looked past me. "And even when they do, you forgive them because they are children and don't know any better."

I looked down at the coarse tan fabric of my jacket. Mrs. Ying's clothes had straight lines and even curves, while mine had all the fits and starts of home sewing. I picked at the waist of my pants. "Do they dress like you? We saw some men in Hong Kong. They wore suits. And the women wore dresses, straighter and made of softer fabric than yours."

"I don't think I am a picture of the current fashion. Some dress like me. Others don't. The men do wear suits."

"What do they eat?"

"Chinese food is very popular right now," she said as she folded a shawl she had pulled from her bag.

"What do you mean?"

"They eat rice or noodles cooked in oil with vegetables and meat."

"Oh." I was disappointed. "I eat that at home."

"They also have this wonderful food called Jell-O. Mr. Ying loves it. It is cool and sweet. It comes in bright colors." Her eyes sparkled with excitement. "It starts out as liquid, but when you chill it in the icebox, it becomes a wobbly solid. It is delightful! You will have to come to my house and have some when you are in America."

As I opened my mouth to ask what an icebox was, the engines shuddered to life. Mrs. Ying nodded toward the stairwell and led me up to a small deck where rows of Chinese pushed against the railing. Mr. Ying joined us. She rested her hand on his arm and said something that made him look at her, his face soft and happy. I smiled at the vision of what I would have in America: the easy smile and smooth movements of someone who had a big enough life.

I watched the smokestacks give birth to a gray dragon's breath that writhed and twisted above us. Brushstrokes of light shone from behind the clouds. As we pushed out to sea, the buildings and noise and crowds of Hong Kong shrank into the expanse of water behind us.

That evening, I met Father and Sterling Promise in the common room for dinner. After we ate our cabbage and rice, the tables were cleared and fan-tan games began to form around us. Some men overturned a bowl of beans, then bet on the number of beans under

71

the bowl. Other men sat alone, drinking tea and staring past the walls of the ship. I watched several pull thin booklets of folded, brown paper out from under their hats.

"What are those books they are reading?" I said to Father and Sterling Promise.

"They are studying for the exam to get into America," Sterling Promise said. "Sit down. We have our own coaching book to study."

"An exam? But we have Uncle's papers. I thought those got us into America."

"Uncle had a paper son."

I remembered Master Yue using that term, congratulating Sterling Promise on avoiding the cost of one. "What is that?"

My father lowered his gaze to meet mine — warning me against too many interruptions and questions. Sterling Promise said, "America has been tricky, not letting Chinese come to America or be citizens. In Hong Kong, they say the Americans have laws like tigers."

"What can you expect from foreign devils?" Father muttered. He rose and left to join a group of men playing cards in the corner.

Sterling Promise watched him go. Then he leaned closer and winked, making my heart stumble. "I know how much you like stories. I will tell you one."

I took a breath and waited.

"It all started in San Francisco nearly twenty years ago. An earthquake caused a fire, and the fire burned the list of citizens the Americans had made."

He paused, and I nodded to show I understood.

"They needed to make the list again, so the Chinese played a trick. All the Chinese in San Francisco went to the government to

72

put themselves and their children on the new list. The Americans asked, 'Were you born in America?' and the Chinese said, 'Yes, of course.' Some of them were lying, but no one could prove it, so suddenly they became American citizens. Then the Americans asked, 'Do you have children?'

"The Chinese thought for a second. A man might have one son back in China or even two there with him in America, but he couldn't pass up this good luck. So each Chinese man told the Americans, 'I have three or four or five sons. All born here, then sent back to China.' And like magic, all the sons are Americans too."

"But I don't understand what this has to do with us," I said. Despite the joy in Sterling Promise's eyes as he told this story, it was nothing like the ones Nushi told.

"Those extra sons, those are the paper sons. The Chinese in America sold the sons' identities to people who want to come be Americans. Sixteen years ago, Master Yue bought a paper son for your uncle so he could go to America and oversee Master Yue's investments there. He became Sung Feng Hao."

"And that is the paper you gave Father? The paper son?"

"No. Because your uncle was admitted once, he has legal papers that say he can enter again."

"And *those* are the papers that you gave Father."

"Yes. He will pretend to the Americans that he is your uncle — Sung Feng Hao."

I tried to imagine my father pretending to be the brother he had resented for so long. "And who are we?"

"We are his children — Sung Sterling Promise and Sung Jade Moon. We can keep our given names because the Americans have never heard them."

"Why do we have to pretend to be people we aren't?"

Sterling Promise shrugged. "The Americans like business, so they let merchants in, and they let them bring their wives and children. Your uncle planned to bring me over as his son, so he made a deal and became a partner in a store that sold Master Yue's fireworks to get his merchant papers. But before the Americans admit us, we will have to prove that we're related." He held up the coaching book. "That is why we have this."

I looked at the thin book, then at Sterling Promise's eager face. "I still don't understand what the coaching book is," I said.

"The Americans know that the Chinese have figured out ways around their laws. They will ask you and I the same questions they asked your uncle about our paper family, the Sungs. They may even call our paper grandfather in to be interviewed. Then they will compare our answers to the Sungs' answers, to your uncle's records, to each other's answers. If everything matches, they will let us in. If it doesn't, they will send us back." He tapped the book. "This is the story that will get you into America."

"I don't like this story. It is built on too many lies."

He shook his head. "It is tempting to live how you do, to kick at the very air you breathe, but what does it gain you?"

I knew the answer — a tight feeling in my chest and a bellyful of bitterness. Sterling Promise smoothed a page of the book for a moment.

"Can I see it?" I said, holding my hand out.

"Be careful," he said. He handed me the thin brown book, ten or twelve pages sewn together with thick thread. The page it opened to was covered with dense writing — a series of questions and answers.

Who got the water and did the cooking? *My mother.*

What direction did the village face? *East.*

How many houses were there? *There are three rows of houses. About ten houses total.*

The questions filled the page, except for a drawing of a house in the bottom corner, sketched as if we were looking down at it from the sky with the roof off. "That is the house the Sung family lived in," Sterling Promise said.

I stared at the page, fragments of a family's story drawn out for strangers. I wondered if this family knew they were getting a Fire Horse. How simple my own story would look mapped out like this. Would someone still be able to see my heartache between the tight lines of characters? The frustration, the kicking and fighting? It would be hard to put all of that on paper.

"Ask me anything about it."

I studied the page. "How many rooms are in our house?"

"Seven."

I counted them. He was correct. "What are the walls made of?"

"Clay. Ask something hard."

"Who were our closest neighbors?" I said.

"The Long family."

"Where is their house?"

"To the west. You could see it from the front yard. What else?"

"What are they like?"

"What are they like?" Sterling Promise leaned over the book and looked at the page. "What do you mean?"

"What are they like as people? Are they good neighbors? Is the wife a gossip? Are the girls well behaved?"

He took the book back from me. "Where does it say what they're like?" he demanded, turning the pages.

"It doesn't. You have to imagine their story," I said.

"Imagine? I don't have to imagine. I only have to know what is in this book." He tapped the page.

"What if they ask something that is not in the book?"

"*Everything* is in the book."

"Not everything," I said, thinking of my own story again.

Sterling Promise looked at me. He was so close that I could smell the cabbage we had eaten for dinner on his breath. "If you give answers that are different from your uncle's, or mine, or your father's, they won't let us in. Our answers have to match, like a family's would," he said.

"Then we may want to practice questions that aren't in the book," I said through gritted teeth.

"This is important, Jade Moon."

I met his eyes. "It is important to me too."

"It is not the same," he said, leaning back. "You just want to leave China. I want to get *into* America."

"That's not true." The farther I got from China, the more I felt America tugging at the ties wrapped tightly around me — its loud laughter, its childlike enthusiasm, its bright Jell-O. I dropped my head.

Sterling Promise examined me for a few seconds, causing the blood in my face to warm.

"What do you think America will be like?" I asked him.

"Your uncle used to say that it was a place where stories began. A place where any ending was possible."

My eyes widened. "Did Uncle like stories?"

"He liked possibilities," he said. "I think America is a land that allows you to walk away from an old life into a better one."

I nodded slowly.

"And you, what do you think it will be like?"

"It will have . . . what do you call it? Getting to live as who you are?"

"Freedom," he said. But he wasn't looking at me.

"That is what it will be. Freedom."

"I wouldn't think you would care for freedom. It would take away all your reasons to fight."

I squeezed my hands into fists. "I don't enjoy the disapproval of Auntie Wu or the stares from the villagers when I am too loud or too bold. I don't relish the gossip of neighbors. I don't want to be married to someone just because he is the only one ignorant enough to take me. And, despite how I behave, even I am not so foolish to think that I can win a fight against the rest of the world."

He nodded, but said nothing.

I had revealed too much. I don't know why all my thoughts had to force their way out of my mouth. "Do you want to study some more?" I asked.

"I think that is enough for tonight. We *all* have to learn the answers in the book," he said, shooting a glance at Father's back.

"Father too? I thought he already had the merchant papers."

"Yes, but your uncle was supposed to be back long before now. Master Yue said the Americans might be suspicious and question him too. They are always looking for lies."

I looked down at the worn brown book in his hand. "Can I keep the coaching book? Just for tonight. To study."

He hesitated.

"You don't want me to ruin everything."

He handed over the book.

"Thank you," I said as I unfolded my legs and stepped toward the stairs. I thought of one more thing I wanted to say, stopped, and turned back.

"Sterling Promise, I won't make you rescue me again like you had to with the firework, or the grocer in Hong Kong. I won't get in the way of your dreams."

He smiled at me. "If that is true," he said, "I'll help you find the freedom you seek."

CHAPTER 11

I DIDN'T SEE MUCH of Sterling Promise or Father for the next few days. Father spent his days on his cot, sleeping or trying to sleep. Sometimes he came to meals, but only to sit listlessly while Sterling Promise taught us the details of our paper family.

"Do you think Father is sick?" I asked Mrs. Ying one night after dinner.

She shook her head. "It will pass. Traveling on the sea doesn't agree with everyone right away."

Traveling agreed with Sterling Promise. He made as many friends on the ship as he had in the village. I had my usual luck with friendships too. The sisters who shared our room whispered to each other when my voice was too loud. The mother and daughter-in-law preferred to ignore me. I spent my time with Mrs. Ying, who, thankfully, found me less intolerable than Father expected.

One morning, I stood on the deck watching the sun cut a sparkling path through the water. I leaned over the railing to look out onto the watery landscape stretched before me. Waves of white slapped against the ship's side, then tumbled away as the ship pushed through the water. The sky swept overhead, then poured into the vast horizon.

Two hands gripped the rail next to mine. "The sea is beautiful, isn't it?" Sterling Promise stood beside me. "Dangerous, but beautiful."

"True," I said, stepping onto the railing to feel the spray against my skin.

Sterling Promise shifted his gaze past me. "You shouldn't do that. People are staring."

I put my feet back on the deck. I had been making a study of the way Sterling Promise straightened his back around Father and Grandfather when he was at our house, versus the loose, swaying motions of his arms when he talked to the sailors at fan-tan in the evenings. He constantly molded himself to mirror the person he was speaking to, but I could not figure out the form he took with me.

When Mrs. Ying appeared beside me a moment later, he lifted his shoulders and pasted a wide smile onto his face. "Good morning, Mrs. Ying. Is your husband at breakfast? I wanted to speak to him."

"Good morning, Sterling Promise. Yes, I believe he is."

"I think I will go have breakfast too," I said, but Sterling Promise had already turned and walked toward the stairs.

"Sterling Promise," Mrs. Ying called. "I believe Jade Moon is going to breakfast. Could she join you?"

"She would not want to," he called back, his voice gentle but firm. "We are going to talk business."

"I don't mind," I said.

His feet pounded the stairs in answer.

Mrs. Ying looped her arm through mine and steered me toward the other end of the deck. "I wonder why he is in such a hurry to have breakfast with my husband. It certainly isn't the food."

Angry tears threatened my cheeks. "It's because I embarrass him. People stare at me. I don't think before I speak, and then I say too much. It is difficult to be what people want you to be." I wiped the tears away. "It will be different when I get to America. There will be more space and fewer lines."

"Jade Moon," Mrs. Ying said, "I know it is difficult to be a woman in China, but it is not easy to be a woman anywhere."

I looked away, running my fingers along the red thread that held Nushi's pouch around my neck. "Sterling Promise says America is a place of possibilities . . . hope. A story that isn't written to the end."

"Sterling Promise said that?"

"Actually, my uncle did."

"It is true. But there is something unsettling about a story that doesn't have its ending yet. The truth is that few Chinese women live freely in America," she continued. "Most stay locked in their houses. Others work in sweatshops like the lowest servants. Those are the lucky ones. Others are sold to men."

"Like concubines?"

"Like prostitutes."

"Oh." My cheeks reddened. "But your life is better."

"The first generation pays a heavy price for entry into America — men and women. My father paid it for me. America is not like China. If you are born in China, it is done. You are Chinese. No discussion. But in America, you earn being an American." We walked in and out of the hard shadows that divided the deck, mirroring the ropes and planks towering above our heads. "Jade Moon." She stopped and waited for me to meet her gaze. "Do you know what your father has planned for you in the new country?"

I shook my head.

"I ask because fathers don't bring their daughters to America. Some men bring their wives."

"I think Sterling Promise convinced my father to bring me," I said. I was still examining this idea, trying to figure it out, so that I could push away the uneasiness of not knowing, not understanding. "Maybe he understood how much I needed to go."

Mrs. Ying narrowed her eyes. "My husband tells me that Sterling Promise has dreams of making his fortune in America."

"That is true."

"I don't think you can trust him with your dreams. He will have enough trouble with his own."

"What do you mean?"

"It is just that . . . it doesn't always seem like the Americans want us there. When my father worked on the railroads, the white men would attack their camps. They even killed some Chinese. My husband cannot deliver the laundry on foot outside of Chinatown. People throw stones at him or scream 'rat' inches from his face." It looked like it pained her to say these things. "Most of us stay within the boundaries of Chinatown. Many stay between the four walls of our rooms or businesses. It wasn't very long ago that the hatchet men were fighting wars on the streets."

"Hatchet men?"

"Yes, brutal men who terrorize Chinatown as they battle over the inches of space and crumbs of power." The wind pushed her skirts tight around her legs. Mrs. Ying straightened her shoulders.

"The Chinese make everything from bamboo. It bends without breaking because it is strong, but flexible. The Americans, they build everything from metal. That takes fire. We are learning to survive in their metal country, but not without sacrifices."

I did not want to hear this. Not from Mrs. Ying. I longed to be sitting with Sterling Promise instead, listening to his stories about Gold Mountain and all its possibilities. "If it is so bad, why do so many people leave their homes to go there?"

"You are right. It is wonderful. Opportunities hang over every doorway and wait around every corner. America will promise you everything you want, but it will also make you gamble all you have to get it. That is the tragedy of it. You will love America. It will break your heart, but you will still love it."

Mrs. Ying put her arm back through mine and started walking again. "And, Jade Moon, find out why they brought you before we land. Women are brought to America either to be wives or prostitutes. You may have dreams, but your father and Sterling Promise have plans." She looked at me for a moment. "Now, are you ready to begin?"

"Begin what?"

"Your English lessons. Someone who has so much to say will need to speak the language."

For the next two weeks, I spent most of the day wrestling with the foreign words, twisting my tongue and lips around their sounds. Mrs. Ying taught me how to change the rising and falling notes of Chinese into the steady beats of English sentences. I was useless at putting words together, but I loved them alone. Mrs. Ying fed me a ceaseless stream of them, as many as I could hold in my head. We started with the things around us. I learned "ship" with its quick halt at the end, "chair" and "finger" that backed into the throat by the last letter. I learned "ocean" and "land" — their long sounds stretching at their middles. I let them all tumble through my lips.

But my favorite words were not always of objects I could touch. I loved words like "home" and "hope," "because" and "begin." I carried those more carefully, whispering them to myself, letting them sit on my tongue like candied ginger. They sounded like words used to cast a spell.

I was also good at learning the paper son story. We studied the coaching book night after night inside the swaying yellow cone of light from a lamp, while the boat creaked and groaned around us. Sterling Promise had been studying the book for months already. He taught Father and me generations of the Sung family. He taught us the rooms in their home and the homes in their village. The Sungs' grandfather, Uncle's paper father, had worked on the American railroad. He traveled back to his home village of Xi San every three years to see his family. We kept our rice bin in the northwest corner of the kitchen, three or four chickens at all times, and a pig or two once my paper grandfather began sending money from America. Our paper grandmother was blind during her last seven years of life, then she died in her bed and was buried in an auspicious spot — east-facing, with a good breeze.

I thought my paper grandmother sounded kind, like someone who would visit a sick neighbor or send her husband to plow the field of a farmer whose ox had just died. I wondered if my paper uncles wrote to her often enough when they were in America. I was even a little sad that I would never meet her. When I said that to Father and Sterling Promise, Father frowned and Sterling Promise shook his head.

None of this distracted me enough from the worry of why I was going to America.

One night, I arrived in the dining room to see Father by himself, leaning against the wall behind our bench, his arms crossed.

"Sterling Promise is coming. He met a man who owns a grocery in Chinatown, and they have been talking business," he said.

"Yes, Father."

We waited silently. After I had twisted and untwisted a loose thread on my pants several times, he spoke. "Are you comfortable with Mrs. Ying? She is looking after you?"

"Yes, she is wonderful!" I said.

"We will land soon. Then you will have to say good-bye."

"I will find out where she lives. She said I could visit her."

"Don't impose your friendship on Mrs. Ying." His nostrils flared, but I knew that I would have Jell-O with Mrs. Ying in America.

I changed the subject before he could forbid me anything. "It is strange learning all of this about a family we will never meet," I said.

"Yes, what a foolish way to decide who gets into a country. My brother . . ." But his voice faded.

"Father, what sacrifices did you make?"

"What?" His face quickly hardened to stone.

"When Sterling Promise came, he said the paper son was to repay a debt, for the sacrifices made."

Father's forehead wrinkled. "My brother left to pursue his own dreams, but he did not consider how the rest of his family would suffer because of them. He was a son who should have had more sons. He was the one Father trained to manage the land.

Everyone in the family must do their duty for it to survive. My duty was to study. To bring honor to the family. I was to be a scholar. When my brother left, I had to return to take care of the fields."

"But if he didn't want to work the fields —"

"What does it matter? His first responsibility is to his family. He rebelled against virtue, against order. Remember that, Daughter."

"Maybe it would have destroyed him, trying to be something he was not."

"He risked the survival of countless generations to avoid a life that was unpleasant for him?"

It was a heavy burden — the burden of generations. I looked over my shoulder to see Sterling Promise moving toward us. "What am I going to do when I get to America?" I asked Father.

Sterling Promise arrived in time to hear my question. "What do you mean?"

"That is not your concern," Father said to me.

"Father, please. I need to know." I was not sure whether to be more scared of what my father might say if I pushed the question, or what he would do if I didn't.

Sterling Promise sighed and said to Father, "Tonight, we need to go over what your brother did in America in case they ask you where he lived or what associations he belonged to."

Father whirled around to face him. "I know what my brother did in America. He brought shame to the family through his selfishness."

After he stormed away, I turned to Sterling Promise. "You have to tell me what he plans to do with me when we get to America."

"Your father *has* to learn this information. Everything depends on him." He flipped through a few pages in the coaching book. "I suppose we could study the layout of the town again."

I yanked the book out of his hand. "Mrs. Ying said that there are only two reasons to bring a woman to America, to marry her or make her a prostitute." He stared at me for a second, then started to tap at his leg with his middle finger. "Is Father going to sell me into prostitution?"

My voice must have been louder than I intended, because six sets of eyes snapped to us and then drifted politely away. Sterling Promise leaned forward and lowered his voice. "Is *that* what you are worried about? Don't be ridiculous, Jade Moon. Your father would never do that. Think of the shame."

I had. "But if he and Grandfather were desperate enough? They have been working to marry me off for years. Maybe this is their only chance to get rid of me."

He laughed. "You do have an imagination."

"This is serious."

"No, it is not. And we should not be discussing it."

I leaned back and crossed my arms. "Then, according to Mrs. Ying, they have arranged a marriage that could bring its own share of misery."

"I don't know your father's plans for you." He straightened. "But is marriage such a horrible fate?"

"It may be for me. What kind of man is desperate or foolish enough to marry me? I heard you tell Auntie Wu that you would never marry such a girl."

"I should never have said that."

"It doesn't matter. You can go where you wish, have any

opportunity within your reach. You have never had to hand your life over to fate, or had your hands tied with tradition."

"You know nothing about my life." He snatched back the coaching book.

"What have you not been able to find a way to get?" I said, the edge of my words sharp.

Sterling Promise looked up. He glanced at the people huddled around their own coaching books or gambling bets. "I will tell you if you stop asking why you were brought here too."

I nodded.

"It's the story of how I got from Master Yue's to your house. The story you asked for before." He paused. "And it's a secret, Jade Moon. Your father and grandfather can't know."

"I won't tell anyone," I said. People did not often share their secrets with me.

He set down the coaching book. "You saw the merchant center of Hong Kong, but I grew up in its slums. My family lived in a single room surrounded by more single rooms, with more people, more filth, more poverty. Fires and disease often ran through the slums, killing everything in their path. My parents and sister died in one of the fires. I went to work for Master Yue and took care of my two younger brothers. When I was ten, both of those brothers became sick and died. I could do nothing to help them. It happened so fast. One of the plagues."

"So you had no family," I said.

Sterling Promise nodded. "Do you know what it is like not to have a family? It is like being a branch fallen from a tree. It may look like freedom to you, but it is no different than the trapped feeling you have. It means you can get nowhere.

"Then your uncle came back to China to meet with Master Yue. He saw the trouble I caused Master Yue and the blows it gained me. He found out what happened to my parents and siblings. I think he knew what it was to be alone. He let me stay in the room he rented from the Yues.

"People told him that he should not adopt me, that death clung to me like wet leaves, but he did it anyway." He smiled a little. "When it was time for him to go back to America, he couldn't take me with him, because he didn't have his merchant papers yet. But he persuaded Master Yue to keep me in the house, learning as much of the business as I could. He said I would be his apprentice.

"When he returned to China last year to get me, he was already sick. He got weaker and weaker until he died. Just like my parents and siblings."

"His death is not your fault," I said.

"But people think it is. They smile and bow politely, but they keep me at a distance." He leaned forward. "If I stay in Hong Kong, I will always be the unlucky boy who carries death with him. No one will do business with me. Bad luck, good luck: It is all a game other people play with your life."

"You don't believe in luck?"

"What I believe isn't important. The foreigners don't care about it, and that is what matters."

"You don't have to carry those burdens in America," I said slowly, nodding. "It is a place where people don't care if you are cursed."

"Exactly," Sterling Promise said. "And that is a very valuable kind of freedom."

"The children at Master Yue's, they looked so hopeless. They looked like the empty firecracker shells scattered around them."

"That is why I am here. I can never go back to that life. I need a new life. The one I had in China was destroying me."

"I understand," I said. For all of his pleasing speeches and ready smiles, he was as unlucky as I was.

He picked up the coaching book, turning to the page we were studying. "You cannot tell anyone about my past, not your father, not Mrs. Ying. It is too shameful."

"I won't," I promised.

I did not tell Mrs. Ying about my conversation with Sterling Promise. I knew that there were more questions buried in his answers, and that my own questions had not received full replies. But now I saw why he was going, and that he had brought me for the same reason. Sterling Promise understood me, and I did not have to fight for that understanding. One of my layers of loneliness, one buried close to my center, melted away.

CHAPTER 12

AFTER THREE WEEKS AT SEA, the ship developed a specific smell — a combination of the cabbage and cured fish that we ate in rotation, and the odor of too many people crammed in a small space. The men spent most of their time on deck or at tables in gloomy corners, smoking and gambling and talking about China. They discussed the crops that wouldn't grow, the rain that wouldn't fall, the Japanese who would not compromise, the foreigners who would not leave. Mrs. Ying and I strolled around their hunched backs, learning new English words or practicing old ones.

In another week, the coast of America appeared. Sterling Promise, Father, and I stared at the land rising from the ocean. "What is it called again, the city we are going to?"

"San Francisco," Sterling Promise said. He pulled out the coaching book. "This is our last chance to study. Did our paper family have a garden?"

"Yes," Father said, starting to look around the deck.

"They had two gardens," I said. "One in front and another in the back."

"How many entrances are there?"

"Three," Father said.

"Four," I corrected.

Sterling Promise nodded. "How many times did Sung Feng Hao enter America?"

Father shrugged and walked away.

"Twice, once in 1907 and then again in 1916," I answered.

"And now a third time," Sterling Promise said.

"And now a third time," I repeated. Sterling Promise's eyes followed Father for a second before he tossed the book overboard.

"Why did you do that?" I cried out, the papers chewed up by the wake of the ship.

"The Americans can never know that we are a paper family. We are the Sung family now. You must only use this name," he said.

A tiny fracture in my heart opened when I let go of the Chan name. But it was a small crack, and I ignored it. I knew that one breath of the air in America, thick with its possibilities, would heal it.

When the boat docked, men in green uniforms, with pale, stern faces, boarded and started to move among us. They shouted directions in Chinese, their American tongues stumbling through the sounds. Those with certain papers were allowed to land. The rest of us were going to a place they called Angel Island to answer the Americans' questions and get the permission we needed to enter. Mrs. Ying picked up her bag and pressed a slip of paper into my hand. "My address. You will visit when you land."

"Yes, thank you."

"And you will not hesitate to come to me if you have any trouble."

I shook my head.

"Good. Then this is not good-bye," she said, smiling through teary eyes. "Jade Moon, it would be wonderful if America could be all you are hoping for."

"It will be," I said.

Once the passengers in first class and those with papers had gone ashore, the rest of us were packed into the lower deck of a waiting ferry. It pulled away from the dock and sped through two arms of land that hugged the bay. By the time we reached the island, the coast of America had faded into a pale brushstroke bleeding into sea and sky.

After we docked on Angel Island, the guards sorted us again — men from women, Chinese from pale — before allowing us off the ferry. Father and Sterling Promise were led away. Sterling Promise blended into the crowd of men until I could see only the top of his cap bobbing down the walkway. Father, trailing him, looked back at me before stepping off the boat.

Once the men had disappeared into a large white building, the guards shouted for us five women to follow. My legs felt unsteady, like the legs of a newborn goat. They expected the movement of the sea. I stumbled down the wide, wooden pathway that led from the boat toward another big white building that stood in the distance.

It was a beautiful island — green grass, and trees with thick trunks and giant palms sprouting from the tops. Thinner, taller trees rose from the coast until they disappeared into a gentle fog that hovered high in the air. The cries of seagulls mixed with the fading whistles and bells of the bay behind us.

I could not see America from where we landed on the island. I could see only the ocean that we came from. I tried to picture what

America was like from my glimpse of the docks and the fragment I saw here. It was big; I could see that. The buildings looked effortless, like the Americans had decided to build there and the land agreed. In China, the houses and rice terraces wore the cuts and scars of the long battle it took to create them. Here, the earth was soft and the wood was new.

The women around me stared ahead silently, the cloth of our shoes patting along the boards. I smiled broadly, looking from one scared face to another. They had kept a polite but cool distance from Mrs. Ying and me during the voyage. "Don't worry, we are here. We have arrived," I said to the old woman who stood next to me. She just clutched her bundle to her chest.

"Follow me," shouted a guard as he turned to enter the door at the front of the building, his voice loud to fill the vast space around it.

One of the sisters gestured back to the trunks sitting at the end of the dock. "Our trunks?"

The guard pointed to the shed they were piled next to. "They go there."

"Yes. Good," I said to him, glad for the chance to share the shreds of English I learned from Mrs. Ying. He must be taking us to where they ask the questions. I ran through the locations of the well and the large trees in the Sungs' village. I reviewed the aunts that lived in the house and the children they brought. I was ready. How long would the questioning take, an hour? Two?

The guard led our group down a hallway and into a large room. The white walls outlined a sparsely furnished space. A metal table stood in the center, next to a solitary wooden desk. A few smaller tables and screens lined the walls.

Two Americans stood behind the table — a man with a long white jacket over his clothes and a woman in a stiff white dress, her hair pulled into a knot at the base of her neck. A harsh smell stung the air.

"Medical exam," the man announced. "To enter America." The notes of his Chinese were flat and unpracticed, coming from the tip of his tongue.

I could feel a collective question form in the room, but we stayed still and silent. The woman in white passed out metal pans to each of us.

"We need stool samples," the man said in Chinese, accompanied by a series of bizarre gestures.

"Stool?" I said.

"Surely not," one of the sisters said.

The daughter-in-law shook her head and tried to hand the pan back. "Not necessary, thank you," she said in Chinese.

The man frowned. "You will not be able to leave. It is the law," he said in Chinese.

"This is humiliating," the old woman said to her daughter-in-law.

The woman directed us to different corners of the room, providing space but no privacy. After a few minutes, one of the sisters, her face red, returned from behind a table and handed her pan to the nurse. We stared, our mouths open. What was this? The American women peered into it, then, holding it at arm's length, paraded it over to the doctor. He disappeared with it through a door.

The American woman began to circulate around the room, scolding us. "You aren't doing anything. You will not be able to enter America if you don't do this."

My heart started to pound. They had us squatting like animals as we filled the pans, which were taken out one by one. I had traveled across an ocean for this? Did they think we were diseased? Too dirty for their shiny America?

Once we had all performed to their satisfaction, we were lined up. One by one, they poked and prodded us, looking at our teeth, tugging at our skin with their metal instruments. When it was my turn, I focused on a brown patch of skin below the man's right ear, where the bottom of his earlobe joined his face. I stared at it, enduring every press of cold metal against my skin. When he lifted my eyelid, I jerked my head away, but he said some words in English, put one of his huge hands on the back of my head, and yanked my eyelid up again. Anger poured into the hole that joy had left in my heart.

"Jump," he said in Chinese.

"Excuse me?"

"To see if your limbs work," he said, grabbing my arm and shaking it. I twisted my arm from his grip and lifted my head, staring above him as I jumped.

When he was done with me, he moved to my neighbor in line — the older Chinese woman who had kept to her bed through our journey here. Now I could see the crooked stance that had kept her confined, one hip jutting awkwardly above the other. The man looked her up and down and then said something to the American woman, who began to pantomime undressing. Terror spread across the old woman's face. Her daughter-in-law whispered, "To undress in front of a stranger. A man!"

"The shame," one of the sisters said sadly.

My chest was as tight as the fists at the end of my wrists. "No. You cannot. Wrong," I said loudly, the English words flying out of my mouth before I could stop them. Every eye in the room turned to look at me, the Americans with confusion, the Chinese with horror and outrage.

"Shut your mouth. What did you say?" the sister next to me hissed. "Who are you to talk to them like that? Do you want to get us all sent back to the boat?"

"It isn't supposed to be this way," I said in Chinese, reaching into my mind for the English words that might make them stop.

"You are nobody to them," she said through her teeth. "If you forget that, they will remind all of us. Get back on the next boat to China if you can't swallow your complaints."

The old woman shook her head and tried to pull away, but the American woman led her behind the screen, speaking soft, meaningless words and showing her gleaming teeth behind painted red lips. From the other side of the screen, we could see the woman's ankles and hear her sobs.

A pile of clothing gathered on the floor — jacket, pants, undershirt. The women around me gasped as the man stepped behind the screen.

I did not know what to think. The cruelty of it hammered inside me. Did the Americans know what they had made her do? We never undressed before strangers. Doctors in China came to a sick room to spread herbs over the bed, prescribe teas, or cut the bad air with knives. They looked at the patient, her skin, her hair. They did not put their hands on the body. The women in our village had children with the help of a female servant. If there was no servant, they had the child alone. It was difficult to imagine why a doctor would need to see a woman naked, but given the choice, many women would rather die of the disease than live with the shame.

After an eternity, the man moved to the table and wrote a few marks on a piece of paper. The pile of clothes disappeared from the floor. The old woman dressed and stepped out from behind the screen. I only saw her red eyes for one second before she cast them to the floor, wringing her hands in front of her.

The rest of the day was the longest journey of all — longer than the trip from our farm to Hong Kong, longer than our trip across the ocean to America. The Americans herded us from room to room, exchanging one of our papers for another. They did not ask us any questions from our coaching books. I understood little of what we did. I did know that this was not the America I imagined. The Americans moved us from place to place with an automated reluctance. There were no easy smiles. There was no loud laughter or bright bowls of Jell-O. By the time they led us into a dining hall, all the hope had poured out of the broken vessel that was my heart.

Long tables stood in neat lines and smells soaked the walls. Bright, large lights hung from the ceiling, but they only illuminated the dinginess of the place — flat gray walls and rough wooden tables standing on scuffed floors. We five new women joined a handful of others crowded around two tables in a corner. Plates of rice and limp, pale vegetables were put in front of us.

We newcomers listened as some of the other women offered advice.

"Now you just wait for your interrogation," one said.

"I have been through two," another said, sitting straighter. "They tried to send me home, but my husband has an expensive American lawyer. I told him that this worthless self should go back to China, that I would be less of a bother to him. But he and my sons are here, and he says it is time for me to join them. So I obeyed, of course."

"The food is always this bad," a third woman said, picking up a green lump from her plate. "You can have people bring you food from the mainland. My husband sends food three times a week."

I turned to the woman to my left. "My name is Jade Moon," I said.

She was staring listlessly at the plate of food in front of her. It took her a moment to realize that I was speaking to her.

"Snow Lily," she said. He voice was almost a whisper.

"How long have you been here?"

She shook her head. "Almost a year."

Impossible, I thought.

When the women had shared all of the advice they could think of, they questioned us. Where in China was your village? What does your husband do? Do you have children? One of the women turned to me and asked, "Is your husband here?"

I considered lying, but I had to lie about so many other things. "No, my father." I stabbed at the rice on my plate.

"Ah, you are meeting your husband, then, in America. Spring Blossom is also meeting her new husband. It was all arranged in China." She nodded toward a wisp of a woman at the end of the table, only a little bit older than me, who gave me a weak smile. Her dark hair hung in a single braid down her back. With her hands resting in her lap, she seemed to curl into herself.

"I am not meeting my new husband," I said.

The woman sitting to my right studied me. "How old are you?"

"Seventeen."

"Then your mother has begun to make arrangements."

"No," I said flatly.

"Of course she has. She just hasn't spoken of it to you yet."

"She died when I was born."

The woman wrinkled her face, no doubt taking in the hair flying out of my braid, my fidgeting hands, my eyes, which were too wide to be called almond-shaped, and my cheeks that were too full and red from years spent by the terraces when I should have been inside embroidering seat cushions. Without a mother, husband, or sons, she knew I was worthless.

I returned her stare. "When I am American —"

The woman smirked. "Little Sister, you are not American. You are Chinese."

"I will be American," I snapped back. The anger strengthened me. I could feel it coursing though me, reminding me why I was here, on this island, in this country.

But most of the women covered their mouths as they laughed. Only two did not laugh — Spring Blossom, who looked at her hands in her lap, and Snow Lily, who seemed unaware of anything said at the table.

"You are not going to be American," my challenger said. "You are going to live in America. Do you think they treat Americans like this?" She nodded toward the guards with their lines of buttons, pockets of keys, and cold faces.

"I am sure they have their reasons." My voice skipped a little with the nervousness I was trying to hide.

The woman leaned forward. "The reason is that they don't want you here."

I was tired. My head hurt. I focused on the worn surface of the table.

"Oh, I see," the woman continued. "You thought they would welcome you." She turned to the other women at the table. "This one believes in her dreams so much that she will spend all of her life asleep."

I rose to find another table where I could sit alone. As I swung my legs over the bench, my arm knocked against my plate. The plate of rice and vegetables slammed into the woman's shoulder and chest and tumbled onto her lap before clattering onto the floor. Everyone in the dining hall stared. Even the guards and kitchen workers watched me with cool curiosity.

The woman stood and faced me. Bits of rice fell to the floor from her shirt. She gripped her fists at her sides, leaned forward, and hissed into my face, drops of saliva flying into my cheeks. "You don't belong here. Don't think I did not hear about the trouble you made at the medical examination," she said, her words quiet but cutting. "You must be the shame of your family if they had to send you all the way to America. If your face comes within reach of my hands again, I will scratch at it until it matches your ugly manners."

The women exchanged looks down the table. It was the same story I had tried to leave behind in China.

After dinner, the guards brought us to a long, narrow room with metal beds stacked along the walls. A stench crawled into the room from the bathroom. I pressed the pouch Nushi had given me close to my chest. The bent old woman had been taken away after the medical exam, and her daughter-in-law, who had taken care of her throughout the journey, looked lost. She took a tattered shirt from her bag and held it to her face, inhaling its smell. One of the sisters from the boat burst into tears. The other sister put her arm around her, leading her away from the group. The strangeness of the place swirled around me. It crept inside of me. Nothing was right — the room too big, the smells too strong. There were too many voices, all high and soft.

Those of us who survived the ordeal of the first day cried that first night, foreign-smelling pillows soaked in tears, the metal beds squeaking between sobs. I wept as silently as I could, clutching close to my heart the red pouch Nushi had given me with the piece of jade inside. I thought of our rice terraces, their beauty and promise built over generations, and I tried to remember that dreams, like terraces, are built one stone at a time.

CHAPTER 13

THE NIGHT WAS LONG and filled with the sounds of strangers' breath instead of sleep. The next morning, women bustled around their beds, combing their hair and dampening their faces. Those whose bunks were near mine moved their belongings to other beds until my bed became its own island surrounded by empty mattresses.

After breakfast, guards escorted us back down the short covered walkway to our sleeping quarters. We filed into the front sitting room. I noticed that Snow Lily lay back down on her bed. Several women pulled out their sewing and gathered in one corner. Another group started to unpack a set of dominoes. No one invited me to join them, their silent disapproval filling the air around me.

"They keep us in here all day. We only go outside once a week," said a gentle voice.

I looked up to see Spring Blossom, the only one who had not laughed when I said I was going to be American. "Well, that is good."

"Why is that good?" she asked.

"I would hate for the women to miss any display of my faults — my temper, my clumsiness."

"Oh," Spring Blossom giggled. "They would be sorry to miss that. Do you also have warts?" she asked. "They would love it if you had a few warts!"

I smiled. "Of course. Someone as unpleasant as I am is sure to have warts."

The laughter tumbled from deep inside our bellies. The other women scowled at us, but it had been so long since I had laughed that it only made me laugh more.

"I admired what you did at dinner," Spring Blossom said. "The way you stood up for yourself."

I let out a snort. A few women turned to stare again.

"You have spirit, fire in your belly. I wish I had more of that."

"No, you don't," I said.

The woman I spilled rice on came out of the bathroom. "Spring Blossom, come show us the slippers you were sewing yesterday. We want to admire them."

I hid my face so no one would see the hurt that would come when Spring Blossom chose the society of all the other women over mine, as she should. How did women always know what to take from you — the thing that would leave the largest hole?

Spring Blossom hesitated. "In a moment, Auntie."

The woman huffed off to join the others.

I turned back to Spring Blossom. "That is very fortunate, your marriage."

"Yes. That is what everyone tells me." A flicker of unease swept across her face. It was quick, like when the wind blows ripples on the surface of the water.

"Do you know the man you are going to marry?"

She shook her head and looked at her lap.

I tried again, making my voice cheerful. "I am sure you exchanged pictures or gifts?"

This time her head did not even move. I could practically hear Nushi scolding me for my boldness. When the silence began to hang heavy between us, I searched for a way to continue the conversation without letting any more stupidity spill from my mouth. Spring Blossom shifted her weight. I was sure she was leaving to join the other women. "Would you like to hear a story?"

She lifted her head.

"Nushi, our servant, always told the Cowherd and Weaver Girl story when I was sad."

Her eyes found mine again. "Yes, please."

Spring Blossom was a better audience than me. She did not interrupt. She let her gaze slip past the walls that surrounded us, tracing the outline of the holes in Cowherd's coat, finding the rainbow of robes in the grayness of the sitting room. Her hand clutched at her chest when Cowherd and Weaver Girl were separated. Her cheeks dripped with tears when they were reunited.

When I had finished, Spring Blossom looked at me. "I wish love was that beautiful."

"You don't think it is?"

"Only in stories."

"Then where do the stories come from?" I asked.

"Deep inside of us, where we must bury what we desire most in order to protect it," she said softly, tugging at the ends of her sleeves.

*   *   *

I did not cry the second night. Or the third, or any of the days that followed. No one could tell me when my interrogation might happen. Most women had been there for weeks, some for months, though Snow Lily had been there longest of all. Some were waiting for relatives to come and be interviewed to prove their stories were true. Others were trapped in cycles of questionings, denials, and appeals. Every night, I tried to recite in my mind all the facts I could think of about the Sung family to keep them fresh and real for me.

The women had created a routine out of the limited activities available. In the morning, we watched the ferry arrive, carrying the guards and translators and sometimes new residents — Chinese, Japanese, Russians, even Europeans, all wearing the same lost faces. The people with pale skin would leave on the ferry that evening or maybe the next day, but the Chinese stayed locked in the barracks.

In the afternoon, some women sewed, others chatted. Hours were lost staring at the walls, listening jealously to the birds outside our window. Tedious chores grew heavy with importance because we had nothing else to do. We washed the same clothes to wear day after day, drying them on lines hung between the beds, then wrapping ourselves in the stiff, stale odor of the fabric.

Whatever we did, guards shadowed every movement. They lurked in the entryway of the barracks. They poked through the deliveries that some women received from the mainland. Matrons sat inside the barracks during the day to watch over us. The guards' and matrons' comings and going startled us back into the reality that we were prisoners, and the oppression of their stares made every move, every word, an effort.

Eventually, the day would end, and then, finally, we could escape into sleep for a few hours.

This routine left the women plenty of time to scrutinize one another's every word and move, and to battle over subtle shifts of power — all that this world of four walls offered. There were the petty, predictable arguments over missing belongings. When the women weren't maneuvering to get the chair with the cushion, they wore through all the wrongs they had suffered at the hands of the Americans, each trying to outdo the others, almost relishing every barbaric act. It pulled them apart and drew them together in a messy, frail patchwork of uncertainty.

I chose to go to the English classes the Americans offered. The woman did not teach the colorful words Mrs. Ying had used to feed my curiosity. Instead we learned polite phrases favored by Americans — "Good morning," "Nice to meet you," "How are you?" The last one we were taught to answer properly — "I am fine" or "good" or "quite good." What honest answer could you give when you were trapped in a prison on an island?

I spent part of my time letting my mind wander to Sterling Promise — his words, his looks. I wasn't sure why I was so willing to let him linger in my mind, other than an urgent need for distraction. I also thought about Father. Now that the novelty of travel had faded, it struck me how difficult this journey must have been for him — away from his land, his home, all the things that he had wrapped into the layers of his skin, and pretending to be the brother who had abandoned him.

One morning a new energy hummed in the air. The other women did not get out their sewing. Instead they sat, staring at the door. "What is happening?" I asked Spring Blossom, who was looking over her belongings, spreading them out across her cot.

"We are going to visit our trunks. They let us get the things we need once a week."

"Mostly, you just check what was stolen from you this week," another woman declared.

An older woman clicked her tongue and shook her head. "Nothing was stolen. You wasted your soap."

"I brought plenty of soap," the woman replied and stomped away.

The first woman turned back to me. "You can get anything you need."

"I'm not sure I need anything," I said.

"Of course you want to see your things. And you can go outside," Spring Blossom said.

I looked at Snow Lily, who was curled up on her bed as usual. At mealtimes, the women tried to get her to eat, but she did not seem to hear them. Sometimes her gaze would snap back to the present, sweep over the walls around her, then drift far away again.

"She won't come," Spring Blossom said. "She hasn't visited her trunk for months."

The door clicked open and the chatter stopped. A guard motioned for us to follow. Outside, the sun on my face breathed life into me. It was not as bright as it had been on the day we arrived. Instead, a layer of gray fog hung in the air just above the tops of the trees. The air was fresh with a hint of the salt and water that surrounded us. It clung to our faces, damp and cool. For a moment, I was not a prisoner. My heart opened a little with the old feeling of possibility.

Our belongings were stored down near the docks. The guards escorted us with their customary aloof distrust. But they didn't prevent us from walking slowly, savoring the sun and sky. When we slipped inside the shack that waited at the end, my eyes had to adjust to the dim light. Only then did I see the trunks and bags stacked around the room.

I soon found my trunk. It looked like it had come from another world. When I lifted its lid, smells of the past wrapped around me — the ginger that always covered Nushi's fingers, the river, the sprouts of rice in the fields. The trunk was not the chaotic mess I'd accused Nushi of packing. She had stacked our belongings in neat layers. On top sat soaps, cloth, and other necessities. When I dug a little, I found some of my clothes, a blanket that I used on cold nights. Below that lay the half-finished embroidery that I had abandoned several years ago. I ran my fingers over each item — my rice bowl, my combs, my slippers from the New Year, my favorite quilt, the one that was my mother's. Almost at the bottom was a box of writing I had done when Father thought that calligraphy might teach my wild mind order and discipline.

Something was odd about what Nushi had packed. I dug deeper, pushing past piles of my tunics, pants, and skirts. I tipped the lid down to make sure that I was looking at the right trunk. What was Nushi thinking? She had only packed my belongings, nothing of Father's.

Then I spotted something unfamiliar — a handkerchief, bright red and embroidered with mallard ducks. It was the kind of handkerchief a woman exchanged with her husband at her wedding, to symbolize her wish to stay together forever, like two mallard ducks mating for life. I pulled at the corner and laid it across my hands.

"A wedding handkerchief," said one of the women, trotting up next to me on her bound doll-feet. "You said you were not getting married."

"I'm not," I said.

"It is beautifully made," the woman said, taking the handkerchief and holding it to the slant of light cutting through the stirred-up dust. "Did you do this?"

"No."

"I did not think so." She held it out to me, and I let the silk tumble back into my hands.

I folded the handkerchief carefully and tucked it into the waist of my pants. I was glad that I would not be here when Father opened the trunk for the first time.

CHAPTER 14

SPRING BLOSSOM AND I NICKNAMED some of the women. There was First Wife, who reigned over us like Angel Island was just an extension of the women's quarters in her family's home in China, making us listen to endless talk about her sons and husband. The woman I spilled the plate onto became Big Teeth, because the permanent scowl she wore pushed her mouth out over her chin, like it was crowded with giant teeth. Everyone called the oldest woman in the barracks Po Po. She rarely spoke, her sorrows etched into the lines of her face. Other names I did not bother to learn.

Women came and went on waves of joy, fear, sorrow. Some were told that they could land and sent down the dock to the ferry. The rest of us were left to wait and wonder.

One day, a guard handed Snow Lily a letter. Her hands shook as he passed it to her. Then she went back to her bed and lay down, clutching it to her chest.

"She is being sent back to China," Spring Blossom whispered.

"How do you know?"

"That is always what the letter says."

My heart started to tremble at the idea of holding a letter someday.

That night, I woke to the sound of the other women rising from their beds. Some had gathered at the entrance to the bathroom; others were huddled in a far corner. I joined Spring Blossom near First Wife's bunk. One of the matrons came out of the bathroom, followed by a guard carrying Snow Lily. She was limp, her chest barely rising and falling. They hurried out of the barracks.

"What happened?" I asked Spring Blossom.

"She couldn't go back," First Wife whispered. "She tried to hang herself instead."

Spring Blossom put her hand over her mouth. Another matron shooed us back to our beds. I stared into the darkness, thinking about what Nushi said — how dangerous desperation can be.

The next morning, the events of the night cast a shadow over the women's quarters. A fog had rolled across the island and settled on it, so we could not watch the ferry come and go. The English teacher did not come, and no guards arrived to let us onto the small walkway outside our barracks. Sewing rested in the most industrious hands. Most of us did not even bother to get anything out to do.

Women sighed. Chairs creaked.

Spring Blossom sat in silence the whole morning, a grief-stricken look on her face. I had sat by her at breakfast, which she didn't eat, and asked her questions, which she didn't answer. Now, just as I was considering shaking some reaction from her, she turned to me. "Tell a story, Jade Moon."

"Of course. What story would you like to hear?"

"Not just for me. For everyone."

Big Teeth's scowl deepened. "I have never been entertained by stories. What can stories do for us, stuck in this prison?"

But the women had already embraced Spring Blossom's request.

"Oh, please, tell us a story."

"I need something else to think about."

"This day will never end if you do not."

I shook my head at Spring Blossom. These women would only criticize any story I told — "Jade Moon, you did not mention the lucky charm he carried with him," or "Jade Moon, that story is not as good if you don't describe the fish they had for dinner," or simply a chorus of "I am a very poor storyteller, but when I tell that story . . ." But when I saw the sad look in her eyes, I found myself moving to the center of the room, and the other women shifted their chairs to face me.

It is important when you tell a story to tell the right story. I studied the women I had lived with for almost three months. Some had the even skin of youth. Others had the soft lines of age around their eyes, eyes that hungered for home. When the women rubbed their hands together in anticipation, they were hands that had sewn, cooked, dug soil, birthed children. Everyone wore the dark shadows of grief or fear. I knew the Cowherd and Weaver Girl story best, and the first words of the story sat on my tongue, but when I looked at the women, I understood what Big Teeth had meant. What would she do with a love story, especially after last night? These women needed a story about people trying to get somewhere impossible. They needed a story about promises kept and broken, a story about sacrificing everything for a chance at something beautiful. I needed that too, and I knew which story I would tell them.

I began, "There once was a woman who could weave cloth that was so lifelike that the roses she wove into the gardens smelled sweet, and the breeze she wove through the branches brushed against your skin."

The women leaned forward, imagining such weaving. Some nodded their heads.

"She was not a wealthy woman. Her husband had died, leaving her to raise three sons. But she worked hard, and she and her sons lived comfortably in a small house on the edge of town. One day the woman went into town to sell a basketful of cloth to a merchant. When she walked into his shop, she saw a painting of a faraway land on the wall. It was like nothing she had ever seen before. In the painting, a beautiful pavilion made of white marble rested at the base of a cliff. Vines twisted up its sides, spraying flowers along its walls. Swaying bamboo surrounded the pavilion, and behind it grew pines, where deer nibbled at soft moss on the ground. Beside the pavilion sat a pool of clear water filled with gold-colored fish."

"It sounds beautiful," one of the women said. The others mumbled agreement, and then looked at me to continue.

"She asked the merchant, 'Will you sell the painting?'

"The merchant shrugged.

"'I will give you all the cloth I made this month for the painting.'

"The merchant knew a good bargain, and he immediately accepted."

"I think she should have haggled more over the price. To pay a month of weaving!" Big Teeth said.

"But think how beautiful the painting was," another woman said.

Big Teeth nodded and rested her sewing in her lap. "True, true."

"It *was* beautiful, but when she brought it home and showed it to her sons, they shook their heads. Their mother was getting old. They would have to accompany her to town from now on to make sure she did not make any more reckless bargains.

" 'You traded all of your weaving for this!' the first son said.

" 'You'd better get back to work. We cannot eat the painting or live in the pavilion,' the second son scolded.

"The third son looked at the painting. 'My brother is right. We cannot live in the pavilion. But you could weave the scene into cloth, Mother. Your weavings are so lifelike! Think how beautiful it would be.' "

First Wife nodded her head, "Ah, she does not seem reckless now. That cloth will fetch a heavy price."

"Exactly," I said. "So the woman took the third son's advice and began weaving the picture into cloth. She worked from early in the morning until the last traces of sunlight faded from the sky. Her first and second sons grumbled because their mother no longer made cloth to sell in town. The sons had to chop firewood to sell instead. But the third son defended her, saying that this was something their mother needed to finish. He chopped twice as much firewood as his older brothers so they would complain less.

"Meanwhile, their mother continued to work on the cloth. After a year, tears started to flow from her tired eyes. After two years, those tears turned into blood that stained the sun in her weaving red. After three years, she finally finished.

"She showed the cloth to her sons, who stood speechless. They could hear the rustling of the bamboo leaves against each other and feel the warmth of the sun on their faces. She laid the cloth on the ground so the heavens could see it, but just as she unrolled the last edge, a gust of wind blew it high into the heavens.

"The woman wailed. She begged her sons to find it. The eldest son said, 'I will find it, Mother. Then we will sell it and be rich.'

"The son traveled for many days before he came to an old woman sitting in front of her house at the bottom of a stone mountain. 'Old woman,' the first son said. 'Have you seen my mother's weaving?'

" 'I have,' the old woman said. 'The fairies from Sun Mountain have taken it. If you want to go there, you must take a rock and break off your two front teeth. Place them in my horse's mouth, and he will fly you over Flame Mountain. There, the fire will burn you, but you must not cry out or you will die. If you make it through that, the horse will take you to the Sea of Ice.'

" 'What is that?' The first son was already losing his courage, and almost too afraid to ask.

" 'At the Sea of Ice, freezing water and blocks of ice will crash against you, but you must not shiver or you will die. Then you will come to Sun Mountain.'

" 'And the fairies will return my mother's weaving?'

" 'First you will have to climb to the top of the mountain. Then you will have to convince the fairies to give you the weaving. They may give it back to you.' She rubbed her hands along the arms of the chair. 'Or they may kidnap you, and keep you as their servant forever.'

" 'I don't want to go through that for a piece of cloth,' the son said.

" 'Of course you don't,' the old woman said. 'Why don't you just take this gold and go home?' "

"Ah, that isn't a good son," several of the women muttered.

"She is lucky to have two more. If she had to rely on that one when she was old . . . ," another said, looking meaningfully at the woman beside her.

I waited. "Oh, he behaved very badly. He took the gold, but he did not go home. He was greedy, so he decided to live in the city.

"When the first son did not return, the weaver woman sent her second son to find the cloth. But after the old woman explained the path to Sun Mountain, he also took the gold and went to the city to live.

"After losing two sons, the old woman did not want to send her youngest son, but he insisted on going. 'Don't worry, Mother. I will bring back your beautiful weaving.'

"When he got to the old woman, she explained what he needed to do. The youngest son did not hesitate. He knocked out his teeth with a rock and placed them in the horse's mouth. The horse flew over Flame Mountain, where the fire licked at the third son, but remembering the cool pool of water in his mother's weaving, he did not cry out. Then the horse took him through the Sea of Ice, where the frigid waters crashed against him. Still, he did not shiver; thinking of the bright sun his mother had woven warmed his skin. Then he climbed Sun Mountain. When he got to the top, he found the fairies sitting at their looms around his mother's weaving.

"He told the fairies that it was his mother who made the weaving, and that he had come to retrieve it. They begged him to allow them one more night with the weaving so they could finish their own cloth. The third son agreed. But early the next morning, when the sun began to rise in the sky, the fairies stretched out their weaving next to his mother's, and it fell short. One fairy, devastated that she would never have such a beautiful weaving, stitched herself into

117

his mother's cloth and disappeared. The third son rolled his mother's cloth up and took it back home.

"His mother felt such peace at having her wonderful cloth back. She took it outside to share with the heavens. Another gust of wind came, but this one did not take her weaving away. It stretched it. The cloth grew and grew until the family's hut disappeared and the weeds from their garden vanished. In their place appeared a white marble pavilion, a grove of bamboo and pine trees, a clear pool of water, and a lovely lady in red. It was the fairy from Sun Mountain. The youngest son married her, and they lived in great joy in the paradise the mother had created.

"One day two men, dirty and tired, stumbled to the gate and peered inside. They were the two older sons, returning from the city penniless. But once they saw that their younger brother had done what they were not willing to do for their mother, they were too ashamed to go in."

The women sat in silence for a few moments. Then the chorus of voices began.

"That story is very true," one said softly.

"Yes, very true," echoed another.

"Sometimes, it seems impossible to hold on to what is most precious," said a woman, shaking her head.

"It would be wonderful to have such a lovely place to call home, wouldn't it?" Spring Blossom said.

"Without invasions or fighting," Big Teeth said.

"Or guards who shout orders no one can understand," another added.

"Free from soldiers who look like children," a woman said.

"And act like animals," First Wife said.

"We all know why she tried to kill herself," said Big Teeth, wiping tears from her eyes. "It sometimes seems like the only escape."

A hush settled over the room.

"I don't know what my husband was thinking, bringing us here," said one.

"I don't know what mine was thinking, leaving us in China for so long," said another.

"Dreams come at a high price," one woman sighed.

The woman next to her put her hand on the woman's shoulder. "And there is no bargaining with luck."

"Thank you, Jade Moon," Big Teeth said, getting up and bowing to me.

"Yes, thank you," said another, and then another.

It felt good, their acceptance. I did not know how much I wanted it.

"Now I have somewhere to go when I feel trapped here," said First Wife, and I could tell that she was sitting in the marble pavilion, listening to the bamboo rustle in the wind.

The next morning, as I scooped rice from the serving bowl, one of the kitchen workers appeared at my side and began to pour more soggy rice from a pan onto the pile. Without looking at me, he said, "Sterling Promise wants to meet you at the hospital."

I looked up at him.

"Don't look up," he said. I dropped my head. "Tomorrow morning. Pretend you are sick. The guard will take you there."

"Why? What does he want?" I asked, but the kitchen worker had already walked away. A guard by the door was staring at me, so I quickly looked the other direction. The matrons had explained the strict rules against communicating with relatives in the men's quarters. We could be sent back to China if we were caught. Still, I felt a bloom of warmth inside at the thought of Sterling Promise taking that risk with me.

First Wife leaned over her neighbor and hissed, "What was that about? Who is this Sterling Promise?"

"The young man we came with. My adopted brother."

"Ahhh, that explains the wedding handkerchief." The women down the table nodded and resumed picking at their food.

"How does it explain the wedding handkerchief?" I asked.

First Wife tilted her head. "Your father is a landowner, yes?"

I nodded.

"And I believe that you are the only child," said First Wife.

"He was already adopted by your uncle," one added.

"So he says," another pointed out.

Their words swirled around me.

"It would an acceptable marriage for a boy with no family," said the older woman.

"And I am sure your father wants to see you married," said First Wife.

"Then you can bring your bad luck to your husband's house," said Big Teeth, the corners of her mouth lifting slightly as she winked at me.

"Seems like a lot of trouble for a match," tried Spring Blossom.

"But for a Fire Horse, like this one . . . ," said First Wife, jerking her chin at me.

"Yes, of course," agreed the older woman.

"A mother-in-law would never allow such disaster."

"But a young man . . . with no family."

"Who could inherit land."

I listened as they picked at my life as if it was a piece of their embroidery, pulling apart the messy bits and tying the ends off neatly.

"Are you saying that Sterling Promise has agreed to a marriage with me?" I asked.

"Unless you have a more pleasant sister he can marry," snorted Big Teeth.

"So that he can have a family? Land?"

"It isn't for your grace and patience," said First Wife.

I shook my head. "How can you be so sure?"

"We are women. We know," said First Wife, patting my hand.

Is this why Nushi packed the wedding handkerchief? Is this why all the things in the trunk are mine? Is Father leaving me here? I was dizzy with all the deception.

I stood up. "Sterling Promise isn't tricking me. He wouldn't," I said, agitated.

"Why would they tell you? They know you will cause trouble," Big Teeth said, shaking her head.

"Marriage is good. It brings you sons," said First Wife. She paused, studying my flushed cheeks. "But love . . . love is dangerous."

The other women nodded, their eyes deep and dark. I looked at Spring Blossom, but her gaze was fixed somewhere far away.

CHAPTER 15

THE NEXT DAY, when the guard came to get us for breakfast, I pointed to my stomach and made a face of pain.

"Hospital," he said indifferently, steering the other women through the door, then locking it behind him. My stomach *was* feeling unsettled. Not because of the gray meat they served us, but because I was going to see Sterling Promise again. A few minutes later, the guard returned, motioning for me to come with him.

I rose from my bed and trailed behind him to another of the island's endless wooden buildings. I followed him up the steps and through the door. Sun poured into the room through a line of windows and settled on a row of beds with white sheets tucked neatly over mattresses. I could smell a wisp of the sharp odor from that first day they examined us.

The guard guided me to a woman in the same white, crisp dress those women had worn the day of my arrival. "Nurses," the woman who taught us English called them. My heartbeat sped up, and I wrapped my arms around my waist. Was Sterling Promise leading me into that ordeal again? After the guard and the woman exchanged a few words, the guard left, and the nurse sat me in a chair before leaving the room.

She came back with a bottle of thick liquid. She passed me a thumb-sized cup of it and went through the motions of drinking the liquid. I was shaking my head at her when Sterling Promise appeared at the door.

My breath caught in my throat when I saw him again. After almost three moons, his hair looked longer, his clothes more threadbare, but his brown eyes still held the same intensity they'd always had.

Sterling Promise did a much better job of having a sore stomach. He held his hands over his middle, his forehead crossed with lines of suffering. The nurse brought him the same medicine, which he took immediately.

Sterling Promise ran through a series of English words with the nurse, ending with "Thank you." She widened her smile. He indicated the beds, and she nodded.

He lay down on a bed. The nurse pointed me to one a little farther down, then left the room. As soon as she disappeared through the door, Sterling Promise rolled on his side to face me.

"What was the medicine?" I twisted the white sheet around my finger. I felt unsteady next to him, like when I first stepped off the boat.

"It won't hurt you. It does nothing." He looked over his shoulder at the door, then continued, "They started my interrogation yesterday. They will probably ask more questions today."

"Oh" was all I could say.

"It is very difficult. They ask questions that are not in the book too." He smiled. It was his real smile, and the warmth from it made me melt. "You were right. I wanted to tell you my answers so that yours will match. If they don't, they will never let me" — I lifted my head to stare at him — "*us* in."

Sterling Promise went through the additional questions and his answers in a low voice. When he finished, we lay there quietly for a minute.

"Are you doing well?" he asked.

"Yes."

The nurse stepped into the room. Sterling Promise rolled onto his back again, and we went silent. She turned down the sheets on one of the beds and left again.

He turned his head and studied me. "You look well."

My chest tightened again. "How is Father?"

"They questioned him last month. I don't think his answers match mine or the paper family. He is why this is taking so long." Sterling Promise sighed. "I have heard that it is more difficult for women. They do not want to let women into America."

"What?" I shot up.

"Quiet! We aren't supposed to be talking," he hissed. "This is what I mean. If you want us to get in, you have to follow the rules."

I felt tears pushing at the corners of my eyes. "What rules? Where are the rules? I would like to see them. They make up the rules as they go along." The funny feeling in my chest was gone, replaced by the familiar fire.

"Of course, they make them up. They are *their* rules. The Americans' rules. And we are in America now. If they make up rules, we have to figure them out and follow them."

I lay back down.

"I am just warning you," he said gently. "They are looking for a reason to send you back."

I stared at the ceiling.

"Jade Moon, if you don't get in . . ."

I didn't want him to say it. "I'm getting in. I *have* to get in."

The nurse walked in again. Sterling Promise hastened to look away from me, but she wasn't interested in us. She was leading Snow Lily to the bed across from me. Snow Lily shuffled slowly across the floor. Her ghost had hung over the women's quarters since the night she had been carried out. It was strange seeing her here, flesh and blood. The distance that used to be in her eyes was gone, but it was replaced with a deep, real pain. The nurse helped her lie down, then tucked the sheets and blankets around her.

Snow Lily started to wail. I could hear in her cries every fear I had of getting my own letter. Her sorrow sat on my chest like a stone, making it hard to breathe. The nurse spoke to her in the soothing tone people use with children. I squeezed my eyes shut, but her cries echoed inside me. I wanted to be anywhere but here.

"I can't stay in this room another second," I said.

"We have to stay until a guard comes."

"Please," I said, pressing my hands to my face.

Sterling Promise was silent. When I lowered my hands, he was staring at me, his forehead wrinkled. "I will get you out of here," he said. He rose and walked over to the nurse. "I feel better," he said to her in English.

"Good, good," the nurse said. Snow Lily released another long wail.

"You need help?" Sterling Promise said, reaching for the glass of water sitting by Snow Lily's bed. "I stay and help." He rattled through a long string of English, moving around the bed, picking up one thing and then another while Snow Lily cried and the nurse shook her head. As she was tucking in a corner of the blanket Sterling Promise had pulled loose, he looked out the window. "Oh, guard. Go or stay? I can stay."

"Go, go," the nurse said without looking up from Snow Lily. Sterling Promise signaled me to come with him. I stood up silently and followed him out of the building. There was no guard in sight.

When we got outside, I took deep breaths and let the sun dry the tears on my face. It felt strange to be on the island without a guard or the other women. I looked over my shoulder. "How did you do that?"

"It was mostly luck. And asking for the right thing at the right time. She wanted us to leave, so it was easy to convince her we could." Sterling Promise seemed to expand in this wider environment. His arms swayed when he walked. His chin lifted higher.

"You look different," I said, watching his long strides. "You look . . . American."

Another wide smile broke across his face. "Yes, I have been watching the guards and the men in the administration building," he said. "I am practicing for when we cross to San Francisco."

We walked down the path to the women's and men's barracks. "The men are still at breakfast. I want to show you something." He opened the men's door.

"I can't go in there," I said. "I have been trying *very* hard to stay out of trouble."

"We are just going into the front room. No one is here right now. They are eating breakfast. You will want to see this."

I looked over my shoulder. "Why isn't the door locked?"

"They aren't as careful if there isn't anyone here to lock up. Remember, they are trying to keep us in, not out." I hesitated.

Sterling Promise held the door open. "I told you, we won't get caught. If you don't want to go inside . . ." He started to close the door.

I put my hand out to stop it. "No," I said. "I want to." I might not want to go inside, but I also wasn't ready for our time together to end.

I slipped into the dimly lit room. The air was thick with the earthy smell that men wear in their skin. Wooden planks lined the walls. Sterling Promise took me down the hall to a small room in the front. It was empty, but the walls were covered with writing in ink or carved into the wooden planks. I walked around the space, running my hands over the characters, reading them.

> *There are tens of thousands of poems composed on*
> *these walls.*
> *They are all cries of complaint and sadness.*
> *The day I am rid of this prison and attain success,*
> *I must remember that this chapter once existed.*

"They are *tibishi* — poems of travelers." I could feel Sterling Promise's eyes following me from the doorway. "They are all over the walls of this barracks, but this room has some of the best ones."

I bent to read another.

> *In the quiet of night, I heard, faintly, the whistling*
> *of wind.*
> *The forms and shadows saddened me; upon seeing the*
> *landscape, I composed a poem.*

The floating clouds, the fog, darkened the sky.
The moon shines faintly as the insects chirp.
Grief and bitterness entwined are heaven sent.
The sad person sits alone, leaning by a window.

And then I understood. The room was a burial ground for dreams. The people in this room had broken hearts like mine.

My parents are old; my family is poor.
Cold weather comes; hot weather goes.
Heartless white devils,
Sadness and anger fill my heart.

"Your father has written one."

"Where?" At home, when the days were long and light tumbled in from the windows, Father and Grandfather often entertained themselves composing poetry at the dinner table. Nushi and I would listen from behind the spirit screen that stood at the door. I used to hold my breath, praying that they would invite me to join them. I composed poem after poem for the moment when my father would call, "Daughter, come recite something for us." In the story I created in my head, when they called me into the room, I recited a poem that left them speechless. I guarded this story, never telling Nushi, because I knew she would tell me that it was impossible, that I should stop reaching for the clouds when I was thirsty.

Sterling Promise took my elbow and led me to the side wall. He pointed to a corner, and when I knelt down, he settled next to me, his leg pressed against mine. I recognized my father's poem written in ink in his neat, exact calligraphy.

I am a thousand li from home,
In a cruel country, where hatred hides behind blue skies
I am the honored guest of tyranny. Trapped in
      his white, wooden buildings,
Dreams here are nothing but wind and fog.

It made me sad to see my father's pain in ink on the wall. "He is so miserable. I don't understand why he came," I said.

Sterling Promise gave me that patient look that I often found myself receiving. "It was his duty. He did it to save his family."

"How much of himself should he have to sacrifice for duty?"

"However much is necessary," he said, tilting his head.

I nodded. I agreed only because I should agree, because everyone had always agreed. But I often wondered why people invoked duty as the reason to keep doing what was destroying them.

"There is one more you need to see." He pointed to a small carving —

It was on the day that the Weaver Maiden met
      the Cowherd
That I took passage on the President Lincoln.
I ate wind and tasted waves for more than twenty days.
Fortunately, I arrived safely on the American continent.
I thought I could land in a few days.
How was I to know I would become a prisoner suffering
      in the wooden building?
The barbarians' abuse is really difficult to take.
When my family's circumstances stir my emotions,
      a double stream of tears flow.

I only wish I can land in San Francisco soon,
Thus sparing me this additional sorrow here.

"It is perfect," I said. Someone had stood in this room, touching this wall, feeling the same turmoil that I was feeling.

"I thought you would like it."

"It makes me feel less lonely."

Sterling Promise grinned. "I know you like the Cowherd and Weaver Girl story. A lot of the poems mention it. Would you like to see those too?"

He did not know that it was the emotions that echoed inside me, not the story. I opened my mouth to tell him, but the warmth of his eager smile stopped me. He was trying to show me something he thought I would like. And I did love the poems. Maybe why I loved them wasn't important for him to understand.

"How did you know I like that story?"

Sterling Promise blushed. "I heard you and Nushi talking about it."

"You were spying on me."

"I thought I could, since you spied on me first. I was sure you would spoil everything."

"I was so angry!" I said, laughing.

"Yes, you made that clear at dinner that night, while you sat there with your nose scrunched up and your bottom lip pushing out. And then clearer when you pushed me in the terrace."

"I behaved like a monster." I sighed.

"I behaved badly too." He took a step toward me.

My face felt hot. We stood staring at each other until my head grew so light I had to lean against the wall. Love seemed closer than it had ever been. I longed to reach out and touch it, to trace the outline of it on Sterling Promise's face. I turned back to the poem. "It is a little bit of a love story. Coming to this country. The promises. The suffering," I said.

"I think it is more the story of heroes." He brushed his fingers against my hand. My heart started to pound. "Jade Moon, if you don't get in . . ."

"I don't want to talk about it." I had to get into America. It held every possibility, every story, even one where someone like Sterling Promise could love a Fire Horse. I was not going to let something this precious slide through my fingers.

"You were telling the truth on the ship. It is not just about leaving China anymore," he said. "You really do want to get into America, don't you?"

"Desperately," I said, thinking of Snow Lily wailing in the hospital.

He nodded. We should leave here before we were caught, but I had to know Father's plans for me. I had to know if this was all worth it. If I did not ask him now, I might not get another chance.

"I have a question for you," I said.

"That does not surprise me." His voice danced with gentle amusement.

"Has Father arranged a marriage between us?"

Sterling Promise hesitated, and his eyes began to calculate.

"Just tell me the truth."

We heard voices in the distance. The men were coming back from the dining hall.

"We better go," he said.

"I am not leaving until you answer my question."

He looked over his shoulder, stepped back, and began the familiar nervous tapping on his leg. "Jade Moon, we will be caught."

I crossed my arms.

"Stop being so stubborn," he said, his mouth tense.

I did not move.

Sterling Promise stared at me, and then he said, "Yes, he has arranged a marriage between us."

"He agreed to bring you to America if you would marry me?"

"Yes," he said impatiently.

I frowned at him. The next question was harder to voice, but I dug it from inside my heart. "Do you want to marry me?"

"Jade Moon, you aren't supposed to be here. They will think we are discussing answers for the interviews." He rubbed his hand on his forehead, but then his face softened. He reached down and held the tips of my fingers. "I would not have agreed if I did not want to."

My whole body warmed, melting with his touch. *Almost* making me forget his gift for saying exactly what people want to hear.

"I wish you had told me."

"Your father did not want you to know. He said you would make things difficult."

That sounded true. I frowned a little.

"Jade Moon, I had to get your father to bring me here. Remember, I was trapped too."

We could see the men coming toward the building with a guard. My heart was pounding. I did not want to be caught here either, but I needed to hear what he would say, to make sure I could live with it. "Is there anything else you are keeping from me?"

But Sterling Promise had his attention fixed on the men coming up the path. "You need to get out of here." He grabbed my elbow and dragged me to the door. He listened for a second. "They are at the end of the walkway. The guard will let you in the women's side." He held my arm firmly, opened the door, and shoved me through it.

I stood staring at his closed door for a few seconds. The voices of the men behind me shook me out of my daze. I moved quickly across the porch to the door of the women's barracks. The guard was already yelling when he came up the steps. I didn't think he had seen me leave the men's quarters, but that didn't seem to lessen his outrage. He grabbed my arm, marched me through the women's door, and pushed me in front of the matron, who came running in to see the commotion.

"I left the infirmary," I told her in Chinese. "I had to."

"Why?"

"Snow Lily was there. The woman who . . ."

The matron nodded and then spoke to the guard. He scowled, but turned and slammed the door behind him.

The matron led me back to the sitting room, where the other women raised their eyebrows. As I collapsed into a chair in the corner, I closed my eyes for a moment, trying to escape the screaming guards, crying women, worried thoughts, and mountain of lies. Inside that darkness, I wrote my own poem.

> *Don't expect a new life to be easy.*
> *Love comes as clouds*
> *Dreams are mostly air*
> *Hard to hold, harder to carry*
> *Somehow impossible to let go.*

There was no room to put it in, no wall to carve it on, nothing to carve with. So I tucked it into my crowded mind.

CHAPTER 16

I TOOK ONE BREATH, then another, and finally opened my eyes and stood up. "You were right about Sterling Promise," I announced.

"Of course we were," First Wife said. The other women continued their sewing.

"He agreed to an arranged marriage so Father would bring him to America. And I am sure Father only brought him to America because he agreed to marry his worthless daughter."

"You are acting like marriage is a bad thing. Everyone wants to be married," First Wife said, turning back to the other women.

"He could be doing this just to get to America, or to inherit the farm, or to gain a family," I said to Spring Blossom.

"Or he could love you," Spring Blossom said softly, taking my hand and leading me to a corner of the sleeping quarters. We sat on one of the empty beds.

"I always hoped for love, fool that I am." I lifted my head and gave her a sad smile. "Do you remember the story of Cowherd and Weaver Girl?" I asked.

"Of course."

"That is what I always thought love would be. A kind of understanding."

"You are very romantic for a Fire Horse," Spring Blossom said.

"Maybe. I also like the story of the kitchen god who throws himself into the fire." We sat silently for a few minutes. "Were you ever in love?"

Spring Blossom's body stiffened. She turned her head away. I knew I was not supposed to ask, but it is difficult to find out about important things when you can't speak of them. I started to get up, to avoid offending her further.

She whispered, "Yes, I was in love."

I sat back down next to her and waited. I did not know if I should continue asking questions.

Spring Blossom looked at her sleeves. I could feel the beginning of the story gathering in her throat. Stories are that way, like storms. If you pay attention, you can sense them in the air.

"My husband was chosen for me almost as soon as I was born. My father's best friend, our neighbor, had a son several years older than me. The two of us played at our mothers' feet. He would bring me leaves and flowers from the fields around us. He had a quick smile and an easy laugh. He would squeeze my hand when our mothers were not looking, and I would bury my face in my other hand and giggle. I remember watching bright orange-and-white fish swim in the stream that ran between our homes. He convinced me to stick my toes in the icy water and try to touch their shiny scales."

"And that is why you loved him?"

"Partly. He was adventurous and daring. I was cautious and shy. But when we were older, our parents kept us apart. It was no longer

135

proper for us to watch the leaves rustle in the wind or lie on our stomachs next to the stream.

"I spent my days with my mother and grandmother. I learned to sew and cook. I learned to listen politely and speak quietly. I learned to sit still so that I would disappear into the background of my father's home. My husband was sent to school. Sometimes his mother would visit us, and she would bring a photograph of her son. When she passed it to my mother, I could catch a glimpse of what he looked like. The pictures showed a much more serious face than the one I knew as a child, but his eyes held the same mischief. It was a relief that I knew some part of him."

"Do you think he saw a picture of you?"

"I wondered. If he did, I hoped they made his heart jump into his throat like the pictures of him did for me."

I knew that feeling, but I kept my mouth shut. This was Spring Blossom's story.

"He was the third son, so after a few years, his parents sent him to study at a military academy. His pictures from that time looked different, his eyes harder, his face lined with ruthless determination. But I thought I could still see my childhood friend. I thought the darkness was only a veil."

"Were you ever married?"

Spring Blossom paused. I waited. When she did not continue, I was afraid that she would not finish the story. She gave a tiny nod.

"His mother visited less and less. I heard my mother and grandmother whispering about the sorrows of having a soldier for a husband, but letters and gifts were still exchanged. The fortune-teller found an auspicious date. My parents sent my dowry to his home to wait for me. I cried at my mother's feet just as I should,

136

and worried that she saw the joy I felt through my tears. I was dressed in red, put in a sedan chair, and carried to my new home. I looked forward to all of the happiness I thought our marriage would bring. I would make his mother tea; I would prepare all his favorite sweets; I would sit with him by the river and watch the fish go by.

"But dreams are fragile things. I wish I had been told that very little from your childhood survives the strain of growing up. The moment I stepped out of the sedan chair at the threshold of my new home and saw him, I knew he did not want to marry me. He did not love me."

"Oh, Spring Blossom."

She grabbed my hand, lines forming at the center of her forehead. "But that I could have borne. I could have loved him and been happy, except that he had become like the clay ground that dries in years of drought and has to be broken before anything can grow there. I was taught how to be soft and gentle, not how to break up the rocky soil of my husband's heart. He rarely spoke to me, and nothing I did pleased him. He sent back the tea I made. He didn't eat the dumplings I cooked. He tossed aside the slippers I embroidered. I watched him bury himself deeper and deeper in his own darkness. He left in the middle of the night, sometimes for weeks. When he came back, he would not tell anyone, even his father, where he had been."

"Did you ask him?"

"I knew," she said, rubbing her wrists. "The warlords in our area struggled over territory, bickering with one another, playing games with our lives without telling us the rules. My husband was one of their weapons. He came home, his face spotted with mud, blood on his knuckles, and that darkness in his eyes. They had turned the boy who lay next to me on his belly by the river into an assassin."

"Why would he join the warlords?" I asked.

"He went to military school with many who were fighting. He wanted a strong China. He would rage about it — the concessions to Western countries that made us foreigners in our own cities, Japan's threat to our safety, people's blindness."

I shook my head slowly. "Were you heartbroken?"

"Love is not the way you think, Jade Moon. Your heart is not full or broken all at once. Pieces heal and break and heal again. My husband was not always unkind. We had evenings when we would talk. He would tell me stories about his school days. I was in love and heartbroken, and everything between. My husband's heart was broken too, but not because of me. While I dreamed of love and marriage, he dreamed of a better China. While I prepared for my wedding, he prepared for revolution. While my marriage was not what I expected, his whole world was descending into the chaos of broken promises and betrayals. I bore my pain, and I would have borne his too if he had allowed me."

"Oh, my friend. I wish you had not had to bear any of it."

Spring Blossom nodded. I reached out and pulled her hand away from her wrist. A series of white scars ran down the inside of her arm. "Did he do that?"

"No. He sometimes beat me. He was angry, and if he was not fighting, he needed a place to put that anger. His blood already ran too thick with it. But what he did to me has long faded. This, his mother did."

"His mother?"

She closed her eyes, then opened them again. "When my husband had strayed too far from his true self, he hanged himself. One of the servants found him. I don't know if he realized it, but he chose one of the trees we sat under as children.

"I think my mother-in-law had thought I would bring peace to her son. He would settle at home with his wife and family. When I could not do that, she blamed me for what he was. I found out about his suicide when she tore into my room, wild with grief. She beat me and ripped at my skin until her screams brought the servants. They could not stop her. When her rage exhausted her, she collapsed next to me, and the servants carried her to her bed.

"I lay there, a bloody mess. The servants would not speak to me or even help me up from the floor for fear of upsetting my mother-in-law. One finally went to my family's house, and my brother came to take me back. I was a widowed woman back in her clan's house, steps away from the door of her husband's family, which was a daily reminder of my failure. My brother decided that a marriage in America would be the best way to push the tragedy and shame of it all away from the family."

"America must be where the cursed find a country," I said.

"I hope so." Spring Blossom looked down at her arms.

The sounds of the barracks trickled back. New arrivals listened while First Wife and Big Teeth passed on their wisdom. Thread whispered in and out of fabric. A child had arrived with one of the women. He was curled into the curve of his mother, who was crying softly.

"You are lucky to be a Fire Horse," Spring Blossom said.

A sharp laugh escaped. "No one has ever called me lucky before."

"I wish I had your strength."

I shook my head. "It is too destructive. Would you have the fierceness of your mother-in-law, only to scar people with it?"

She looked at her hands.

"Do you still love him?"

She nodded.

"How?" I said. My voice had a harsh note to it that made Spring Blossom press her lips together.

"You can love someone as many ways as water falls from the sky. Sometimes it falls with thunder and lightning; other times it falls silently. Sometimes it falls as cool snow, and other times hard balls of ice beat down. If you want the water, you don't get to choose how it falls."

"You don't get to choose?" I said.

"No," she said.

Two days later, the guard called my name. He led me to the administration building and through a winding series of hallways to a room where three men sat. One was older, with white hair, white skin, and a fleshy face. His lips peeked out from under a bushy mustache. The other was younger with dark hair and wire glasses framing serious eyes.

The third man was Chinese. He wore one of the suits that Sterling Promise admired. I tried to give him a smile, but he just stared. A woman sat in front of a small machine on a table, her fingers dancing across its buttons as we spoke.

"Sung Jade Moon," the Chinese man said. I nodded. "This is your interrogation to determine the status of your application for entry into America."

First the man with the mustache spoke in English, then the Chinese man echoed the question in my own language. Some English words were familiar, but I was grateful for the interpreter. When I spoke, he repeated what I said. He smoothed out the sharp notes of my Chinese, melting them into soft English.

But I didn't have to know the words to hear the suspicion in each question. "Did your father have brothers or sisters?"

"Yes, three brothers."

He raised an eyebrow. "No sisters. Don't you find that strange?"

Even when lying, being called a liar stings like a smack across the face. "I believe there were two children who died before they were two years old. Both girls."

"Your father is the oldest child, yes?"

I nodded.

"You need to speak your answers so we can record them," the Chinese man barked at me.

"Yes, he is the oldest."

"He claims to be born in America, yet he knows no English."

"He was sent back to our village to live with his aunt and uncle, to learn the language and traditions of our country. He didn't return here until he was a young man. I think he learned some English then, but when he came back to China, he forgot much of it."

"Yes, why was he in China for two years on his last visit?"

"I believe business kept him there."

My palms were moist, and my tongue tripped and stumbled over the lies I'd memorized.

"And why is he coming here now? With you and your brother?"

For this question, the truth would do as well as any practiced lie. "My father does not share his reasons with me."

"You and your brother were born in China and lived with your uncle and his family there."

I nodded. The translator lifted his head and frowned. "Yes," I said. I could feel the Fire Horse rearing up inside me as I met his stare.

"How many times a year were letters received from your father?"

This was one of the extra questions that Sterling Promise had told me about. "Three," I said.

"Your father says that he wrote two letters each year. How do you explain that?"

"Some years, two. Other years, three," I snapped. I must have used the voice that Grandfather said made him deaf, because both the Americans jerked their heads up. I cursed the knot in my stomach.

It was not a very auspicious beginning. Over the next three days, they asked me enough questions to fill ten coaching books. Sometimes I knew the story. Sometimes I had to make up parts to fill holes the coaching book had left. I told myself it was just a story I was telling to Nushi or Spring Blossom, not one that would determine the rest of my life.

"How many streets does your village have?"

"How many houses are in your village?"

"How is the front room of the house furnished?"

"And your father, who are his business associates in America?"

"Did your family have servants in China? How many?"

"Where is the rice bin kept in your house?"

"Which direction does the door face?"

"Is there a clock?"

"Where is your father's business in Chinatown?"

"Does he belong to any associations?"

I answered question after question until Uncle's and the Sungs' stories spun in my head. Lying made me thirsty for the truth. I wanted to touch the edges of my face and arms. Was I still myself, or were the Americans crafting me into someone else? Someone they would prefer to have in their country, someone with a big family, whose grandfather helped build the American railroads. Someone with small dreams that could squeeze between what the Americans wanted. Dreams that wouldn't cause a fuss. The answers I gave brought me one step closer to America, but they also pulled me away from myself.

By the last day, they had unraveled and examined every thread of the story I had woven for them. I was lost and trapped inside the story at the same time. I wanted my own story. Why didn't they believe that if I had left my home and traveled over the ocean, I needed to be here? Why couldn't I tell them how hard it was to live in China, how people broke off pieces of you to make you fit? Why didn't they want to know what it was like being a Fire Horse, full of a strength and power that only destroyed everything I touched?

"Do you have anything further to add before the hearing comes to a close?"

I looked around the room at the Americans. They stared back, their expressions blank and bored.

Before I could stop myself, I said, "Yes."

Everyone waited.

"What is it?" the translator said, pushing his chair back to leave. I hesitated. "I . . . I want . . . Don't you want to ask anything about me? Why *I* came to America?" I regretted the words as soon as I spoke them.

The translator passed my question to the men in suits.

"We know why you are here," the man with the mustache said as he opened a folder and read from the papers inside. "Your father is using his merchant status to bring his children to America."

"That is not why I came to America," I said softly.

The translator did nothing with my words, letting them hang, meaningless, in the air. The woman began stacking papers. I was preparing to stand when the younger, dark-haired American spoke. I recognized the English word "why."

The translator glanced at him, and then turned to me. "Why did you come to America?" he said in Chinese.

The man with the mustache shook his head and said a few words, but the younger man waved his hand and leaned forward, waiting.

"People tell me that America is full of possibilities. A place where you can dream a life for yourself and it forms around you. That will never be true for me in China." I paused and looked at the younger man's kind eyes. "I came to America because I want a place where I don't have to hold everything in so tightly," I said. "A place I can breathe."

"A place where you belong," the younger man said after my words had been translated.

"Yes."

"It may not be the way you imagine."

"I know. The people here expect so much from your country. It cannot be everything." I wanted to tell him about the poetry on the walls of the men's barracks and the tears on the pillows in the women's, but those weren't my stories to tell. "But what other place makes such promises?"

"True," the young official said. "I hope you find your place, Sung Jade Moon." He rose and nodded toward the door, so I stood and followed the guard back to the women's barracks.

CHAPTER 17

FOR WEEKS, I HEARD no further news. Sterling Promise did not ask to meet me again. New women arrived; other women left. Snow Lily did not come back. One day, First Wife was allowed to land. She bragged about her husband and her sons and how they would fuss over her even though they shouldn't bother, but her lips trembled slightly as she said good-bye. Other than that, nothing changed, until everything changed. Perhaps that is how it always is in prisons.

We had watched the ferry pull away from the window and then returned to the sitting room when the guard entered. "Sung Jade Moon," he called. The women's faces jerked toward me. My stomach tightened into a fist. I waited for him to say I could land, or to frown and give me the letter that sent me back to China. I was surprised when instead he signaled for me to follow him.

The guard led me through the doors of the administrative building, his boots clicking along the tile floors with quick determination until he stopped at one of the waiting-room doors. He slid a key into the lock, and the door clattered open. Sterling Promise and Father sat across from each other in the center of the room.

I entered, then heard the lock click into its slot behind me. Sterling Promise, elbows resting on his knees, held his head in his hands. My father sat still and straight, staring at the wall across from him.

"This is a bad sign," Sterling Promise said in a low voice as I sat down beside him. "If we passed the interrogation, the guard would tell us. They would not need to bring us here."

"But if we failed, wouldn't they have sent a guard with the letter?"

Sterling Promise nodded. "And if they were going to question us further, they would never put us together like this."

Father pressed his hands flat on his thighs. Sitting, it was hard to tell, but I might have grown taller than him over the past three months.

"How are you, Father? Are you well?"

"I want to go home," he mumbled. "I am tired of this prison that calls itself a country." His face was thin and his hands seemed more delicate. Even his skin looked more transparent.

The metal door rattled as it swung open, and the guard gestured for us to follow. He led us into a small, dimly lit room with wooden walls and a heavy table in the center. An immigration official in a suit sat at the head of the table. The young official from my questioning sat next to him. A translator situated himself across from us. I stole a look at Sterling Promise and was surprised to find him staring at the older official. He gave Sterling Promise a small nod. Sterling Promise relaxed back into his chair.

The older official began speaking in that rolling English, a language that makes it difficult to tell good news from bad. I gripped one hand in the other, trying to hold the panic inside my skin. But I was too jittery to decipher enough of the words to understand.

Finally, the translator began. "We have reviewed your answers in your interviews and compared them to the transcripts of your relatives' interviews. Two of you" — he looked at me and Sterling Promise — "gave satisfactory answers. But you, sir . . ." He looked at Father. "You claim to be a legal citizen, but your answers were incompatible with the others'. You don't know any of your business associates or even your own address in San Francisco. We cannot confirm that you are Sung Feng Hao as you claim."

He paused to shuffle some papers. We stared at the man. My heart was pounding, and pressure gathered in my head.

"Despite this, we have decided to admit Sung Sterling Promise. He seems a suitable immigrant with merchant connections."

"What?" I said.

The young official turned to the older one and said a few words that weren't translated. The older one shook his head, his face tightening.

"This doesn't make any sense. Why would he be allowed in, but not us?" Father demanded.

"You have not proven any relationship to the Sung family," the older man said through the translator.

"But I have papers," my father protested.

"Papers we can't confirm are yours," the official pointed out. "And we cannot allow your daughter in if she is not under your protection."

The young official leaned forward. "You can appeal our decision if you think it is unfair," he said, looking directly at me.

"Yes, I was about to mention that," said the older official.

"We need to discuss this," Father said. The translator nodded and said something to the Americans.

"You may talk over your situation here," the older official said.

After the men filed out of the room, I turned to Sterling Promise. "What did you do? How did you get them to let you land?" I asked.

"I answered their questions correctly," he said, but his finger had started to tap his leg. I looked at it. Sterling Promise covered one hand with the other.

"No." I shook my head slowly. "You did something. You took advantage of an opportunity."

"I warned you that it would be difficult," Sterling Promise said, staring at the shiny surface of the table. "I am staying. I have business to do for Master Yue. And I have nothing to go back to."

"But our agreement," Father said, glaring.

"I will honor our agreement. I will return to China in one year."

"Hmph," Father grunted, turning away.

"Are you talking about the marriage?" I asked.

"What marriage?" Father demanded. He followed my eyes to Sterling Promise. "You told her!"

Sterling Promise met his glare for a moment, then looked down. "I had no choice," he mumbled.

Father shook his head. "You will get married in China because you are coming back to China with me," he said.

My heart lurched forward. "I am not."

His voice was quiet. "Yes, you are."

I tried to calm the fury swirling inside me. "Father, I will do my duty and marry Sterling Promise, but I will do it here in America. I am going to appeal. If Sterling Promise is allowed to land, I should be too. I can stay with Mrs. Ying. I have earned the right to stay as well."

"The right to stay?" Father stared at me. "Ah, I see. You did not tell her that part," he said to Sterling Promise, his voice sour and angry. He turned back to me. "You were never going to stay. You were going to marry and come back with me, even if we were all let in."

I felt like I had been punched in the stomach. I looked at Sterling Promise. "I was never supposed to stay in America?"

"Jade Moon . . ."

"Why did you bring me all this way only to take me back?" I asked my father.

"We brought you to ensure that you were married in the end. Sterling Promise had no guarantee that I would bring him to America if he married you in China, and I had no guarantee that he would come back to marry you if I took him to America first." He explained it coolly, like he was planning where to build the next terrace. "You know we can't trust him. He makes promises as easily as a mountain makes a shadow."

I blinked away the tears springing into my eyes. "You . . . you knew how much I needed to come to America," I said to Sterling Promise. "And you were going to send me home? You are taking away my only chance at freedom."

"Women are no use in America," he said halfheartedly.

My father pounded his hand on the arm of his chair. "I knew you were tricking us. You knew they wouldn't let us in."

"And you tried to keep us all out," Sterling Promise said.

"Ha! Adopted son of my tricky brother. You think I didn't know you were lying from the beginning."

"I did everything I promised to do." Sterling Promise looked at the door. "You did not have to bring Jade Moon. I told you it would only cause trouble and heartache."

"So you never wanted me to come?" I asked him.

"Lower your voices. They may still be listening."

"Why would we care if they listen? You are the only one getting to stay!" I was almost shouting.

Father crossed his arms and leaned back in his chair. "I don't understand why the Americans did not send us all home."

"That was *your* plan!" Sterling Promise said. Father pushed his lips together. "You tried to get us all sent back. We have been stuck on this island because of you. I need to be here! And I made sure that I would get to stay."

"What do you mean, you made sure?" I said, staring at him.

Sterling Promise was silent.

Father looked at both of us. "Of course I want us to go back to China. My land is there, my father. Our ancestors. Your places are there too."

Sterling Promise turned his face away. "You don't know where my place is."

I shook my head slowly. "I will never have a place there. You know that, Father."

"Quiet! This was a fool's journey. I am returning home." Father's words clicked with resolution, just like the guard's boots. "Daughter, you will join me. Sterling Promise, if you honor your word, we will see you in a year."

I tightened my grip on my chair, trying to lock up the last of my fears. "No, Father," I replied.

"You cannot stay. I forbid it." My father waited for me to yell, to fight. Then we would both see that I could never survive on my own.

I stayed still. I kept my voice steady. "Yes, I can. The man said that I could appeal the decision."

Father snorted. "How do you plan to do that?"

I did not have an answer. Sterling Promise looked down at the table. After a few seconds, he rose from his chair. "I am going to get my papers," he said, pulling open the door. I stared at him. He did not look back.

The door shut behind him.

"I am glad we are rid of him," Father growled.

"We are not rid of him. You have arranged a marriage between us."

"Once we return to China, we will never see him again."

"Did you try to get us sent home?"

"Yes, it is where we belong. When Sterling Promise told me on the boat about the interrogation the Americans gave, I thought it would be easier to get us all sent back. Of course, this country is bad luck for Chinese. Whatever you wish for, they keep out of reach, and whatever you don't want, they thrust at you with both hands."

"Why did you come?"

"I was being a dutiful son, obeying my father."

"And in your plan, my duty was to marry and return to China?"

"After a year or two here. Enough time to have a grandson."

"Why not just tell me about the arranged marriage?"

"I don't have to tell you anything."

"I know you don't have to, but why wouldn't you?"

"Your grandfather and I knew you would make difficulties."

"Because I am a Fire Horse."

"Because you believe in love."

"I thought you did too . . . once."

Father looked down at his hands.

"I would not have returned to China with you," I said.

"We would have told you we were going for a visit. Then we would not come back here."

I remembered Nushi telling me never to return to China, all my things in that trunk, the wedding handkerchief. She knew. The women knew. Only I was doomed to blindness.

We stared at each other. The steel in my eyes reflected the steel in his. "I am not leaving," I said, my voice shaking. "I will stay here, in America."

"We are going home." Father's hands were in fists on his lap. His words bore their way through clenched teeth.

"No, Father. I can't." I thought of Nushi and the strength it took for her to pack only my belongings, the strength it took for her to tell me never to return. I thought of Spring Blossom and the stillness of her scarred arms. I thought of the jade around my neck — sharp and strong, without cutting. I had to be that.

"We will leave in two days. I will be back in my fields in time for the harvest."

He rose, but I put my hand on his arm to stop him. He stared down at it. I could not remember the last time we touched. I measured my words carefully before I said them. "Father, listen. I am not leaving. I will make my own arrangements."

The words I said terrified me. Voices in my head cried out, *How? What will you do?* My father turned toward me and paused, half-standing, half-sitting. He searched my face, then collapsed back into the chair.

"You can't stay," he said quietly, looking at the veins in his hands.

"Yes, I can. The man said —"

"No . . . Daughter . . ." The anger had drained out of his voice. "I will be alone. You would abandon your father with no one to care for him when he grows old?" He paused. "You would leave me, just like my brother did?"

"Father . . ." I choked on the word, a sob escaping my throat.

"I know you think I am trying to bar you from love." His face softened slightly. "Did it ever occur to you I was trying to protect you from it?" He waved a hand. "You can marry whom-ever you choose. It doesn't have to be Sterling Promise or Fourth Brother Gou. Marry for love if that is so important to you. I will settle it with your grandfather." He sat up straighter in his chair and resumed his authoritative tone. "I will adopt your hus-band as my son. He will inherit the land. You will raise your sons where you grew up. Nushi will help you raise them. You would like that."

I would like that. In my mind, I ran with my children across the fields. I watched them spread out on the kitchen floor, playing games around the stove. We chewed on sugar cane in the morning and counted stars at night. And the five-year-old, nine-year-old, twelve-year-old Jade Moons inside me wanted the life that Father was describing. They wanted to work beside him, to talk to him over bowls of steaming rice in the evenings, to read the newspapers that drifted into town from Hong Kong. These children of my past clamored for the promise of that lost love from my father. It would soothe years of heartache.

But the new woman inside of me, the one just beginning to grow, knew that while it might heal my past, it would never give me a future. It would not open up a world where I could move and stretch freely. The children protested, *No, that would be nothing. Go back to China. You would be happy, loved.* I resisted, stuffed them down inside. I knew that I would have to sacrifice giant pieces of myself if I returned, and all the love of my father, a husband, children, would never fill the hollow shell of me that would be left.

Both of us had our heads bowed, staring at our laps. I knew that he had finally offered me everything, and for that I was grateful. But he was still asking me to give up too much. "Father, I wish you would appeal," I said gently. "You could try to stay here, with me."

"It is a prison." He spit the words out, his voice bitter and sharp.

"Yes, but so is China . . . for me. Here I can smell the freedom. It drifts in on the wind. The guards carry it in on their coats."

"You smell the sweet perfume of lies and false promises."

We sat next to each other, staring at the wall across from us.

"I hope you aren't counting on any help from Sterling Promise. He will leave you to rot here. He will certainly never marry you." My gaze dropped. "It is a bad match anyway. You are a Fire Horse, and he is a Wood Snake. You are too headstrong, and he is too selfish."

"I know."

"You will disgrace me by staying," he said. "I will have to tell everyone that you died here."

I gripped his hand, but he turned away and pushed his chair back. Rising quickly, he crossed the room and pounded on the door to be released. The guard opened the door and led Father away.

I covered my face with my hands. America, its promises, had to be worth it. I had nothing else to bargain with — no marriage, no family, no name. I had handed it all over to fate for the sake of a little air to breathe, some space to move, the chance to look people in the eye. What else could I give the Americans? What had Sterling Promise offered that I hadn't? Then I remembered what he could give them, and it made me furious.

After a few minutes, the door opened. And there, with a set of papers in his hands, was Sterling Promise.

CHAPTER 18

The guard shut the door. Sterling Promise let a half smile waver on his lips. I crossed my arms and stared back.

His smile tightened as he crossed the room and sat down next to me. "This is for the best. You don't know how difficult it will be, what trying to survive in America will make you do."

"I guess it made you use the money Master Yue loaned you."

"What?"

"That's how you got in, isn't it? You bribed the official. I don't care. But I want you to find a way to get me in too."

"I can't."

"Can't or won't?"

"You don't understand —"

"Have you ever considered that it is *you* who doesn't understand?" My voice grew louder as I spoke. I had controlled my anger as much as I could for one day. "You, who know the way a person stands, the words they use, the things they want, the stories they love. How could you not see how much I need to escape China?

And how could you not understand my curses? You know all about trying to escape curses."

"Jade Moon, it is not me who is keeping you here. It is the Americans."

"You are saying you can't find a way to get me out of here. Like you did at the infirmary. Like you've found a way to get out of here yourself."

"It would involve time and money."

"So there are ways."

"Of course, but —"

"But you won't."

The gentleness drained from his eyes, but his tone remained soft. "It isn't practical. I am here to see to Master Yue's business."

"And I can be terribly inconvenient."

"Yes, you can. I saw the way you interfered when you were at his house."

"I brought bandages and water to children who had to work for a man who beat them, starved them."

"You can't control yourself. If you come to America, you will want to interfere again. It is too risky. Jade Moon . . ." He sighed. "If you can just wait for a few years, I will have my fortune and my merchant papers. I will be respected and successful, and it will not be so impossible."

"You know what is impossible? Fitting into the life I have in China," I spat.

"You think that living in America is going to give you the freedom you long for," he said, "that you will not have to kick at the walls of a prison anymore. Those walls may stretch and shrink, but they will always be there. You can never have the complete freedom you imagine. So instead you will destroy yourself, trying to kick down one wall after another." He reached out to take my hands, but when his fingers brushed mine, I jerked away.

"Despite all that, Jade Moon, I will still marry you. That is what I have been trying to tell you. When I return to China in a year or two, we'll have the wedding ceremony and you can come to America with me then." I could see his face through my angry tears, and I wondered why I had ever let myself care. "You are so irresistibly stubborn," he chuckled. "I know you will give me no end of trouble, and I will spend half my life making up for your blunders, but I can't help that I love you."

His words cleared the tears in my eyes, but I had to breathe deeper into the hollow space they left in my chest.

"Marrying me would be too great a burden," I said. "Just get me across to America now. Then you will never have to see me again."

"What . . . Why would I do that?" he said.

"Because you know it is what I want. You know because it is the same new beginning that you are seeking,"

Creases rippled across his brow. "You don't want to marry me? But I thought . . ."

"I won't have my father's lands. He considers me dead," I said. "Which releases you from your promise to him."

There was a flicker of surprise in his eyes, but his forehead smoothed again and he said, "Is that all?" He brushed a tear from my cheek. "It doesn't matter. I didn't want to be a farmer. You can wait for me in Hong Kong."

My father was right. Sterling Promise would let me rot here.

"So you will not help me find a way to get to America," I said, needing to hear it from him.

"No," he said. "But what does that matter? We will be like Cowherd and Weaver Girl. Separated except for once a year. That will be our love story." He lifted my hand and pressed it between his.

"Except you will be the only one in heaven," I snapped, jerking my hand away. I took another deep breath. "I know what you think of me. You are right that when people look at me, they see a wild woman, too sharp, with a touch of the ridiculous. You may think you love me now, but that will end, tomorrow or the next day, whenever the winds of fortunes change. I can already hear the resentment creeping into your voice."

I lifted my head. I wanted to hurt him, not with the wild bucking of a Fire Horse, but with a calculated cruelty, meant to push him as far away as I could. Far enough that he could not hurt me again. "But do you know what I see when I look at you? I see a shadow of a person, who shifts and changes to suit whoever he is standing in front of. If I am too much, you are too little — a kite without a string, a lantern without its own light. You are nothing but smoke and shadows. I would never marry such a man."

Sterling Promise swallowed. "That is what you think of me," he said. He bowed his head. "It would be difficult to have such a husband. The wife of such a man would be greatly burdened."

"Some might say cursed," I said.

A guard entered.

I stood. "Go to America. Make your fortune. You don't have to compromise this time. You can find a love that is more convenient."

Sterling Promise looked away. We did not say good-bye.

*　　*　　*

I cried through my first evening on Angel Island, and I cried through my last. The women moved in wide circles around me. They weren't sure what had happened, but loss and devastation seeped from my pores, and it was too risky to be close to someone so unlucky.

Big Teeth put her heavy hand gently on mine. Her skin was as rough as a worker's in our fields and covered in the same dark patches. She read the pain in my face, and, after a moment, patted my hand and left to sit with the other women. Only Spring Blossom sat patiently by me while the tears ran like rivers down my cheeks. Soft, sad tears for my crushed heart. Angry tears that burned. Bitter tears that I could not live in America. Tears that I would not survive in China. Tears because I might love Sterling Promise; tears because part of me hated him. Tears because I had finally held love in my hand, only to discover how hollow it was. All the tears I had swallowed on this island spilled out of me this one night.

After letting me empty my eyes, Spring Blossom asked, "What happened, Jade Moon? You are going back to China?"

I shook my head.

"You are allowed to land?"

I shook my head.

"You can appeal."

"And stay here another six months? Another year? Until every drop of hope is squeezed from me?" I glanced at the women's bathroom and shivered. "I can't let that happen. My father has to return, but Sterling Promise is allowed to land."

Spring Blossom nodded. "I have heard of that. Families separated."

"He bribed the official." I shook my head again. "Nothing is the way it should be."

"So Sterling Promise is breaking his engagement to you?"

"No, he will marry me. But he refuses to help me enter America." My laugh bit the air. "He does not love me after all." I paused. "Or if he does, he does not love me enough."

"Jade Moon, you are going to have to explain what happened."

I told Spring Blossom about the meeting. I told her about Father, how he had planned to fail the entire interrogation and take us all back to China. I told her about Sterling Promise, who agreed to marry me, but only if I would return to China, where he would visit when he could.

"He said we would live like Cowherd and Weaver Girl."

"Is that what you want?" Spring Blossom asked.

"It doesn't matter what I want. Everyone uses me to get what *they* want."

"It may not matter to them, but it matters to others. It matters to me. It matters to Nushi. Are you going to base your life on the fact that people care about you, or the fact that they don't?" Spring Blossom said. "Both are always true."

"Do you think Sterling Promise cares?" I did not want the words to come out, but they did.

Spring Blossom thought for a moment. "He loves you in the best way he can, but he thinks he can bargain down the cost of your love. If that is enough, then marry him."

I paused, trying to calm my tears. "I want love to be offered with an open palm. But I've never seen love like that before."

"Except in stories. And there is a magic to believing in something you have never seen." She held her hand out to me, and I laid mine in hers. "Now, what will you do?" she asked in her steady voice.

My shoulders slumped again. "I don't know. I am only good at slamming my fists and making people's heads hurt." I looked at Spring Blossom. "I am just a Fire Horse."

She squeezed my hand. "Did you know that there is another ending to the Weaver Girl story?"

"I am sick of love stories."

"This one isn't a love story." Spring Blossom smiled. "In this story, Cowherd and Weaver Girl are not in love. He tricked her into marrying him, just like in the other story, but in this one she never forgave him for it."

"That sounds familiar," I said.

"He kept her magic robe so she could not return to heaven. Weaver Girl constantly plotted how she would get home. Every day, sometimes three or four times a day, she asked her husband, 'Where is my magic robe?' But he refused to tell her.

"One day, the faithful ox who helped Cowherd trick Weaver Girl grew ill. Before he died, he gave his master one last piece of wisdom. 'When I am dead, cut off a piece of my skin and fill it with sand. Then take the ring from my nose and slide it over the hole where you put the sand. Carry it with you at all times. One day, when you are in trouble, you will need it.'"

I leaned forward. This was not Nushi's story.

"A few years went by. Cowherd carried the ox skin with him everywhere. Weaver Girl continued to badger her husband to find out where he hid her robe. She asked him every day, even waking him up when the skies were dark and the rest of the world was asleep."

"She is persistent," I said, sniffling.

"Yes, and it worked. The constant questioning exhausted Cowherd. One night, as he was slipping into sleep, Weaver Girl whispered the question in his ear. She could not believe it when he mumbled the hiding place half to himself. Before he even realized what he had done, Weaver Girl jumped from the bed, snatched her robe from its hiding place, leapt onto a cloud, and flew away back to heaven where she belonged.

"Cowherd, cursing his weakness, chased after her. He flew up to heaven with the help of the magic ox hide. Weaver Girl saw her husband following her, the man who had kept her out of heaven for so long, and she took a hairpin from her hair and drew a river in the sky to cut off his pursuit. Cowherd used the sand in his bag to create a bank to cross over. When Weaver Girl drew another river, he could not go farther because the bag was empty. He flung the ox ring at her. She hurled her weaving shuttle at him."

"I like this Weaver Girl," I said. "I wonder why Nushi never told me this version of the story."

"The Emperor of the Sky heard all the commotion, so he sent a messenger to make peace. Now the couple stands on opposite sides of a river of stars."

"Do they still meet once a year?"

"Of course, because they are married. But here is what is important — Weaver Girl got to heaven on her own, even though Cowherd tried to stop her."

"That's right." I let this new story settle in my head. "I don't know. I don't have a magic robe."

"Ah . . . perhaps it is just hidden."

"Nushi said once that desperate people are dangerous." I looked across the room at the group of women keeping their distance. "I wonder who brings more bad luck — an orphan or a desperate Fire Horse."

Spring Blossom smiled. "I wonder."

I spent the first half of the night dissecting every word Sterling Promise had let drop from his lips. I turned them this way and that in my mind, looking for the love I had imagined. The scent of it, the flavor was there, but nothing else.

Then I decided, if there was nothing to hold on to, there was nothing to lose. I spent the rest of the night building in my mind the steps I would have to climb. With each I became more terrified at my own daring, but there they were, laid out for me. And, if I was lucky, they would take me all the way to America.

CHAPTER 19

FIRE HORSES AREN'T DESIGNED to bend rules. They're designed to break them.

The next morning, I stared through the crisscrossed metal of the window to where the ferry pulled into the dock. It melted through the fog, more like a dream than metal and wood. What would happen to me? Would I end up on the floor of some shop making fireworks, or living in a slum crowded with sickness and death? How many tricky grocers were on the streets of America, waiting to have me arrested?

Before the guard called us to breakfast, I went over the plan with Spring Blossom.

"It is risky," she said.

"Maybe impossible," I replied.

"You could lose everything."

"Luckily, my 'everything' doesn't amount to much," I said. "Ah, but it does include one thing." I lifted the wedding handkerchief from under my pillow. "This is for you."

"I can't."

"You must. There is no wedding for me, so you should have it for yours. Otherwise I will just have to leave it here." She took it from my hand and held it to her heart. "Don't worry. I will be fine."

She nodded, and her thin arms wrapped around me, squeezing me with surprising strength. Then she turned and fell in line with the other women on their way to breakfast.

Sterling Promise had taught me how to get to the hospital, something he would soon regret. I lay down in my bunk and held my stomach. When the guard leaned over my bed, I murmured weakly, "Sick," hoping that my English would help me as it had Sterling Promise.

A wave of surprise crossed the guard's face, then he nodded and left me behind in the barracks. I was hoping he would trust me enough to leave the door open, but he did not. Language only goes so far. When he returned, he walked me to the hospital, where a different nurse with the same wide smile sat at the desk.

"Sick," I repeated.

Her face lit up with pleased surprise, then softened with concern. She rattled off some words, but most went beyond my vocabulary. I shook my head.

"New," she said, pointing to herself. "No Chinese."

I nodded.

"Fe-ver?" She touched her hand to her forehead. It was a word I didn't recognize. "Pain?" She wrinkled her forehead and made a hurt look.

I put my hand over my stomach. "Here."

"Good, good." She seemed thrilled with the whole exchange. "Bay-bi?" she asked, cradling her arms in each other and rocking them back and forth.

I looked at her a moment, trying to decipher her actions. "Oh, baby! No. No," I said, eyes wide.

"Okay." She sat me in a chair against the wall. "Medicine," she said.

I nodded.

Now, I just had to ask for the right thing at the right time. I sat still and stared forward. I could not leave too soon . . . or too late.

The woman moved to a cabinet and rummaged around the bottles and boxes. After a minute, a man came in, the one in the white coat. "Doctor," the Americans called him. He held out his hand and said something to her. The nurse returned to the desk, shuffled some papers, and handed him a stack. He shook his head. She flipped through the papers and handed him a different stack.

I sat up a little.

The man pointed to four men coming up the path to the hospital, followed by a guard. The nurse nodded and dug through a drawer. The doctor fired a few more words at the nurse, then stomped past the desk to one of the rooms. The nurse frowned, staring after him.

I shifted, and my chair squeaked. She looked up and hurried back to the cabinet. When she found the medicine, she brought it over and I drank it immediately. "Thank you," I said, mimicking her sympathetic smile.

The doctor poked his head out of the doorway and yelled something. The four men from the path came in the front door and gathered around the desk. The next few minutes were a rush of broken English and frustrated Chinese. The nurse handed out a set of papers, then took them back and gave the men different ones. After a few more minutes, their guard waved to the nurse, turned around, and walked down the path. The men continued to speak all at once and in rapid Chinese to the nurse, who just shook her head.

I stood, hoping this was the right time. When the guard was far enough down the path, I pushed myself back in front of the nurse. "Better," I said, smiling. "I go with guard?"

"Oh, yes," the nurse said. She waved her hand at the door, then went back to dealing with the men. I took a breath and walked out the door of the hospital without a guard, just as Sterling Promise had taught me.

Once on the path, I had to focus. I listened for the chatter of the women returning from breakfast or the rumble of men's voices going there. I wished that I had paid more attention to the dictated rhythm of our movements. I could see shadows in the front windows of the women's barracks. They were gathering their sewing for the day.

I searched the windows of the men's barracks. With the bright sun, everything inside was buried in shadow. I walked slowly toward the covered porch, trying to copy the easy comfort I had seen Sterling Promise use. A part of me wanted to take the door that led to the women's barracks, lie down on my bed, and still my rushing heart. I toyed with the thought, enjoying its predictability, before brushing it aside. I put my hand on the door that Sterling Promise had taken me through, then listened and turned the handle.

It was open, just like last time. I slipped in, shutting the door behind me. I took two hesitant steps before I heard voices — deep, low voices, speaking Chinese. The men had not left for breakfast yet. My heart plunged into my stomach. Leave or hide? I cursed myself for not taking more time in the hospital. I cursed the men for being so slow. What were they still doing here?

"Out! Out!" a voice boomed from down the hall. I could open the door and go back to the porch, but where would I hide there? A guard would take me back to the women's side and lock me in. And even if I managed to conceal myself on the porch, they might lock the door behind the men. I had to stay inside.

Gathering my courage, I dashed into the small room across from the door — the room with the poems that Sterling Promise showed me. I pushed myself into the corner on the same wall as the door and held my breath. The men's voices drew closer and closer. I could hear the men passing the doorway, their shoulders brushing against its frame. I squeezed my eyes shut.

A voice I recognized drifted into the room. "They gave me my papers last night. Finally, I can begin my life in America. There is nothing keeping me here." The seeds of tears stung my eyes a little, but I smothered my hurt in anger, then wrapped it in desperation, so buried I could not reach it.

The line of men seemed to pass for hours. Then the voices faded, and no new ones took their place. I started toward the door of the room. The sleeve of a green uniform came into view — the guard. I gasped and jumped back to my corner. The footsteps stopped just past the doorway. I waited and waited, sure that his face would peer through the frame.

When the door snapped shut, I exhaled. Then I heard the click of the lock. I was stuck in the barracks until the men returned.

I was going to be caught. I was going to be sent back to China. Why was I so unlucky? I slid down the wall and put my head in my hands. What made me think I could get to America? I could not even get out of the building.

I sat in that room of broken dreams, my own crumbling around me. But something about the poems brought me solace. I was not the first to have my hopes crushed, and I would not be the last. I lifted my head and ran my fingers over the grooves made by the characters on the wall. On the women's side, there was not a room big enough to hold all of our hurt and disappointment. It is a good thing we women learned to swallow our sorrows. They would have spilled out into the world and drowned us all. I breathed in the hope of the people who had been in that room — people who had come to America with the same plans and illusions that I had, some of whom had gotten to land in Gold Mountain, some who had been sent home.

I took another deep breath. At least I knew the men were gone. I needed to get what I came for and find a way out. It was risky. I had not seen any of the men's barracks except this room. I did not know where their beds were or if they left a guard behind. After a few seconds, I forced myself forward and through the doorway.

A long hallway ran outside the door. I followed it until it opened into a sleeping quarters longer than the women's quarters and crowded with more beds. The whole place had the strong, sharp odor of men. The walls were dingy. It wasn't messy; it was temporary, less settled than the women's quarters. I scanned the room for Sterling Promise's bed. Clothes hung on lines stretched from the rafters of the ceiling and between the bars of the beds, but nothing looked familiar. I crept down one row, searching the shoes and clothes. One man's belongings blended into another's. Just as I was beginning to despair, I came to a bed that was free of clotheslines, with a bundle sitting in its center, an American hat next to it. Sterling Promise was leaving today. His things would be packed.

This has to be it, I thought. I pulled at the corners of the bundle with trembling fingers. When it fell open, I saw papers — one with Sterling Promise's picture on it. I knew I had found what I needed.

Then I felt the hairs lift on the back of my neck. A shadow fell across me. I combed through my brain, searching for a logical reason that I was there in the men's barracks, rooting through Sterling Promise's things. There was none. I turned, ready to meet the scowl of a guard.

CHAPTER 20

THE EYES BURNED, and the mouth was drawn tight. But it was not a guard.

"Father," I said.

We stared at each other, neither of us moving or speaking. I *had* grown taller than him since we left China.

"I can explain." I held my hands out to him, pleading. They shook.

His eyes shifted. Now he was staring through me. "I must be seeing ghosts." He turned his back to me.

He was not raising the alarm. He did not want to know what I was doing there. He was just going to ignore me.

Father lay down on the bunk below Sterling Promise's. He was so thin. His clothes swallowed him. I knelt beside him. "Are you feeling well?"

Silence.

"You won't tell anyone I was here, Father?"

Silence. It stung, but it was an old wound, so the pain was dull.

"I can't go back to China."

He turned away from me.

"I am sorry. For everything. But I have to do this."

He lay there, his face to the wall, motionless.

"I know you are ashamed of me. I am ashamed of myself right now. I wish for once you would try to understand."

He did not reply.

I stood up. I was truly dead to him. More tears stung, but this was no time for crying. I wanted to talk to him, convince him that I could not return to China, demand that he look at me. I wanted to shout until he did. But I didn't need another battle.

I returned to searching Sterling Promise's bag through blurry eyes. I looked at the papers, foreign letters creating foreign words, full of stamps and signatures. I did not know which papers I needed, so I took all of them. I knew that I was destroying his dream for my own. It was selfish, unfair, and everything I had accused him of doing to me. It was also the only way.

I needed just one more thing from Sterling Promise. I dug deeper into the bundle. My hands touched something soft. I pulled it out — pants, the kind the Americans wore and, folded neatly below them, a jacket and shirt. It was Sterling Promise's suit, the one Uncle had given him. The one he had brought all the way from Hong Kong to wear in America. I rummaged for something else to wear but found nothing. I sighed. I would have to harden my heart. Father still faced the wall. I pulled on the pants and shirt, fumbled with the buttons, and slid my arms into the sleeves of the jacket. I looked around for a place to hide my clothes. There was only Sterling Promise's bag, so I buried them in the bottom and retied his bundle. The sleeves of the jacket hung to the middle of my hands. The extra length on the pants pooled onto the top of my slippers, but not by much. I tucked the papers into the waist of the pants, took his hat, and stepped back from the bed.

"Good-bye, Father."

"At least I do not have to feel shame for such a daughter," he said. I pulled the thin gray blanket of the barracks over his shoulders. "Or perhaps it is you who are ashamed of me."

"Father, we are all doing what we must to keep ourselves as whole as possible."

"Ah, you are hoping to find freedom for yourself. I should have known. Did you ever imagine that the walls you are so determined to destroy might be protecting you from even greater dangers?"

I could not think of that now. I had the papers. They were a heavy burden. For the first time it occurred to me that it might not have been easy for Sterling Promise to steal my dreams either.

I slipped into the bathroom. Spring Blossom's scissors hung on a piece of thread around my neck, next to Nushi's pouch, which held both my jade and the scrap of paper with Mrs. Ying's address. I hacked at my thick braid of dark hair. When it fell into my hand, I tucked the clump of hair in the pants pocket and pulled Sterling Promise's hat over my uneven locks. We all looked rough after months on this island.

I went back to the front door of the barracks and tried the handle. It did not move. I heard the jingle of keys. I froze, my stomach twisting. As the knob turned, I darted back into the poetry room and called on the people who had left the carvings there to protect me. I heard the door swing open.

The guard's footsteps clicked halfway down the hall. The door to the barracks was unlocked. If I could only see what direction the guard was looking, I would know if I could escape or not.

"Sung," he called. He must be looking for Father. A pair of feet shuffled from the barracks.

"Hospital," the guard said.

He led Father down the hall, past the room that I was in. They went through the door. I waited. There was no click. *They lock people in, not out*, I reminded myself.

I left the men's barracks and flew past the dining hall, toward the administration building. If someone just glanced at me from a distance, I could be a translator in my American suit. Only my uneven hair and panicked expression gave me away.

Finally, I reached the long pathway that led from the administration building to the ferry. The ferry still sat at the dock, and I watched the new immigrants walk down the long ramp toward the island. Guards buzzed around the dock, separating the arrivals. The men were being hustled down the path to the hospital. Two women, clutching small bags and clinging to each other, continued along the pathway toward me.

I could hear the boots of a guard pounding behind me. "You. Not here," he said in broken Chinese.

I put my hand at my waist and pulled out my papers, ready to show them to the guard. But when I summoned the courage to look up, he was headed toward the two women, who answered him with confused faces. He gestured with his hands for them to go into the administration building. They looked at each other.

"We must," one said.

The other woman nodded.

I still had the papers in my hand. In his picture, Sterling Promise stared straight at the camera. His mouth was flat and serious, but he could not keep the smile from his eyes. I pulled my hat low and hardened my expression.

The guard caught sight of me. He marched over, jerked the papers from my hand, and glanced at them. My heart sank as my legs tensed. I would run to the ship if I had to. I would jump in the ocean and swim to America.

"Dock," the guard said, pointing down the path. "Boat."

I nodded. I flew along the line of boards that led to the ferry. My blood was hot and pounding. I was steps away from the boat.

"Stop!" I picked up my pace. It was the guard's voice. "Stop!" I walked faster. I might still be able to get lost among the passengers and crew.

I jerked back as a hand grabbed my shoulder. The guard spun me around.

"Your papers." He held the papers so close to my face that they sent back my breath. Sterling Promise's picture stared at me. I took them in my hand. As soon as I had, the guard turned and stomped back down the dock.

I handed my papers to the guard on the boat, who hurried me on with impatient American words. My legs wobbled under me. I had to sit. I thought I might faint. The boat's horn vibrated through the thick air. The deck was not as crowded as before — five or six groups of men, some Chinese, some American.

The wind carried voices, men's voices. The commotion grew until some men rounded the corner of the administration building.

Two guards were holding back a crowd of Chinese men. Two more guards ran from the path that led to the barracks. More poured from the administration building.

Still the group of Chinese men swarmed toward the dock. My chest burned, and I could barely swallow. This was it. They would drag me off the boat. The man leading the crowd was Sterling Promise.

"My papers were stolen," he shouted to a guard, whose face was washed with anger.

"Yes, my papers were stolen too," the other men echoed.

"There is a thief in the barracks!" Sterling Promise said.

"Yes, a thief, a thief!" The men kept repeating the complaints that Sterling Promise was making. There were at least twenty, maybe twenty-five of them echoing his pleas. They looked hopeful, waiting to see what trick he was trying to pull. Maybe the trick could work for them too.

Sterling Promise's mouth was drawn tight. The guards pushed the men back, yelling at them, their faces filled with frustrated confusion. I moved behind the line of men that had formed on the deck, ducking down slightly to peer between the brim of my hat and the shoulder of the man in front of me.

A guard waved his hand at the boat. One of the Americans on the ferry shouted something to another American in uniform, and the boat began to pull away from the dock.

Sterling Promise stopped and grabbed the arm of one of the guards. He shook the bundle from his bunk and pointed to the ship. Now that the boat had pulled away, the other men onshore lost hope that they could talk their way onto it and began to drift back toward the buildings. The guard jerked his arm away from Sterling Promise and pointed to the barracks. Sterling Promise shook his head and continued to dig in his bag. I had never seen him so angry. I had finally knocked off the polish that coated his actions. It did not feel as good as I imagined it would.

The guards grabbed Sterling Promise and started to drag him down the path. Suddenly, he stopped fighting them. When his arm fell to his side, it was clutching the clothes I had left in his bag. Maybe now he understood.

CHAPTER 21

THE BOAT PULSED FORWARD in uneven jerks, swaying and pitching as I gripped its side, staring into the misty air. Bells clanked blindly in the fog. Wind whipped the water. Drops of cold cut into my cheeks. I had done it. I was going to America.

A pattern of rooftops climbed through the mist. I pulled the clump of hair from my pocket and dropped it into the water, watching the dark strands scatter. Maybe some would make their way back to China — tiny travelers like the dandelion seeds that I used to send on journeys with my breath.

The fog drifted past us and broke apart on the land, its ghosts wafting onto the shore. The shoreline sharpened, became more real. As we got closer, I could see people scurrying around the docks. Chinese men in their American suits and a few pale-faces waited. Cars and carts eased themselves through the chaos. I did not want to blink for fear that I would lose sight of America and never find it again, like when you try to hang on to a beautiful dream. This would be the place, a place of possibilities, a place where I could look into people's eyes.

Blurred shadows anchored the boat to the dock and disappeared into the fog. I could hear yelling from the shore, but the strong winds carried the shouts away before I could understand them. I followed the other passengers to the plank that poured us onto the dock. A line of guards was letting people off one by one.

"What are they doing?" I asked the man next to me, dropping my voice and trying to smooth the stutter of nervousness from it.

"Checking our papers," the man said.

"Probably trying to cheat us," another man mumbled.

"Or they think one of us did steal papers," a third man said.

My throat tightened as I gripped Sterling Promise's papers. I peered around hats and heads, stretching my neck to see what exactly the guards were doing, but the wall of men blinded me. I had never been in such a crowd of men — their low voices, their earthy smells, their rough movements. Bodies pressed against me, pushing me toward more bodies, the corners of suitcases knocking against my legs. The itch to run flared in the soles of my feet.

A layer of the crowd shifted. I could see two guards in the familiar uniforms carefully examining the men's faces and documents before stepping aside to let people pass onto the dock. Would they read the tale of what I had done in the worried lines on my brow? They would not even need to do that. They could read it in the papers in my hand with Sterling Promise's picture on them. With fewer than five men in front of me, I had to think of something.

"They *are* trying to cheat us," I said to the closest men. They turned to look at me, listening. For a second, surprise stopped me, since I was just a worthless girl. But the wrappings Spring Blossom had helped tie around my chest cut into my skin, reminding me that they saw a young man standing before them. "We have followed their rules. We tolerated their prison." My voice grew in strength. "We should not have to show these foreign devils our papers." I whirled around to face the man who had been complaining earlier. "You agree with me. Cheaters and thieves! All of them." My voice was loud enough now to attract the attention of the guards and a few people on the dock.

The men did not hush me. They did not laugh or taunt me. A boldness swelled inside me. Then, in the silence, their faces turned to stone. And I realized that dressing as a man did not make as much difference as I thought.

"I am proud to show my papers to the Americans," the complaining man announced, looking around nervously. "I have nothing to hide." And with that he pushed past the three men left in front of me, holding out his papers.

"Don't start trouble," the man behind me snarled. "If they take us all back to that prison, you will be sorry."

The rest stayed dangerously silent, scowls on their faces. Their anger was different from the anger of women — quieter, thicker, darker. As a woman, people had insisted I stay silent. These men dared me to speak again. One man now stood between me and the guard. My lungs took shallow, quick gulps of air. I looked around for an escape, but there was only the guard and man in front of me, the men behind me, and Sterling Promise's papers in my hand.

I spotted two Chinese men staring at me from the dock. One — shorter, older — leaned against one of the poles with the slack rope wrapped around it. The other, tall and closer to my age, stood next to him, black hair stuffed under a cap and hands deep in his pockets. He held my gaze. His face was friendly. It was the only face that matched the welcome that I hoped I would have in America.

The older man shouted at me, "The devil is after you. You better run, Little Brother." He turned to laugh with the younger one, who only nodded slowly.

I was out of ideas, so I took that one. I exploded past the guard's shoulder, slipping through hands that struggled for my arm. Shouts followed, words I did not understand, and they only made me run faster. I ran blindly, pushing past blurs of people through unfamiliar streets, turning down every path, twisting my way free of the hollers and footsteps behind me. Someone pulled at my jacket. I stumbled back for a moment, then shot forward again, through a crowd of people in front of a building, down one street, then onto another.

The wooden buildings by the waterfront grew into taller brick buildings. The odor of fish faded and the wind softened. My legs ached, but I could feel my old life at my heels. I kept running up roads that bent sharply to the sky, only to peak and dive back down. I slowed my steps, the fear draining from me. Panting, I sucked in the chill from the air.

That is when I realized how lost I was.

Stores with big square windows filled with signs I couldn't read lined either side of the street for a block. In one shop, narrow links of sausage hung from hooks behind the glass. Waxy wheels of white and yellow sat below them, with slices cut out revealing their creamy insides. Another shop, its windows filled with bags of dark beans, smelled of earth and spices, a rich smell. Everything was wonderful . . . and terrifyingly unfamiliar. If I looked at too much, I got a dizzy feeling, like I would drown in the strangeness of it all.

A pale-faced woman hummed as she swept her front steps with a broom, clouds of dust swirling at her skirts, her face relaxed into faraway thoughts. I watched her for a few moments, wondering how I could show her the paper with Mrs. Ying's address. The

English words it would require struggled to arrange themselves inside my head: *Hello, I find friend. You help?* I pulled out Nushi's pouch and took one hesitant step, then another.

When I got close to her, the woman stopped and stared at me. She placed one hand on her hip; the other still held the broom. Her mouth dipped into a frown. I quickened my steps, passing her, but I could still feel the heat of her suspicion pressing against my back, pushing me on my way.

Two doors down, a pale-faced boy about my age walked toward me, his chin and chest forward. He shook his fist in the air and started yelling at me. I did not know the words, but I understood the warning. Two more boys followed him — more pale-faces, more foreign words. My mind struggled to find something to say. I looked around for help, but the woman with the broom was nodding along with them. When I moved to run, one of the boys slid in front of me. Another blocked my next step. I froze, looking from one boy to another, watching them fill the space around me while my heart pounded against my chest.

One stuck his nose close to mine. I stumbled back into another of the boys, who pushed me forward. I caught myself before my chest flew into the boy in front of me. Then two more pale hands shoved me. Blood flooded my face, making it red and hot with rage.

"Stop it!" I shouted.

The boys laughed a low, sinister laugh. Then one said a few words, mimicking my Chinese, stretching his eyes into thin slits with his fingers.

I had escaped guards, my family, and an island of fog and tears. I was in America, as far from China as I could go, disguised, distant from my past and myself, and yet I was still ridiculed. The smirks of Auntie Wu and the frowns of my grandfather had followed me.

Saliva gathered in my mouth and I had to concentrate to keep from spitting it in the boy's face. I could not believe that this was America. It had to be the place I imagined, because I had nothing else.

As the boys caught the scent of anger welling up inside me, their fingers curled into fists. They stopped yelling and an eerie silence settled over us. Then I saw one of their arms twitch. I stood my ground, preparing myself. I had never fought with my fists before, and that made a small part of me a little scared. The rest of me was ready.

A hand grabbed my arm. I tried to snap it away, but I was yanked backward through the small circle. Someone else stepped behind me to allow my passage. *Two more*, I thought, and set my teeth and jerked my arm from the grasp. Surprise and then fear replaced my rage when I saw the young Chinese man from the docks.

"I'm not going back," I said.

"Run!" he said.

I took one step, but one of the pale-faced boys now gripped the top of my arm, and he was leaning back, holding me there.

The younger Chinese man called to the older one, "Do something."

"The police are coming," the other yelled. "Leave him here."

Fear shot through me. I gave my arm another jerk.

"I'm not leaving," the young man announced.

"The police are a block away, Harry. I'm not telling your father that I let you get arrested."

"The police!" I shouted. "They are coming for me?"

"Fool," the older one growled. "The police aren't interested in you." He glared at the cluster of boys in front of him. "I told you we should not follow him," he said, then calmly pulled out a gun and shot it in the air. I started to run.

CHAPTER 22

When I looked over my shoulder, my pale-faced attackers were chasing us with lazy strides, waving their fists. The young Chinese man called Harry ran beside me, calling out, "Chin, let's go. No more fighting with the Italians today."

They led me on a twisted path through roads and alleys. Buildings loomed over us as we ran through their shadows. On a deserted street, Harry slowed down and looked around before taking the gun from Chin and dropping it down a sewer grate.

"That was a waste," Chin grumbled.

"You know Father will replace it," Harry said.

Chin's face just darkened.

"Where are we going?" I asked.

Neither one answered. Then, as we continued to walk, the smells that I had run to the edge of the world to escape found me. It was the raw, thick odor of freshly skinned meat that I detected first — heavier than it had ever been in our kitchen, but still familiar. Behind that was the smell of onions piled in straw baskets. Then the clean scent of parsley wove its way between the two. Soon, fragments of Chinese conversation drifted in the air. When the final alley opened onto a busy street, I saw clusters of Chinese people peering into stalls framed with baskets of colorful fruit. Red lanterns dangled in front of stores, and Chinese characters painted boldly on windows announced laundries and groceries. Ducks hung from their necks in the windows while live chickens pecked at the floor in cages below. Merchants in white aprons covered with remnants of the day's chores leaned against door frames. My skin blended with the shades of others'.

"This is America?" I said.

A smile broke across the younger man's face. "This is Chinatown. I'm Harry Hon."

"Harry?"

His smile brightened. "An American name. This is Chin."

There was silence.

"Oh . . . yes . . . of course," I stammered. I opened my mouth to give my name and then realized that I didn't have one. I could not use my real name, not until I found Mrs. Ying. I could not use Sterling Promise's name either, not if the immigration guards knew what I had done. My mind was heavy with the lies I had told, so I named myself with the only bit of truth I could find. "My name is Sung Fo Ma."

"Sung Fire Horse," Chin repeated. "You owe me a gun."

"Chin, leave him alone. He just got here," Harry said.

"I bet all of your family is back in China thanking their ancestors that you are far away." He moved to block my path. "Let me guess. They probably sent you straight from the farm. What does your farm grow?" I opened my mouth to respond, but he continued, "I know: poverty. Terrace after terrace of poverty. You are here to make money. Send it back like a good son."

I just stared at him. I did not know how to explain why I was here.

"You weren't two steps off the boat before you needed us. You see what it is like. You can't survive on your own," Chin said.

"He is trying to ask if you have a place to stay," Harry said, his voice free of the hard tones of Chin's.

"Or money?" Chin said. "You do know you'll need money?" An ugliness controlled his face that did not come from his features; it came from the expressions they settled into — the meanness in his eyes, the tension in his jaw, the snarl below the surface of his lips.

I pulled the slip of paper with Mrs. Ying's address from the pouch around my neck and handed it to Harry. "My friends, the Yings — I am staying with them. Mr. Ying owns a laundry."

"I can take you somewhere better," Chin said. "You would have a place to stay along with money, respect."

"Working for you?" I asked.

"Working for the tong."

"The tong? You want me to join an association? What kind of association?"

"One that provides protection. We're all like you. Sent here with nothing."

I shook my head.

"You need the tong. You've been through Angel Island. You know the Americans won't help you. They wish we would all go back to China. The police don't care what happens to us. In the tong, you would have brothers to keep you out of trouble. Watch your back."

I was familiar with trouble, and it was staring me in the face. "No, thanks."

"Then I guess we helped you for nothing," Chin said. Harry held the paper out to me. Chin shrugged. "I'm sure you know exactly where this address is."

"Wait." I looked at Harry. "I don't have the slightest idea," I admitted.

Chin snatched Mrs. Ying's address from Harry. A grin crept over his lips as he studied it. "Harry can take you." He swung his arm over Harry's shoulder and said something in his ear. They muttered back and forth until Harry looked at the ground.

Chin looked at me. "I was just telling Harry to be extra careful. It's getting dark, and the streets can be dangerous. See you around, Fire Horse."

Harry was already walking the other direction. He was silent, so I kept my thoughts in my head as long as I could, imagining what Mrs. Ying's home would be like and how I would tell her what I had done to get here. "Have you ever eaten Jell-O?" I asked.

Harry shook his head, but didn't look up.

"Mrs. Ying told me about it. It is American food. It is supposed to be sweet and slippery."

Harry's only answer was the slow shuffle of his long strides. Eventually he turned out of the series of alleys we had followed to stop in front of an abandoned building. Boards crisscrossed over each other, blocking the door. A thick layer of gray grime and dust coated the windows, but not enough to hide the empty room behind them. White paint flaked from the glass, but I could still see the Chinese characters. They spelled YING LAUNDRY down the side in giant letters.

"I guess your friends left," Harry said flatly.

I pressed my hand to the window. My head twisted and spun with emotions. "She gave me this address less than four months ago. Where would they go? Why wouldn't she write to me?"

Harry kicked at a rock. My father must have been right. I had been just a bother to her. "What am I supposed to do?" I said to the empty room behind the filthy window. Father was right again; this love of America *could* destroy me. Why did I think I could escape my curse here?

Harry shrugged. "Chin wants you to stay with him. He has a house with some other guys."

Heat swelled in my face. "I can't." I was dressed in Sterling Promise's suit, but I knew the secret it hid.

"Why not? Where else do you have to go?"

I shook my head, struggling to hold an ocean of tears inside.

"Chin isn't so bad."

"I can't!" I yelled.

Harry took a step back. I was losing my balance, emotions pushing up from the depths. Everything I planned had turned to dust between my fingers.

"Chin's right. You are going to need people here. A family."

I pressed my hands to my face and tipped my forehead to lean against the glass. "You don't have any idea what I need," I said. I could hear Harry's feet scrape against the pavement, but he did not walk away. I dropped my hands, my face burning. "Leave!" I shouted, spinning to face him.

He froze. I took a step toward him, fists by my side.

Harry opened his mouth, then closed it. It wasn't his fault. I knew that. But all the fight I had boiled to the surface with my fear and despair. I took another step forward, and he backed into the alley and disappeared.

I peered again into the window of the laundry, searching. There were a few lines of dust along the wall, an abandoned cloth in the corner. I turned, slid down the wall, and put my head in my hands. The bitterness of it all swelled under my wrappings. I was hopelessly lost, a fugitive, friendless, alone. More alone than I had been as a Fire Horse and outcast of the village. More alone than living with Father and Grandfather. If Sterling Promise could see me now, he would have his revenge.

Cold crawled from the bricks that I leaned against, through the suit I wore, and below my skin. My stomach was knotted so tight that I could not breathe. Even with all my anger and fear, I couldn't ignore the realization swelling inside of me — *I* had done this. I had ignored the warnings about how difficult it would be. I had shoved Sterling Promise and Father away when they offered different paths. I had kicked down all the walls and found that there wasn't freedom behind them. There weren't possibilities. There was nothing.

I looked down the street. Harry's figure was fading into the darkness. I knew I couldn't live on dreams and stories. I had tried.

I pushed myself up and raced after Harry. Falling into step next to him, I sniffed. "You're right. I need help."

Harry nodded. "First, you need a place to stay."

"I don't think I can . . . ," I started, trying to explain that I couldn't stay with Chin and his boys.

"You can stay with me. My father's house," he said, rescuing me from my discomfort. "Don't worry, Little Brother." He put his hand on my shoulder and shook it gently. The easiness had returned to his voice. "There are opportunities for the men who come here. My father will help you."

"Your father can't help me," I said.

"Of course he can. He is a powerful man in Chinatown. He runs businesses. You can work . . ." Harry's voice trailed off. He stopped walking.

"What?" I followed the direction of his stare to a figure approaching us — a young man, shorter than me and Harry, but thicker, like Chin. His eyes were buried in a round face, set in dark circles, and perched above a crooked nose. He looked like a rat.

"Harry Hon. An unexpected honor," he said. "Not skulking around in alleys today?"

I scowled. He had a casual cruelty that I recognized, no different in men than it was in women. Auntie Wu had it. Some of the women on Angel Island had it. The Italians I had run into today had it.

"What do you want?" Harry asked.

Rat Face leaned in close to Harry. I took a step closer as well. "I have a message for Chin."

"What's the message?"

"That son of a pig and a dog can go die in the street if he thinks we will let him cheat at our fan-tan tables again," he said.

Harry shifted to the side to try to pass. Rat Face blocked him, his greasy nose inches from Harry's. Inside me, a slow boil of anger began. "He had to. You know why," Harry said, the faintest tremble in his voice.

"It doesn't sound like you're going to tell him. Maybe I'll give you a busted lip to remind you."

"You don't want to do that. My father —" Harry began.

"Your father? Why would you tell your father? Sure, he runs most of the gambling dens and lotteries in Chinatown, but don't you think he feels enough shame already to have you as a son?"

"Let us pass," I said.

Rat Face leaned close and sniffed. "I could smell the stink of the ship you came over on from a block away. Why don't you crawl back to China and into the stalls where your ancestors raised you?"

How many people needed to tell me that I didn't belong here? The corners of my vision shrunk until all I could see was his fat head, and I lunged at him and shoved him to the ground. My feet kicked wildly. Nothing hit him very hard, but the blows were fast and hard to escape. He scrambled up, only to be met by the wild flinging of my fists. I thought of the poems in the room in the men's barracks, the ones that promised revenge, and I pounded at the new cage I had built for myself. If I had to fight for every inch of America I set my feet on, I would.

Hands gripped my arms and pulled me back. I yanked myself free and hurled myself toward Rat Face again. "I am not going back," I shouted.

"People are staring. They will call the police," Harry hissed in my ear.

Suddenly my vision expanded again. I was panting, breathing in with deep gulps. Harry still had a hold on my arms. I looked around at the people who had stopped to stare. Rat Face pushed his chest into mine. Harry tried to step between us. "We are going to get arrested," he said.

"I don't care," Rat Face growled, shoving him out of the way.

"You will when they deport you," Harry told him, squeezing between us again.

Rat Face stopped. "You better stay away from me," he said, sticking his finger in my face.

"That should not be difficult. The boat you smell on me doesn't drown out the gutter I smell on you," I said.

He jerked forward. Harry grabbed my arms again as I lunged toward Rat Face. "We *all* need to get out of here," Harry said.

"Let me go," I said. Fighting gave me a solid feeling, and anger was a familiar friend.

Harry's grip tightened. "I don't want to get picked up by the police after today, and I don't think you do either."

"I don't have anything to lose," I said, lurching at Rat Face, who stumbled before he plastered the smirk back on his face.

"Your friend is crazy," Rat Face said.

"Is this how you are going to repay me for my help?" Harry asked me.

He was right. "Fine," I said, letting him drag me away.

CHAPTER 23

AFTER A FEW BLOCKS of walking in silence, my heartbeat steadied. "You *are* a little crazy," Harry said.

"A little?" I said, my voice rough with the angry tears I had swallowed.

We stopped at a pair of thick, elaborately carved doors. When Harry opened them, a giant pale-faced man filled the gap. The face was rough and scarred. A combination of red, brown, and gray hair sprang from his head, and his mouth frowned over a broad, fleshy chin. I grabbed Harry and yanked him back.

Harry looked surprised, then a smile broke across his face. "It's Neil. He works for my father. Protection."

"Protection from what?" I asked as the man allowed us past him.

A voice boomed from a doorway at the other side of the room: "Protection from my enemies." A man wearing an American suit stepped forward, his gray hair slicked back. "Even you have been in America long enough to know how easy it is to make enemies."

"Hello, Father," Harry said. I heard Neil close the door behind us.

Mr. Hon continued to study me. "This must be the young man who caused the scene at the docks."

My head jerked in surprise, which made the corners of his lips curl into a smirk.

"I keep many eyes on the streets of Chinatown. There is little that happens here that I don't know about." I smoothed the front of Sterling Promise's suit nervously. "You have had an impressive beginning," he said. "You still have the flush of fighting on your cheeks. I remember that feeling. You are called Fire Horse, I believe."

I nodded. I hoped that was all he had heard about me.

"Many eyes, Fire Horse. Don't forget," he said.

"I won't," I said.

"You will bring good fortune. I see it in your face." He stepped aside but continued to study me. "You can clean up for dinner upstairs. There are clothes in the guest room. My son will show you."

I nodded again, and Harry led me across the entryway. He turned to the pale-faced man called Neil and spoke in English. Neil mumbled a string of English words I didn't recognize and lifted a newspaper to his face.

"Neil says you look like trouble," Harry explained. "But trouble for one can be luck for another."

Passing from the bare entryway into the Hons' house was like lifting the lid on a trunk of treasures. The home shone with riches. Ivory pieces rested on silk laid across thick, elaborately carved tables. Mirrors and paintings inside pearl-inlaid frames crowded the walls. A hallway led to a large room that still managed to be stuffed with lounges and chairs. Doors opened to still more rooms.

I caught only glimpses of them, but enough to see they boasted the same wealth of furnishings. "The second floor has the guest rooms," Harry said, starting up a flight of carpeted stairs. "The third floor is mostly for the servants."

"Will your mother be at dinner?" I asked. Meeting Mr. Hon had rattled me a little, and I wanted to know how many more people I had to fool.

"She died when I was younger."

"Oh, I'm sorry." And I was, because I knew the hole that left, but I was also a little relieved.

Harry pushed open a door to a room where a bed made of dark wood sat against the wall, heavy with thick, embroidered blankets. He opened a wardrobe standing next to the bed. Inside sat shirts, jackets, and pants neatly folded.

"You can take whatever clothes you need."

"Your father keeps piles of extra clothes around for people who escape guards and don't have anywhere to stay?"

"He likes to be prepared," Harry said.

"For what?"

"For everything. You'll see. He'll make plans for you too, soon." He left me to change.

When I stared at myself in a small mirror on the wall, I saw chopped hair, a thin face, and a deep exhaustion. I barely recognized myself. My name, my family, my clothes — I had left it all behind. I hoped that soon, I would have carved away enough of myself to fit . . . somewhere. Anywhere.

Once I had washed my hands and replaced Sterling Promise's suit with a fresh shirt, jacket, and pants, I went downstairs for dinner. Harry and his father were already seated. The Hons' dinner table was large, too large after months of banging elbows against the women at Angel Island. A woman brought out several trays piled high with noodles and rice, as well as bowls with chunks of fish floating in warm broth. There was no Jell-O — nothing unfamiliar, in fact. I could still have been in China, except for the fact that people were speaking to me.

"You are from Guangdong province?" Mr. Hon asked, pushing a heavy plate of dumplings toward me. "I hear it in your speech. What does your father do?"

"He and my grandfather grow rice."

"I grew up on a rice farm along the Pearl River Delta," Mr. Hon said. "You have to be determined to farm rice properly. Every step is a battle — against time, against weather, against the land itself."

"Yes, sir."

He chewed a bite of pork as he studied me. "That is how America is too — a battle. You will be a good influence on my son, I think."

My chest collapsed with relief. "I am grateful for your son's help today. Without him, I would still be lost."

Harry smiled, lifting his head for the first time since we sat down to eat. "Fire Horse was in North Beach, about to fight a group of Italians, when Chin and I found him."

"My son was no help there, I'm sure," Mr. Hon said, snorting. "What do you expect from a Rabbit, especially a Water Rabbit? Plenty of luck but no fight."

Harry stared at his plate.

Mr. Hon returned his attention to me. "But you — a Fire Horse. A sign for bold, strong boys. You are young too. You still have plenty of time to make a name for yourself before you get married. What are your plans now that you are here?"

I opened my mouth, and for the first time, there was not a single syllable inside it. I just shook my head.

"We will find something for you to do," Mr. Hon said.

"What is your business?" I asked.

"I have many businesses." He leaned back. "Mostly I help the tong protect people."

"It seems that people need protection here," I agreed.

"I knew you would understand. You would fight if someone you cared about was in danger. You would have fought today for your own safety."

"It is very easy for me to find reasons to fight," I said.

"What else can you do when you are under attack? When I first arrived here, there were many Americans who wanted the Chinese to leave. We developed ways to achieve justice and protection in our community through the tongs. Those were great days for the tongs. The Chinese controlled Chinatown. The tongs could offer something the Americans could not — a place for the Chinese to go when they were in trouble, when everyone else had turned their backs. Now, the Americans want to take that away." He scrutinized me again. "I will tell you something else. The tongs can be great again, with the right leader. There are only two left to fight it out for control of Chinatown, ours and the Sen Suey Yings. I believe you met one of them tonight."

Rat Face? I didn't want him running Chinatown.

"It is a turning point. But I think I have a plan to get the better of them. Nothing I can talk about now, but perhaps when things are more decided."

I nodded. "So you run the tong?"

"I run the businesses of the tong. The gambling houses. The

lotteries. Among other things. And I handle the police when they try to get involved."

"Why would the police be involved? A lottery seems a harmless business."

"It is. The tong is only a threat to Americans who would cheat us, police who would bully us, and even some Chinese who would betray us." Mr. Hon leaned toward me. My strength had never been measured as he seemed to be measuring it now, calculating its quantity and quality, then weighing it against his own. "But the Americans will never understand the Chinese. The lottery is an excellent example. They call it immoral." He shook his head. "It is part of the Chinese character to seek good fortune, to hold it in your hand. We give men the chance to master a piece of the unknown. You came here seeking fortune, seeking control over your fate."

I nodded. So had my uncle. So had Sterling Promise.

"Of course you did. Everyone does. Then you find out that no one wants us here. The lottery is chance to pinch off a tiny fraction of the luck we are all seeking. Why take that away from people?"

A series of chimes rang through the house. Harry and his father rose.

"Good night, Fire Horse. Tomorrow, we will find you employment," Mr. Hon said, disappearing into another room.

My eyelids were heavy, and I had to drag my arms and legs up the stairs to my room. Harry shuffled beside me. "My father will certainly help you," he said. "You are just what he wants me to be."

"My father would prefer you," I said.

"Maybe fathers are destined to be disappointed by their sons. "

"Or daughters." The words spilled from my mouth before I had measured them, but Harry's face kept the same easy expression.

"With daughters it doesn't seem as important. They don't carry the weight of the family on their shoulders."

I could have told him about the burdens daughters bear, but I was too weary from carrying them. At my door, Harry shrugged. "I am sorry we did not find your friends, but I am glad you decided to stay with us," he said.

He started down the hall, but before he slipped into his room, I called, "Harry!"

"Yes?" he said.

"Thank you."

Harry smiled and closed his door.

I undressed and unwrapped the bindings that Spring Blossom had helped me with that morning on Angel Island. It seemed like a lifetime ago. I rolled the thick cloth and tucked it under the pillow, then pulled on the loose shirt and pants that had been left on the bed by invisible servants. These servants had also taken away Sterling Promise's suit. Fire Horse was glad it was gone, but Jade Moon, who stubbornly had not abandoned me, missed that token of her old life.

I washed my face and hands in the basin in the corner and lay down on the bed. My hands settled over my stomach so that I could feel it rise and fall, and know that I was in there somewhere, inside all the fragments of lies and stories I had built around me. Images of Father with his back turned and Sterling Promise's defeated shoulders on the dock flashed through my head. I reached into the collar of my shirt and pulled out Nushi's red pouch with the jade inside. Gripping it in my hand, I tried to squeeze her wisdom from it. She'd said that jade was sharp without cutting, but I seemed to be doing a lot of cutting lately.

Maybe because I wasn't Jade Moon anymore. Jade Moon did not get to speak at dinner. She was not allowed to land in America. Jade Moon did not have a place to stay or any friends here. And I did.

I went to the window to throw out this last piece of my old life, but when I tried to pull it open, it wouldn't budge. I jerked at it until my fingers ached and sweat gathered on my forehead. I ran my hands along the edges, and that is when I felt them. Under the top of the curtain, boards were nailed into the frame, holding it shut and trapping me in the room.

Strange. Hon could be keeping his many enemies out. But I knew prisons, and this felt a little like a prison. I guessed I was not as far away from my old life as I had hoped.

I closed my fist around the jade and collapsed into the bed. When I woke the next morning, my fingers were numb from clutching it all night.

At the first rumbles of activity in the house, I pulled the wrapping out from under the pillow and stared at it for a moment. I wasn't supposed to be wrapping it around me today. I was meant to be at the Yings. I would do this again today, and maybe tomorrow. Then what? I wondered how long Mr. Hon would let me stay.

Mr. Hon and Harry were already at the table for breakfast, untouched bowls of rice in front of them. I stood in the shadows of the doorway. They did not notice me.

"Do not embarrass me."

"No, Father." Harry returned his hand to his lap and tucked his chin down.

"To be cursed with such a son. It is very lucky, this arrival of Fire Horse."

"Yes, Father," he said.

"It may allow you to take more responsibility. Perhaps you will not waste everything I worked for after all."

I had heard versions of this conversation in my own home in China, and I did not need to spy from corners anymore, so I stepped into sight. Mr. Hon straightened his back; Harry lifted his head, one side of his mouth beginning a weak smile.

"Come, have breakfast. My son and I were just discussing the lessons that I arranged for you today," Mr. Hon said, rising to leave. "We were discussing your bold stand against the Sen Suey Ying boy last night."

"Rat Face?" I said as I took the bowl of rice Harry passed me.

Harry and Mr. Hon stared at me. Jade Moon was not the only one who said rash things after all. My cheeks reddened. But out of the silence exploded a sharp, rusty laugh. Mr. Hon slapped his hand on the table, and delight spread across his face. Harry shrugged.

"Rat Face. Yes, that is very good." Mr. Hon rubbed the white hairs that sprouted from his chin. "Oh, to have that youthful outrage in my blood again! I arranged for fighting lessons for you first thing this morning. Then you will run the lottery numbers with Harry. Afterward, Harry will help you with your English."

Fighting lessons? English lessons? What for? Things had never landed in my hands easily. But I just said, "Thank you, sir."

He nodded. The corners of his mouth turned up slightly. "Your anger is good, but it must be focused and correctly executed if it is to be of any use."

I wondered who would use it.

CHAPTER 24

After breakfast, Harry and I stepped into the front room. The man called Neil sat in the entry with a newspaper across his lap, looking even scarier than he had the night before. I was heading for the door to the street when Harry stopped. Neil stood, his chin lifted, bright green eyes set under wild, dark brown eyebrows shot through with strands of gray.

"Neil is going to teach me to fight?" I hissed to Harry, who nodded.

"I can stay to translate for now," he offered.

I smiled at Neil, hoping my good luck getting along with people would continue: It didn't. "He doesn't look happy about this," I whispered.

"He's not," Harry said.

"Should I bow? Shake hands?"

"I don't think he likes it when people look at him."

I dropped my gaze to the floor. "What am I supposed to do?" I asked Harry.

Neil circled me with his arms crossed. He reached out and lifted one of my hands, yanking my arm out to its full length as he studied it. He said something in English, and I shook my head. Only a few of the words sounded like anything I had learned on the ship or on Angel Island. I looked at Harry. "Is he going to hit me?" I asked.

He shrugged.

Neil spoke again. My stomach started churning.

Harry nodded. "He wants you to do a few exercises to see how strong you are. I'll show you." He got down on the floor and showed me how to push my body up on my hands. I lowered myself obediently and began. After just a few repetitions, my arms burned with the effort. I completed as many as I could, but Neil did not look pleased.

Then I had to lie on my back and sit up, bringing my head to my knees over and over again. I was better at this one, but still not good enough to pull the smallest amount of satisfaction from Neil's face.

When I stumbled to my feet, Neil strode over. He shook my arms, which were still burning. He slapped my stomach with his giant hand, and I jumped back. Finally, he sat down and put the newspaper in front of his face again.

"That was the lesson?" I asked Harry, a little lost.

"I'll explain what he wants you to do later. Come on," he said, opening the door to the street.

"So what do we do now?"

"We continue the exercises and run numbers for the lottery."

Running numbers was perfectly named. It involved following Harry as he raced through alleys to the back doors of groceries and laundries. He would disappear inside a store for a few blissful seconds while I leaned against the wall, struggling to gulp air into my lungs. Then, too soon, he would push open the door, tuck a packet of papers inside of his jacket, and take off again.

The soles of my feet ached, my lungs burned, and the muscles down my legs throbbed. I cursed the angles of the streets, which rose to sharp peaks, then fell only to rise again. We ran up and down alleys guarded by brick walls and high windows. When I was a few steps behind Harry, which was most of the time, I could see his fluent, easy pace in front of me. His body seemed designed to run through the alleys — his long legs stretching over the pavement, his arms swinging effortlessly at his sides. Sometimes he would look to make sure I was still behind him, and I could see the light in his face. It seemed he could run forever, and I thought he might, when he pulled to a stop at a nondescript door.

"Are . . . we . . . done?" I said, my heart pounding heat into my face.

Harry stood next to me, his breath already starting to steady itself. He smiled and patted my shoulder. "You did well."

I tried to glare at him, but it was too exhausting.

Harry knocked on the door. A small panel slid open. "Morning, Sam," Harry said. A bolt loosened inside the door, which cracked open just enough to let us slide through. Harry led us up a flight of stairs and down a dark hallway to another door, where another pair of hands opened another bolt. Harry opened the final door into a narrow room. It was a dark, dusty space, empty except for a long table that stretched the width of one side. Four men stood behind it, protected by a wire screen. Harry took the packets from his jacket and handed them through a thin gap in the wires.

"You're later than usual," the man said to Harry as his fingers unwrapped the packets and flew through the papers inside. The man wrote a figure on a piece of paper, which he passed back to Harry.

Harry jerked his chin over his shoulder at me. "I had company."

The man nodded. "You're still the first one here." He peered over his glasses at me. "So he must have made you run."

"We don't have to run?" I said.

"It's actually discouraged, because it might draw attention. Harry knows every inch of the alleys and basements in Chinatown. If you weren't with him, the police would have picked you up and searched you."

"We're not *supposed* to run?" I repeated, glaring at Harry. "We could get arrested for running?"

Harry handed the man a pile of bills and stuffed the remaining ones in his pocket. "True, but now we have time for lunch before we pick up the results."

He led me down another flight of stairs, across a different alley, and into a noodle shop. We sat down.

"About the running," Harry said.

"Yes, let's talk about the running. Did Neil even tell you to make me run?"

Harry looked at the table. "He had me run when I trained with him."

"You trained with Neil?"

"Briefly. Until he realized I didn't have the smallest drop of fight in me. He said if I got in trouble, I should just run. I don't think he meant it badly, but Father was furious."

"You *are* fast."

He relaxed. "My father hates the fact that his son runs numbers. But he lets me because it is the only thing I seem to be good at. He wants me to learn other aspects of the business, but every time I try, I bring nothing but shame to him."

"What do you mean?"

"Last month, I was at one of the gambling houses. Father sent me to observe the dealers and watch for cheating. Rat Face and other Sen Suey Ying boys started coming. They would set down a dollar. If they won, they would reveal the ten hidden underneath. If they didn't, they slid their dollar off the table and replaced it with one that did not cover a ten-dollar bill."

"What did you do?"

Harry leaned forward. "Nothing. Can you believe it? I did nothing. Father was furious. I was the coward he always says I am, but it seemed so pointless to confront them. There were six or seven of them in the gambling house. What was I going to do? But he still blames me for his shame from that."

"It's not your fault they cheated."

"No, but it's my fault that I allowed them to get away with it. He wants me to lead the tong back to its days of glory and power." He started to pick at the table. "Chin kicked the Sen Suey Ying boys out, then sent our boys to pull the same trick in a few of their gambling houses. Father got his money back. He always gets back what is his. I swore to myself that next time, I will not stand by and let anyone cheat us. I will do something, no matter what it costs."

This world of men was a strange one, I thought. If you were wronged, not only could you do something about it, but you were *supposed* to.

"I'm sorry you hate the running," Harry said, "but it is the only chance I have to get out from under my father's scrutiny for a little while. Do something I am good at."

"You found some freedom."

"A little. My father's eyes are everywhere." He shrugged. "So if you could not mention it . . ."

"Of course." I leaned back in my chair. "What do you do with your freedom?"

"I sit here. Sometimes I explore the alleys and basements. I look for faster routes."

"Do you ever go outside the alleys? I would love to see more of Chinatown."

Harry shifted a little in his seat. "It probably isn't a good idea."

"Why not?"

"People might see us — soldiers from my father's tong, soldiers from another tong. The police," he said, but I could tell that he was tasting the idea, rolling the possibilities of it through his mind.

"We could try it, slip in and out of these alleys you are so familiar with."

He pressed his lips together.

"Don't you want to see if you can get just a little more freedom?"

Harry hesitated. "Maybe one or two streets. On our way back."

I smiled. The months on Angel Island had made me hungry for walking, for the joy of air and sun against my skin.

After our meal, we stepped from the alley into a very different Chinatown, a bright, colorful one where red lanterns danced in the breeze. The darkness and fear that had muddied my vision the night before were gone, and I could see the vibrant life that filled the streets. Leaves trailed down from balcony gardens. We passed twisted iron gates and giant light poles with dragons coiled around the tops. Small shrines sat with sticks of incense standing up in front of them, trails of smoke lifting from their stems.

I stopped in front of a window piled high with cages of ducks and roosters. A man looked back at me from behind the cages, and I gave him a small smile. He crossed his arms and spread his stance. I turned away, not sure how I had offended, only to catch two men huddling with a man selling incense, all of them glaring at me from under the brims of their hats. Caught in their stare, I didn't see a mother coming out of a bakery. I almost collided with her. I tried to apologize, but before I could, she swept her child into her arms and scurried across the street.

I was accustomed to looks of disdain, but what were these looks doing here in America?

Harry saw my distress. "It is like my father told you. They have lost their appreciation of the tongs. Corrupted by the Americans." He stared straight ahead.

"How do they know?"

"They know who my father is. Plus, there's your suit."

"Other people in Chinatown wear suits."

"Yours is dark enough to blend at night. You wear a jacket that's loose enough to hold a gun, a few knives, maybe some padding in case you get stabbed. It's a tong suit."

I looked at the clothes I had been so grateful for yesterday.

"We better get back. We need to pick up the lottery results."

I scanned the street. These people did not look at me like I was cursed, but like I was cruel — a harsher look, where disapproval was mixed with distrust and seasoned with anger.

"Yes, let's get back," I said.

CHAPTER 25

It took me only a few days to discover the rhythm of the Hon house. It ran to the beat of rules and schedules designed to ensure safety and compliance. Harry taught me how to read the clocks that hung in every room — their circles of long and short lines — so that I could work myself into the household's pulse. The front door was unlocked at precisely seven in the morning, when Neil arrived. Neil came ten steps inside, newspaper in his hand, and sat in a chair across from the door. Meals began and ended at specific times. He rose to leave at ten at night. Mr. Hon then locked the door with a key he kept on a chain and tucked into his pocket. Nothing would open it until Neil's coming in the morning.

Every morning I would go down to the entryway and do as many of Neil's exercises as I could. Then Neil would point at the door, and Harry and I would go out to run the numbers, have lunch, then wait for the winning numbers to be drawn and pinned to the board at the lottery house. The numbers were hand-copied and passed out to the runners. We took them back to the shops to share with the ticketholders, and then returned to the Hons' house at the precise moment we were expected. Harry spent the rest of the afternoon in his father's office and the evenings with me, teaching me English.

Harry was an excellent teacher. He helped me organize the words floating in my head. I started to fit them together. A table could be a large, heavy table. A book could be a thick, leather book. Eventually, I could say that the thick, leather book sat on the large, heavy table. If I made progress linking more and more words together, Harry would teach me some of the colorful phases Neil used.

" 'You're doing it arseways.' "

"What does that mean?"

"He usually said it when I was messing up. So I heard it a lot. And 'bollocks.' I think it means stupid."

"Bollocks," I repeated, rolling the word on my tongue.

"He doesn't like 'gits.' And if he's really mad, he yells, 'Stop acting the maggot.' "

"I like that one."

"Wait until you hear him say it."

I did more of Neil's exercises in my room at night until my body collapsed in bed. Sometimes I was too tired even to undo my wrappings, and I would wake up with deep impressions of them along my chest. I liked the drained feeling Neil's training left inside me, almost as much as I hated the smug look on his face when he sent me away each morning. I was determined to prove to him that I could learn to fight.

Days passed. Then weeks. Enough time for the days to shorten and cool in Chinatown. Enough time for Father to return to China and plant his feet firmly in the dark soil of the terraces again. Enough time for Sterling Promise to move his life back on a path that didn't include the inconvenience of a Fire Horse girl. With the household's customary efficiency, his suit had been cleaned, pressed, and placed in the wardrobe that I drew my clothes from. I buried it under as many of the Hons' shirts and pants as I could.

I got used to being locked inside at night. I got used to the windows that were nailed shut. I even got used to deepening my voice. The rules and schedules were like the thin string that Nushi had used to mend patches in our clothes. One thread was easily broken, but when you wrapped one on top of another, on top of another, suddenly you couldn't move. I had found only misery at the end of the paths I blazed myself. It was easier to take a path that was laid out in front of me, so I followed every plan Mr. Hon made for me.

One morning, I did my exercises for Neil, rose, and headed for the door. Neil said something in English that I didn't understand. Harry tugged on my arm to stop me.

"What?" I said.

"I believe Neil thinks you're ready."

Neil said something else, but I only caught the word "fight."

"I understood a couple of words, but . . . ," I said to Harry.

"I'll translate," he said.

Neil stomped his feet on the floor, planting them firmly. I stared at him. He stomped again, looking like an angry bear. He threw his hands in the air and pointed at his feet, then pointed at mine. Eventually, he reached down toward my feet. I took a step back, but his long arms pulled my feet farther apart and planted them on the floor, his giant hands covering them completely as he muttered a string of angry English.

I exchanged a glance with Harry. "Under your shoulders," he translated. I nodded.

Neil started to bounce on his feet, moving quickly, gracefully, his weight shifting, his body cutting different angles in the air. After a few seconds of watching, I tried bouncing around a little myself. I could feel the new muscles from the exercises I had done spring to life.

Neil twisted up his face like something smelled bad, settled both feet on the ground, then lazily swung an open palm at my jaw. There was only a fraction of his strength behind it, and I jumped back, but my neck still snapped to the side on impact, and a throbbing began along the lower edge of my cheek. As I rubbed the sting, anger pricked at my skin.

"What was that?" I demanded.

Neil said something.

"He said you have to move faster," Harry said. "And don't look at your feet. Your feet are not going to hit you."

"He could have just said that without the smack." The hit had sent heat through my blood.

Harry put his hands up. "I am just translating."

I took my stance again. I had barely lifted my fists in front of my face before Neil slapped me a second time, turning the heat in me to fire. He said something else.

"He said that was better." Harry smiled nervously.

"He's not teaching me anything. I think this is just an excuse to hit me." I glared at Neil, hoping he saw the spite in my eyes, the shadows of anger, bitterness, and outrage. But when I met his steady glare, I knew the swirling tangle of emotion in me would not pierce even one layer of the strength in him. That just made me angrier. I had dodged two of his swipes, so I decided to get in one of my own. I swung at Neil.

In one smooth motion, he swept my legs out from under me, pressed my face to the floor, planted his knee in my back, and let loose a string of angry words.

"He says not to do that again," Harry said.

"Harry, I'm getting the feeling you aren't translating everything," I said.

"Neil's English is tricky."

"Try," I said through gritted teeth, my face mashed to the floor.

He listened for a moment to Neil's speech. "You are all trouble and no fight. All stubbornness, no strength," he said.

"And?"

Harry sighed. "He said worthless Chinks wash over American shores like trash these days."

Neil lifted his knee and stood over me as I struggled to rise. He grumbled another string of words while I rubbed the spot in my back where his knee had been. I looked at him. He planted his feet and crossed his thick arms. I searched for the anger in him that would feed mine, but I saw only strength and disgust.

"Don't worry," said Harry. "He hates all of us, the Chinese. My father just thinks it's safer to have a white bodyguard. We'll talk to Father. He'll —"

"No, Neil's right," I said. Neil had strength — the kind of strength that made you safe. Even with his face twisted and hard, his eyes remained steady. I only had the kind of strength that made me dangerous. I cupped my hands together and bowed to him.

"I'm a git. I did it all arse-backward," I said in English.

A moment of shock crossed Neil's face, then the scowl returned. He stomped back to his chair and put his paper in front of his face.

Harry gave me a small smile and patted me on the shoulder. "I think he's starting to like you."

So the new rhythm of my mornings began. Harry did not have to translate the names of the moves Neil taught me. Neil's constant shouting of words like "jab," "straight right," and "uppercut" burned them into my memory. He was also fond of using gestures to communicate, most of which ended with a smack to the side of my head. After thousands of punches, repeating the motion again and again, my shoulders ached, my wrists were sore, and my stomach trembled — but Neil was satisfied with my form. We moved on to combinations of punches. These started quickly and then slowed their rhythm, building walls and creating holes.

I loved the fighting lessons, the English lessons, running the streets, learning the workings of a lottery. I was like dry soil getting its first rain. I soaked it all in as fast as I could, fearing it would end in a moment and I would still be thirsty. My head was full of new words to make me American. My body was filled with new moves to make me strong. Unfortunately, my mouth was still full of lies.

Every morning after my training with Neil, Harry and I still ran numbers. The air was getting colder and the running was getting easier, but even though I spent most of lunch recovering my breath, I did not ask Harry to leave his basements and alleyways again. I knew it wasn't the police or the tongs that he hid from.

But one morning, two months into my stay with the Hons, we stepped out of the alley that led to the noodle shop and saw Chin turn in at the other end. Before he could catch sight of us, Harry yanked me into a narrow passage that led to a wide street.

"What are you doing?" I said.

"Chin can't know we finish running the numbers early."

"Why not? The lottery agents know. The noodle shop owner knows."

"My life is not their business. They aren't going to tell my father."

"But Chin will," I said, nodding. "Then we better hurry." I walked toward the line that separated sun from shadow at the threshold of the alley.

"Wait. I can't."

I peered over my shoulder. Chin would soon pass the opening where the two alleys met and spot us. "Look at a spot just in front of their foreheads."

"What?"

"You don't want to go in the street because of the looks people give you, right? The trick to avoiding their looks is to stare at a spot just in front of their foreheads. Their faces will blur. You won't see their gazes."

He hesitated.

"Trust me," I said, shoving him gently into the street.

We slipped between crowds of people, getting a few looks. When we were a block out of the alley, a worn leather ball rolled up a hill, came to a stop at my feet, then rolled back down into the arms of a boy just one or two years younger than me. Another boy called to him, and the first boy dropped the ball and ran it over to the other, dancing it between his feet as he went. They entered a bright building. Big windows lined its first floor.

"What is this place?"

"The YMCA. It has sports and English classes."

"What sports?"

Harry shrugged. "Basketball, soccer, track."

"What's track?"

"Running."

"You would be good at that. Have you ever tried it before?"

"No," Harry said.

I wandered toward the window, drawn by the open smiles and easy movements of the people inside. A group of boys piled their book bags and coats in the corner, then went to join the two with the leather ball. They did not look like they had windows that were nailed shut. People probably didn't pull their children closer when they passed. It was an island of the America I'd imagined. "We should come here after we run the numbers," I said. It was difficult to imagine any tong soldiers there, squinting in the bright light, scowling at the laughter. "Does your father have eyes inside?"

Harry released a hard laugh, his warm breath clouding the chilly air. "No." He stared in the window. "This is a new Chinatown. It is a Chinatown he doesn't believe in."

I took a step closer. "I don't think this Chinatown believes in him and his tong either."

Harry's shoulders tensed.

"Harry, I know, you don't want to hear this. But look, this is what life outside the alleys looks like. They look —"

"Happy," he finished.

"And free," I added.

"People don't hammer them with scowls when they pass," he said.

"Or think they are only capable of harm," I said.

"It would be nice," he said.

"What would be nice?" Chin said, suddenly standing between us. He had crept up behind us while we were talking.

My mind scrambled for an explanation that would leave Harry his number running and freedom. There was none.

Chin lifted the collar of his jacket against the wind. "You must be done running the numbers. I'll tell your father that you can help out with more tong business. I think he will be pleased," he said.

Chin was right. Mr. Hon made the announcement at dinner. "Harry, you will not be running the numbers anymore."

"Not at all? But —"

"You will take on new responsibilities with the tong. This comes at just the moment I was hoping you could take over some business with our friend Lo and his girls."

"Who will run the numbers? Fire Horse?"

"No." He looked at me. "You will have more time for your lessons with Neil. I may have some business for you to take over as well."

"What business?"

"I will let you know soon."

"Sir, I still have a lot of trouble understanding Neil."

"My son can still translate, for a little while."

I saw the walls closing in on Harry, locking him in place. And I had the vague feeling that walls were being built around me too. I brushed the thought aside as quickly as I could.

Neil started the next morning with a series of punches that he had taught me. I swung at his meaty hands, shifting from one foot to another. I liked the motion of striking, the powerful force that started in the feet, moved through the shoulder, and sprung out through the knuckles. As we trained, I thought of Chin taking away Harry's freedom. I thought of all the laughing faces in the village. I thought of the nights I had spent in the kitchen alone, ignored by my father and grandfather. I thought of Sterling Promise and the lies that he had told me. My eyes narrowed, and I punched harder and harder at the air, little grunts escaping, baby versions of Neil's growls.

Neil said something to Harry.

"He says that you are too angry. He says you can *have* anger. Anger can focus you, make you strong. But you can never *get* angry. If you get angry, the other guy wins."

I dropped my fists down by my sides and let the ghosts around me fade. Neil dropped his hands as well and growled a few words. I was getting better at understanding him. It was a matter of finding the important words among the curses and colorful phrases and focusing on those.

"He said —" Harry started.

I held up a hand. "No, I think I understood. He said he would see if I could punch, but I thought —"

A flash of movement. Then pain exploded across the left side of my face, and my neck snapped to the side. I swayed back and forth, lights dancing in front of my eyes, a hum in my ear, and the taste of blood in my mouth.

"He said he would see if you could *take* a punch," Harry said.

I blinked the lights away and stretched the muscles of my face. Blood pushed energy through my veins, leaving a pounding in my heart and tension in my muscles. After one last shake of my head, I balled my hands into the tight fists Neil had taught me and lifted them to guard my face.

"You're pure useless as a fighter, but at least you got the guts to take a punch," Neil said. He didn't smile, but he stopped frowning for a moment.

"Did you understand?" Harry asked.

I nodded. I looked from Neil to Harry and back again, still keeping my fists up. Neil reached out. I flinched, lifting my fists closer to my face. He brought his hand slowly to my shoulder and patted me gently with his paw.

"That is enough for today," he said and sat back down.

CHAPTER 26

MORE DAYS PASSED, more weeks, more months. I got used to standing in Neil's enormous shadow and the rhythms of his speech. I stopped flinching at the low murmurs that came from deep in his throat when he was unhappy. The fighting connected us. It forced us to share space and air, to develop a rhythm and trust as we hurled punches at each other.

Harry was kept in his father's office from breakfast to dinner, no longer allowed to waste his time running numbers through Chinatown's alleys.

One night at dinner, Mr. Hon asked, "How are your lessons with Neil going?"

"Well," I said.

"Good. I have plans that I want to start before the New Year."

The New Year was a week away. I shouldn't have been surprised. There was a burst of sweeping and cleaning throughout the house. From the window in my room, I could see women carrying blossoming lilies and quince home in the evenings. Salted and candied plums, bean cakes, and melon seeds appeared in dishes scattered around rooms and at dinner. The day before, Chin walked in eating lychee nuts from a roll of brown paper. But I didn't want to see all of this.

It had been a year since I sat outside our home in China with Nushi, listening to her tell the Cowherd and Weaver Girl story. A year since Father and Grandfather had tried to marry me to Fourth Brother Gou. A year had passed since Sterling Promise arrived in my life.

Harry had been in his father's office all afternoon, which left me training with Neil until he grew tired of me. My arms ached, and there were bruises along the side of my body where I had carelessly let my guard down for a split second. Neil was showing me how to wrestle a man to the ground, when suddenly he reached down and patted the wrappings along my side. I froze.

"Ah now, what's that?" he asked.

I could feel panic squeezing my heart. I had to close my eyes to steady myself.

"Is it one of those shirts you people wear in fights? The padding?"

I knew what he was talking about — the padded shirts that some tong members wore to slow the progress of bullets and knives. Some were simply a thick quilting. Others had a layer of woven steel links inside. I nodded.

"Did Chin give it to you? The one with the mean puss?" He pointed to his face. I nodded again.

Neil reared back and slammed his fist into my stomach. I buckled over, nausea sweeping over me. "Pure useless," he said.

As I crawled to my feet, my head dizzy, I stumbled a little. Neil's hand reached down. I grabbed it and let him pull me up. Then I took my stance again and readied myself.

He shook his head. "You don't stop when you're hit. You don't stop when you're knocked down. You fight long past the time any sane man would. You know nothing about fighting, but you are definitely a fighter."

"Is . . . that . . . good?" I asked in English, pushing the words out with each exhale.

He thought for a moment. "People who fight like that are usually fighting more than what's in front of them, so I guess that depends."

"On what?"

"On if what you are fighting is worth it."

Neil went into the house and came back with a second chair. He sat it down across from his and gestured for me to sit.

"It is time for you to learn some strategy."

"Strategy?" I said, shaking my head.

"Using your head more than your fists."

"Why?"

"You can't just punch everyone," Neil said. "Did you think that was all fighting was?"

"Nooo . . . ," I said. "There's blocking and holds . . ."

"And thinking," he said, tapping his head. "People who don't think, get themselves killed. When you walk into a fight, you have to calculate."

"Calculate?"

"Look around," he said, pointing to his eye. It was funny when Neil mimed his words. I shook my head, pretending not to understand. "Look. Look," he said. Now he put his hand on his brow and scanned the room.

I held back a smile. "Oh, 'look.'"

"How many people there are. Where you are. Are you blocked by four walls or out in the open?"

"It matters?"

"It depends on whether you want to run away," he said.

"Why would I run away?"

"So that you can fight another day. Sometimes, Fire Horse, it makes sense to run. There's no shame in it."

"But —"

"Let's say I wanted to kill you." He put his hands on his knees and leaned toward me.

I nodded. That wasn't hard to imagine.

"Would you come find me?"

I shook my head.

"When I found *you*, would you rather fight me on the streets or in a room?"

"The street."

"Why?"

"I'm faster. You're strong, but if I . . . I . . . move faster you can't hit me."

"That's right. A real fight isn't about knocking someone out. It is about surviving. You might survive by hitting your opponent, but you might survive by just wearing him down. Draining his resources. Or you might survive by running. Fighting is only useful when it gets you what you want."

I thought of Sterling Promise. He had told me something like that once, ages ago. "How did you learn to fight?"

Neil hesitated. "My father taught me. I was a bit of a trouble-maker, with a nasty temper."

"But didn't the fighting get you in more trouble?"

"Fighting doesn't get you in trouble. Getting angry does. Not having control does. Fighting teaches you that control."

"In China, I was told not to fight," I said.

"You can't ask someone with fight in them not to fight. You might as well ask them to rip out their own heart. Besides, I had to fight. It was tough for Irish families in America. We fought for everything."

"Yes," I said. "I can understand that."

He looked at me, his brows folding into creases that buried the scars between his eyes. "Boxing has always been the sport of the underdog." He picked up the paper and pointed to the pictures of men starting at me from its pages. "Irish, Jewish, German, black, you name it. They come here and they fight for every inch of freedom."

We sat in silence. His words burrowed into me, into places I had forgotten, where my dreams of America and its freedoms had cowered.

Neil leaned back and continued the strategy lesson. He taught me how to evaluate a room. He taught me how to add up the strengths and weaknesses of an opponent and match them with my own. While he was explaining the use of barriers, Mr. Hon came into the room.

"Why aren't you fighting?" he asked Neil in English.

Neil stood but did not answer. "Neil is teaching me strategy," I said, also in English.

"Why would you need to know that?" he mumbled, pulling out his watch. He switched back to Chinese. "Chin and Harry are expecting you in the main room." He walked through the room and up the stairs.

When I started to walk away, Neil grabbed my arm. "That man just wants you to fight. He doesn't care if you get killed. I'm teaching you to survive."

I nodded. He dropped my arm, sat back in his chair, and lifted the paper to his face.

"Wait," I said, grinning. "Does that mean you care if I get killed?"

Neil kept his paper up. "Get out of here. I can't listen to your blathering all day."

CHAPTER 27

HARRY LOOKED UP when I stepped into the room.

"Mr. Hon has a little job he wants us to do," Chin said.

I turned to Harry. "What is this about?"

"More responsibility," Chin answered.

After dinner, we walked into the evening, past the parade of dragon lamps and curved pagoda rooftops. I tucked my hands in my pockets to guard them against the chill. The main street was emptying, so only a few people frowned as we passed. We stopped in front of the door to a laundry.

"Someone needs to tell me what we are doing here," I said.

Harry stared at the sidewalk and shuffled from one foot to the other. Chin said, "Harry is going to offer this man an opportunity, and you and I are here to make sure he takes it." He pushed through the door. I frowned at hearing myself paired with Chin.

Inside, packages of clothes wrapped in brown paper waited in woven baskets to be delivered. Planks of wood leaned in the corner next to a shelf with shakers of water, ready for the next day's ironing. Washing troughs lined the back wall. A man stood behind the counter, moving coins from one pile to another with one hand and writing in a large ledger with the other. When he saw Chin, he lifted his shoulders and tightened his lips. It looked like the beginning of a fight.

But based on what Neil had just taught me, it was a terrible place to fight — crowded with baskets and bottles, and shelves of folded sheets and towels. It was a place where strength or luck would win over skill. Someone like Neil, who could knock a person out with one punch, might do well, but I wouldn't, and I suspected Chin wouldn't either.

"It is nice to see you," the man said to Harry. But the forced sound of his words betrayed him.

Chin pushed Harry forward. "I hope your business is doing well," Harry said.

The man muttered a response.

"You have been a loyal member of the tong for many years, and it has always protected you," Harry said, his voice tense.

The man looked up. "Say what you came to say."

Harry shifted from one foot to the other. "We require your store for our lottery business. People buy their tickets here, and a runner picks up the tickets and —"

The man slammed the ledger shut and coins rattled down the table. "I know how the lottery works."

Harry swallowed and continued. "Chin will send one of his boys to run the lottery in your back room. If the police come, all you will have to do is warn them, and they will disappear."

"That is just what I need. Hatchet men in my business." He looked at Chin, then his eyes shifted to include me. The accusation stung. I wasn't a hatchet man, one of the brutal men Mrs. Ying said terrorized Chinatown. Hatchet men like Chin did not carry bad luck in their skin; they mined it from the tragedy around them and directed it to their own ends. I had never wanted to admit that this was what Mr. Hon was training me for. Every time that thought slipped into my conscience, I slammed it back. But now someone had said it out loud. It was in the air around me. Chin moved forward, but Harry shook his head.

"First I allow the lottery, then you hide slave girls in my back room, then you start to run games at night. Before long, the police come and arrest me. *I* lose my business. The tong, they just find a new laundry."

"Nothing will happen —" Harry began.

"Where did you run the lottery before?" the man demanded.

"What?" Harry said.

"What happened to the last place?" he repeated.

I looked from Harry to Chin to the laundryman. Everyone's shoulders were tight. Chin took a step forward. The laundryman moved quickly, pulling a revolver from below the counter and holding it with two trembling hands. Chin yanked his own revolver from under his jacket. The laundry owner was behind the one piece of furniture that could block bullets. I looked for an escape, but Chin blocked my path to the door. This was going horribly wrong.

Harry raised his hands. "We don't want any trouble."

Chin held his gun steady, and a dark smile flickered across his lips. He wanted trouble.

My heart started to beat faster. I had not come all the way from China to become the hatchet man Mr. Hon wanted me to be. "This is a bad idea," I said to Chin. He flexed the muscles in his arms. I turned to Harry. "Convince him," I hissed.

"How?"

Chin and the laundry owner stared at each other. I grabbed Harry's arm to pull him out of the way, but when I did, the laundry man's arm stiffened and the gun moved to point at Harry. "I can't lose my laundry. I have a family in China," he said. I could barely hear the words for the desperation screaming from them.

Harry nodded. That seemed to be all he could manage.

"Chin, put your gun down," I said, struggling to keep my voice steady.

He did not look at me. "You'll run the lottery from here," he said. "You owe it to the tong."

"What about my duty to my family?" the laundryman yelled at him. "Go ahead and shoot me. It will only prove what bullies the tongs have become. You don't protect anyone but yourselves."

"No one needs to shoot anyone," I said.

"We have talked enough," Chin said, taking two steps toward the counter, keeping the gun leveled at the owner. Chin was someone who fought. He was not a fighter. It was up to me.

"Wait," I shouted, my mind working quickly. "There is a way this can work for everyone."

"I didn't bring you to make peace," Chin growled.

I ignored him and looked at Harry. "This man needs to make money. Your father needs to hide the lottery. What if the tickets came in the laundry? Players tuck them inside the pockets of clothes going to be cleaned." I turned to the laundryman. "You can't be responsible for the things people leave in their pockets." I was trying to get everything out before the dizziness I was feeling overwhelmed me. Shifting my stance slightly, I mimicked the man's lifted chin and shoulders. "After you collect the laundry for washing, you can put the tickets in the trash by the back door. A runner can pick them up from there. Everything still works like a laundry. If the police come, they would find nothing more than a pile of old lottery tickets left in people's pockets. You might even get some extra business. The winnings get packaged with the laundry and picked up the next day."

"It's a good idea," Harry said.

"You don't have to fight everyone," I said to Chin, my heart stumbling a little at the familiar sound of the words. He didn't move. "He has a gun pointed at Harry," I hissed.

Chin growled but lowered his gun. The laundryman let his gun drop too.

My head felt light. Harry's shoulders relaxed.

"I'll consider it," the laundryman said. "Now, get out."

Harry and I moved willingly toward the door. Chin hesitated. "I'll have to discuss this with Mr. Hon," he said before he stormed into the night.

Harry and I walked back home in silence. When we got there, Mr. Hon was in the front hall talking with Chin in a low voice. "I'll take care of it," he said. "Harry, come with me."

"Mr. Hon, if there was a problem, it is my fault," I offered.

"Then we'll have to talk about it in the morning. Right now, I would like to speak to my son."

Harry followed him into his office. I spent a sleepless night going over the evening in my head — the laundryman's desperation, Harry's fear, Chin's anger. And me — hatchet man. Is that what I had turned into? Perhaps. But I was in America, and at the very least, I did not have to be what others told me I was.

When I went down to breakfast the next morning, Harry sat alone at the table. "Is your father angry?" I asked.

"I can't tell."

I sat down and started to eat. After we chewed for a few moments in silence, he said, "Why didn't you want to fight last night?"

"He had a gun. I'm trying to learn not to fight when I know I will lose."

Harry stared at the table. I took another bite.

"It was smart, what you did," he said. "I know it probably saved me."

"Don't thank me. Thank Neil. He taught me," I said.

"Neil taught you to persuade people?"

I laughed at the thought of Neil trying to explain how to manipulate people without hitting them. "No, that was Sterling Promise," I said. His name flew off my tongue like it had been waiting there for months.

"Who is he?"

My smile faded. "We traveled together. He was skilled at talking people into things."

"It is strange hearing you talk about people from your past. You never mention people from China."

"Would you clear away your past if you could?" I asked.

"Maybe some of it. The parts when I brought shame to my father."

"When we ran the lottery tickets, I always liked watching them clear the winning numbers from the drawing the day before," I said. "Everything is possible again. Everyone is a potential winner. That is what coming to America is for me."

Harry opened his mouth, but before he could speak, a servant entered and announced that Mr. Hon wanted to see me in his office. I looked at Harry, who just shrugged. I rose and followed the servant into a room that reminded me of a more elaborate version of my father's study — carpets lining the floor, leather books in tidy rows behind glass doors. Chin was already there, glaring at me. Mr. Hon regarded me coolly. He opened his hand, inviting me to sit in a chair across from him.

"Chin was just telling me about your meeting last night," he said.

I nodded.

Chin turned his dark eyes on me. "You should have kept your mouth shut, Fire Horse. The soldiers of the tong are there to enforce what the tong decides, not make decisions on their own."

"He was going to shoot you. And he was going to shoot through Harry to do it," I said.

Mr. Hon looked at Chin, who shifted in his seat. "That man was a coward. He would not have shot anyone," Chin insisted.

"Can you be sure?" Mr. Hon asked. "You can risk your own life, but you're never to risk the life of my son."

"I can't do my job if I have to negotiate with everyone who pulls out a gun."

"True," Mr. Hon said. "And I agree that Fire Horse did not make much of a soldier."

Chin grunted his enthusiastic agreement.

"How did Harry do?" Mr. Hon asked.

"He —" Chin started.

"He didn't lose his temper and pull out a gun," I interrupted.

Mr. Hon looked a few times from me to Chin. "Would you like to be a soldier for the tong, Fire Horse?"

I was pretending to be many things, but my whole body rebelled against this one. "I would not."

Mr. Hon's face was still and hard. "It is a great honor to be asked."

"There is no honor in what Chin does," I said.

Chin's face reddened. "He would be worthless as a soldier. Worse than worthless, dangerous. You can't trust him to follow orders."

Mr. Hon nodded. "Last night did not go the way I expected."

Chin leaned back in his chair and folded his hands, a satisfied smile flickering on his lips.

"I understand if you want me to leave," I said, starting to rise.

"That doesn't mean it went badly, though." Mr. Hon signaled me to sit back down. "I have another plan." He paused. "Harry must take over leadership of the tong when I am gone. I will not have it fall into other hands after all my work. It is his duty. But he lacks the fight and the fire that he must have to protect our family against its many enemies. Fire Horse, you seem to have just the elements he needs." He looked at me like I was supposed to understand more than what he was saying. "Perhaps you would be willing to help him."

Chin stiffened.

"You would be his friend, his defender, his protector. You would be like a brother to him — a younger brother," he said, making sure I knew my place.

I hesitated. "A younger brother who fights his fights."

"There would perhaps be fights to fight, but you would have more discretion in fighting them. You will gain from this too. Family members are loyal to one another. They don't allow anyone or anything to interfere with that loyalty. Someone that loyal to my son would enjoy my utmost protection."

I did not think I wanted his unique style of protection. "What if I refuse?"

His face hardened again. "I do not recommend that. You will be back on the streets with no friends, no family, and no papers. Do you think the Yings will take you in after you have lived under my roof?"

The shock of his knowledge of the Yings must have registered on my face.

"Of course I know about your friends. I keep a close eye on everything that goes on in Chinatown, especially when it involves my son." He folded his hands. "In fact, I probably know more than you do. They are still in Chinatown."

Neil told me that a fighter is most vulnerable when he is off balance. If Mr. Hon was trying to catch me off balance, he succeeded. "The Yings are here in Chinatown?" I stammered.

"I had Harry take you to their old address," Chin said, grinning.

A chill swept through me. I thought I had chosen my place here at the Hon house. It was my only option, but I chose it. Now, I found out it was chosen for me too.

"Do you think you can go to them now?" Mr. Hon said. "Even if they were foolish enough to want a troublemaker like you, they couldn't take you in. It would offend me. It would open them up to attacks from Rat Face and his tong. Then there are the police, who would happily put them on the first boat back to China with you. I don't think you *can* refuse my offer, Fire Horse."

I shook my head slowly. "I don't think I can either," I said.

Was the world full of traps and cages, or was I particularly good at falling into them?

CHAPTER 28

MR. HON DISMISSED CHIN and me from his office. It was time for my training with Neil, so I followed Chin to the front entryway. Neil glared over his newspaper as Chin stomped into the room, spun around, and put his face close to mine.

"I should have let those guards take you back to China, Fire Horse," he said, the words washed in a bitterness that made the back of my neck tingle with warning. "It's just too easy for you."

"Easy? You think this is easy?" My voice rose, filling the room.

"Everyone falls over themselves to help you." His lips curled up with disgust. "Harry, the son of one of the most powerful men in Chinatown, chases you down. Then his father takes you in." He jerked his thumb at Neil, who set his paper in his lap and stared. "Gets his monkey of a guard to teach you to fight."

"You may want to choose your words more carefully," I said, stepping forward. "I've taught Neil a little Chinese."

Chin looked at Neil and lowered his voice. "I'm watching you, Fire Horse."

I longed to punch Chin. But willful, reckless action had gotten me to the place where I was today. If I was trapped, it might be because I had burned bridge after bridge getting here. I stood and let him shove his shoulder into mine as he walked past me.

"You better keep both eyes on that one," Neil grumbled, lifting his paper again and turning a page. "What did Mr. Hon want?"

I moved to sit in the chair beside Neil. Mr. Hon wanted to tie me up into his routines, his schedules, his plans. He wanted to make me into something hard. He wanted to take away all the possibilities I had risked everything for. Neil had taught me to calculate, to look for the possibilities. Maybe he would know what to do.

"He wanted to give me a . . . I think you call it a job," I said. "Neil, do you . . ." I searched for the word for a moment. "Do you trust Mr. Hon?"

"No," he said, keeping his eyes on the paper.

"Do you trust Harry?"

"Harry is nothing like his father."

I turned to him. "Do you trust him?"

"No."

"Do you trust me?"

"I trust you'll get to the point soon, or I'll knock it out of you."

I took a deep breath. Neil might be the only person in this house who didn't want anything from me. He might even want me gone himself, which might be the kind of help I needed. "And you? Can I trust you?"

Neil folded the paper and placed it in his lap. He leaned forward in the chair, resting his elbows on his knees. "Say what you want to say."

238

I hesitated, forming the words. I hated the stickiness of this life. It was like walking though spiderwebs. I could not shake the feeling of the lies even when I wasn't tangled in them. "I am not who you think I am."

He sat up straight. His mouth hardened.

"I . . . I came here as someone else."

Neil's face relaxed. "Of course you did. That's what all the Chinese do."

"Yes, but I didn't just lie. I stole someone's . . ." I picked up the newspaper and shook it.

"Papers. I'm sure you did. This isn't confession. And if it was, the priest would be half-asleep." He stood, pressed one hand into the other to pop his knuckles, and walked to the center of the room in three long strides. "Take your stance. We're wasting time."

Neil threw slow punches at me, letting me loosen the stiffness left from yesterday's practice and find my rhythm.

"That's the brilliance of fighting," he continued. "There's no deception in a good, clean fight. Just one man standing in front of another man. Everything that matters is in front of your face." He began a series of fast jabs. I raced to block them until the last one made contact, rattling my jaw and sending sparks into my left eye. Neil slowed the rhythm of the punches again, but widened their range.

"What if one of the people fighting isn't who they say they are?" I asked, moving my head to avoid an uppercut to my chin.

"It doesn't matter. Rich or poor. Irish or Chinese. Cop or criminal. You can change the story a thousand times. You'll still be using the same two fists and the same two feet God gave you." He blocked my left jab.

The air was thick with the smell of two fighters, blended breaths, sweat, skin. "What if one of the fighters is a girl?"

"Why would you be fighting a girl?" he said, faking a punch to my ribs to try to get me to drop my hands.

"*I'm* not fighting a girl," I said, looking at him through the tunnel between my fists.

Neil stopped. It was the first clean shot he had ever given me.

"Is it joking you are?"

I dropped my fists and shook my head.

"A girl?"

I nodded.

"You're not. . . . You can't be. . . . All the punches you've taken." He blinked a few times and took a step back. "The shirt that Chin gave you?" He pointed to his chest.

"Chin didn't give it to me."

"Ah, Mother o' God!" He grabbed my arm, then dropped it like it burned him. "Are you trying to get yourself killed?" His pale skin had gone paler.

"I had no choice."

"Fire Horse . . . ," he said, shaking his head.

"Jade Moon."

"What?"

"My name is Jade Moon."

"Your name will be on a headstone if Mr. Hon finds out about this." Neil rubbed his hand over his face. "Chinawomen have those little feet. They're quiet. They stay at home."

"Not all of them."

He pushed me toward the door.

I started to pull back, trying to ignore the embers of fear that Neil's reaction was stoking. "I want to leave. I want to stop. But as a girl, I am . . ." I searched all the English words I'd learned for the right one. "Cursed?"

"Cursed?"

"I think it means no luck."

"I know what cursed means. I'm Irish!" I could see red veins pushing from under the skin on his forehead. "If you have any bad luck, it's only because you're determined to find it."

"I was a joke in my village. My father is so ashamed of me, he tells people I'm dead. The man I loved . . ." I struggled to keep the tears out of my voice. ". . . tried to leave me on Angel Island."

"How is that bad luck? You left your village. You got to America. Luck is about surviving trouble, not avoiding it. You might be the luckiest person I know."

I stared at him, speechless for a moment.

"But even you don't have enough luck to stay here," he said. "So, you'll be needing to leave."

"How?"

"Sometimes the best place to escape is in plain sight."

"In plain sight?"

"I have an idea. You'll leave tomorrow."

"Can we finish the lesson?"

His mouth dropped open. "I'm not punching you now!"

"Why not?"

"You're a girl!" he said, throwing his hands up. "I'm going to be in confession for days trying to explain this."

We heard a door open from across the next room. "Neil," Mr. Hon called. We both froze. "Neil, get in here."

Neil leaned toward me. "You keep your mouth shut about this or I'll break your face." He turned, stopped, then punched his fist into his palm. "I can't break your face anymore, but I'll break someone's face, and won't you feel sorry!" His shoes pounded against the boards of the floor as he left. I heard him mumble, "First Chinaman I can tolerate turns out not to be a Chinaman at all."

I didn't see Neil for the rest of the day.

Mr. Hon met Harry and me at breakfast the next morning. "Harry, you and Fire Horse are going down to the docks today. Chin will meet you there," he said.

Harry nodded. "I won't fail."

Neil came in, and Mr. Hon looked up.

"I need to talk to you," he said to me. He looked at Harry and Mr. Hon. "About some new drills, since we won't be fighting today."

Mr. Hon waved his hand, excusing me, and I followed Neil. He opened the door and stepped into the street.

"At the dock today, a policeman is going to arrest you," he said, his voice low.

"This is how you help me?"

"It isn't real. He will take you to Miss Donaldson. She runs a mission home that takes in Chinese *girls* — girls who have been sold to brothels or bad men. Mr. Hon won't think to look for you there."

"He'll look for me?"

"Mr. Hon always gets back what is his."

Harry had said something like that before. "I'm not his."

"I don't have all morning to stand here chatting," he said, the growl returning to his voice.

"Can't I just run? Disappear?"

"I'm not sending you to a sewing circle. Miss Donaldson is filled with as much vinegar as you are. She rescues slave girls. She stares down hatchet men. You're both lunatics."

"Lunatics?" I said.

He put his hands on my shoulders, forcing me to look him in the eyes. "And fighters."

I looked at Neil. "How will the policeman know me? Do I introduce myself?"

"He knows you are going to the docks today. He is going to ask any Chinese he sees where they are employed. Chin and Harry, they'll lie. You tell him you work for Mr. Hon. That is how he will know who to take with him."

I nodded.

"If Mr. Hon thinks you are arrested and gave his name, he won't want you within a hundred yards." His voice softened. "Go back inside. We don't need anyone getting suspicious. Everyone knows I don't have two words to say to you."

"Thank you, Neil."

Neil nodded, the tight corners of his mouth melting away for a moment.

Harry clenched and unclenched his fists on the way to the dock. I pulled my hat low over my face to hide the relief of escaping the

Hon house. Each step was lighter and easier. I could feel the strings around me unraveling. It would be good to be Jade Moon again. Tomorrow, I would not have to wear Mr. Hon's tong suit. I would not have hide a hundred truths and tell a thousand lies.

The docks stretched behind a wall of activity. Boats eased their way up to the piers and waited while men and women bundled in hats and coats poured from them. Men in immigration uniforms strolled through the crowds. Crates were stacked beside coils of rope. Stalls teetered against each other in long lines.

Harry led the way to where thick poles stood upright in the water. It was exactly where I saw him the first day I arrived. His black hair escaped from under a gray cap, while his face was tight with anxious energy. We watched a ferry pull closer. I wrapped my arms around myself to guard against the wind.

I had come here to find freedom — that rare kind of freedom that allowed you to be yourself. I had gambled everything for that chance, and I could not be sure that I had won. In some ways I could be truer to pieces of myself, my willful strength, my outspokenness, my wildness, but I was still shoving other parts into darkness. I watched the Americans move around the shore, their heads lifted, their smiles quick and easy. But I did not feel part of their world.

"What were you and Chin doing at the docks the day I saw you?" I asked.

Harry refused to look at me. "We were looking for new soldiers for the tong. It was one of the jobs my father had me try. I messed that up too." He shuffled from one foot to the other. "There is something I should tell you about that day."

"The Yings are in Chinatown. You took me to the wrong address on purpose. I know. Your father told me."

Harry hung his head. "I am sorry. I thought I had to."

"For your father?"

"Partly. And for me. You make my life . . . less impossible."

Any anger I felt toward him dissolved. He was just as trapped as I was. "What are we picking up?" I asked.

Harry kept walking, his face stiff with determination. "Not what. Who."

"Who?" I asked.

"A girl. My father showed me a picture," Harry said.

"Why would we pick up —"

But the boat pulled into the dock with a loud blast of its horn, and my head whirled into a spiral of panic and fear. It was the Angel Island Ferry.

What if Sterling Promise was on the ferry? Sterling Promise, who could ruin everything just as I was about to escape? Sterling Promise, who betrayed me. Sterling Promise, who I betrayed. I searched the faces of the men. If he was there, I wanted to see him first.

But he was not among the passengers. It was a different person who could betray me. When Harry nudged my shoulder and nodded to the final passenger stepping onto the dock, I followed his stare to Spring Blossom.

CHAPTER 29

"THAT'S THE GIRL?" I said, my throat tight. "Are you sure?"

He looked at her for another moment. "It's her," he decided.

"Why are we picking her up?" Maybe Mr. Hon knew her betrothed.

"My father is selling her," Harry said. "To a friend. He will marry her."

"Why would your father be involved?"

"It is the way the tong supplies women to the brothels. My father explained it to me. It is very clever. That way if the woman runs away, her husband just goes and gets her and brings her back to the brothel."

"You are selling her to a brothel?" I tried to silence the alarm in my voice. "When?"

"We'll deliver her to her betrothed from here. He will marry her and then take her to Mr. Lo."

The urge to hit Harry, grab Spring Blossom, and run swarmed over me. There were dozens of streets shooting off from the docks. We might be able to make it.

Then I saw them — Chin's men. They waited in the shadows, more used to dim rooms and dark alleys than the bright sun of the docks, but their presence brought me back to my senses. Spring Blossom and I didn't have anywhere to go, and if we got lucky and made it two blocks before Harry or Chin's men caught us, one of Mr. Hon's many eyes would surely see us.

Spring Blossom looked around — confused, lost, tugging at her sleeves. She could give me away as easily as Sterling Promise could. I followed Harry toward the dock, tipping my hat lower still on my head.

I stepped behind Spring Blossom before she could spot me. Harry hesitated a moment before bowing in front of her. "Welcome to America, Spring Blossom. I will take you to your betrothed. He is anxious to make you comfortable after your long delay."

Spring Blossom must have smiled her soft smile, as Harry answered with his own warm one. I knew this was what his father wanted him to do, and I knew he was too weak to resist, but I still wanted to knock his teeth straight into his throat.

Harry turned and started to walk toward the city. I fell in step behind Spring Blossom and nudged her gently. When she saw me, her head jerked with surprise. Recognition lit in her face, but I shook my head. She lowered her gaze toward the pavement, a smile playing at her lips. My heart was wrenched with the tragedy of what they were going to do to her, but underneath that was the warmth of walking next to someone who knew me, truly knew me.

"Chin should be here," Harry said nervously.

I scanned the docks and spotted him talking to a giant of a policeman two docks away. An unsettled feeling crept under my skin, but I still knew what I would do. I tugged at Harry's arm and nodded toward the pair. His face darkened.

"Go see what you can find out," I said. "I'll watch her."

He nodded, his face full of nervous concentration. As soon as he walked away, Spring Blossom whispered, "I wondered if you had made it. I am so happy to see you! They made the biggest fuss when you disappeared. The guards tore through your things. They yelled at us, but we did not understand what they were saying. Some of the women were angry that you caused trouble and disobeyed your father."

I could imagine the sharp clip of their words. *Willful, disobedient girl. Raining down bad luck on the rest of us.* Maybe they were right.

Spring Blossom whispered, "You still have to dress as a boy? I almost embraced you!" She giggled. "That would have been shocking. How long will you have to dress this way?"

"Not much longer," I managed.

I watched Harry pick his way down the dock, staying behind the crowds until he was just a few feet from Chin. Then Chin turned from the policeman, a satisfied smirk on his face.

"Listen. We don't have much time," I said. "There is no husband."

"What do you mean?" Her voice shook on the last words.

"Your brother has not arranged a marriage. I don't know if he realized it, but he has arranged a sale."

"A sale? What has he sold?" she said carefully.

"You. To a brothel."

Spring Blossom gasped. "How could he?"

"He may not have known," I said.

She tightened her hold on her sleeves until her fingertips turned white. "He knew," she said.

The policeman spotted Harry and waved him over. Harry hesitated, then went to join Chin.

I kept my head forward and my voice low. "The policeman — he is here to take me somewhere. Somewhere safe. He has to take you instead. He will ask a question in English — who you work for. You have to answer."

"What do I say?"

"Mr. Hon."

"And I will be safe?"

I nodded. The policeman finished with Harry, and he and Chin walked toward us. The policeman would spot me next. He would come over, and Spring Blossom would escape.

But he looked right over me, then turned away. Every muscle I had tightened.

Chin and Harry arrived. "What was that about?" I asked.

"Just a brute of a policeman asking questions that are none of his business." Chin glared at me. "Scared he'll come arrest you, Fire Horse?"

"No, hoping," I muttered.

"What did you say?" he growled.

"Nothing."

Chin gripped the collar of my shirt. "I don't want to hear a word from you. I don't care how determined Hon is to have you protect his son. The sight of you makes me want to slit your belly from end to end. If you get in my way again, like you did at the laundry, I will make a ghost of you before the New Year."

I felt Spring Blossom's horror beside me but kept watching the policeman. I couldn't bother with Chin's threats. Every ounce of my will went toward forcing the policeman to turn around again. Finally, he looked over his shoulder, past Chin, to me and Spring Blossom. I held my breath until he directed his steps our way.

Chin turned to see what I was staring at. He dropped my collar and stood on the other side of Spring Blossom.

"Should we run?" Harry asked him.

"With the girl? We can't. Pretend you don't speak English," he commanded me. He gripped Spring Blossom's arm. "The police here, they take girls and lock them up. They do terrible things to girls. You don't want to go with him," he said to her. I saw fear flash across Spring Blossom's face. As the policeman got closer, she looked around the dock nervously. I prayed she would trust me.

The man stopped in front of the three of us. Spring Blossom stood like a statue, with just the slightest tension in her cheeks where the muscles clenched the teeth together.

"Who do you work for?" he said, looking straight at me.

"Mr. Hon," Spring Blossom said in a clear voice.

The policeman shifted his gaze to her. I clamped my mouth shut, holding back my tears. He didn't expect a woman who looked like a woman, but he only hesitated a second. The knowledge of where he was taking her won him over — what was the difference between a girl who looked like a boy and a girl who looked like a girl?

"You are under arrest," he said to Spring Blossom flatly. "You will have to come with me."

When he reached for her arm, Chin realized what was happening. "She just . . . ," he sputtered in Chinese.

"She just landed," Harry said in English.

"Oh, so you do speak English," the policeman said. His words had the same sloping ups and downs as Neil's. "I have my orders. Or would you *all* like to come with me to the station?"

Chin's face twitched with indecision. He was not up against someone from Chinatown who he could bully and intimidate. This man was twice his size, and carried with him the confidence of having twice his rights in America. For once, I was glad. The man looked at me for a moment. I let my hand slip off Spring Blossom's wrist as he shepherded her out of our circle.

It was done. Spring Blossom was safe. Chin sent two soldiers to follow her, but they could report only that she had been taken away in a police car. A deep sadness settled inside me. I yearned to be in a car, going further and further from this life.

When we got back, Mr. Hon met us in the front entryway, anger exploding across his face. "How did you mess this up?" he yelled at Harry.

The blood drained from Harry's face. Neil appeared beside Mr. Hon. I could feel the anger rolling off him at the sight of me, like the steady, silent crash of waves in a storm.

A familiar flash of movement swung across the corner of my eyes. I jumped to block Mr. Hon's arm, but before I could, Neil pinned my arms behind my back. Then there was an even more familiar crack, and Harry was crouched on the floor, holding the side of his face, while his father towered over him.

"Father, please . . . ," he begged. "I don't know what happened."

Mr. Hon's face had shifted from anger to disgust, and my heart ached that Harry had to see it. You can't blur some faces enough. Mr. Hon leaned forward, his nose almost touching Harry's. "I don't want to catch sight of you again. Do you understand me? You are no longer welcome here. You wander your alleys. You hide in the shadows like the worthless coward you are."

Neil had had a good plan, a lucky plan. But now sparks were flying from it, burning everything they touched. I thought I saw a way through. I opened my mouth, preparing to tell Mr. Hon that it was my fault. "Mr. Hon —"

Neil jammed his giant elbow into my side, crushing the air that would have formed my next words. He refused to hit a girl, I thought, but didn't feel bad about bruising one. He said in a voice of eerie calm, "Mr. Hon, we'd better tell the buyer."

Mr. Hon arranged his jacket, masked his anger with a neutral expression, and turned and walked back toward his office. "Fire Horse, I want to see you," he said.

I stood silently by Harry as he rose.

"You should go," he said softly. "He will just get angrier." He put a hand over his face. "I don't know how it happened. I have to leave."

"I'll go with you."

"I want to be alone." He walked away. At the door, he turned around. "You don't need to make me feel better. I know I'll never be what my father wants. I'll never be you."

Was it impossible for one tie to loosen before another snapped tight? For one crack in my heart to heal before another broke open? I followed his slumped shoulders to the front door. I was about to step into the street with him when I felt Neil's hand grip my arm. He slammed the door behind Harry and spun me to face him.

"What are you doing here?" he growled, his face a red map of veins and fury.

"I had to help the girl," I pleaded.

"So you're a bit of a missionary now?" He rubbed his meaty hand over his face. "You're going to have enough trouble saving yourself."

"They were going to sell her."

"That's their business. It is long past time to fight. You need to run."

"She was my friend," I whispered. "From Angel Island."

His mouth hung open. "The girl today?"

I nodded. "I could not let them sell her."

"How many more friends do you have?" he said, crossing his arms.

"Not many."

He studied me, still furious, but he had that shallow crease between his eyes that meant he was worried. "You think you're being strong, but you're just being stubborn."

"Or stupid," I said, lowering my head.

"Crazy Chinese girls, putting their noses places they're likely to get cut off," he fumed, walking toward Mr. Hon's office. "Hurry up. This is not the day to keep Mr. Hon waiting. And you better keep your mouth shut."

CHAPTER 30

MR. HON WAS ON THE PHONE, shouting into the mouthpiece. "We have gotten people out of jail before. Call our contacts in the police! See what you can find out."

He slammed the phone down and switched to English for Neil. "Mr. Lo wants the girl tonight. He has been anxious for months. There were too many delays getting her off that island. You are both coming with me. We have to make some excuse until we can retrieve her."

"There is no reason for the boy to come. I can handle it," Neil said.

"This is part of the business." He pounded his fist on the desk. "Fire Horse, you will watch and learn. If my son can't handle these affairs, you will have to. You're the only piece of good luck we've had lately. You will be more than Harry's brother. You will be my son. It will be easier to control fire than create it."

Neil tensed. It sounded like the promise of something I once wanted desperately — a family who valued me, a place to belong. But I wasn't the fool I used to be.

Mr. Hon unlocked the front door and led us through the dark streets.

The yellow lights of windows stared down from above. Chinatown shut its doors as soon as the evening shopping was done. The windows at street level were covered with boards to keep out the bullets that sometimes still flew from tong guns.

We had walked half a dozen blocks when Mr. Hon stopped at a door, knocked, and spoke a few words to a face behind it, then waited impatiently as fingers struggled to pull the thick wood open. He led us up a narrow flight of stairs to a hallway. Then we walked through a second and third door that had only another long hallway and a watchman between them. From there we entered a large room lined on two sides with a series of curtained doorways. Men and women sat on couches, resting in the shadows. Hushed voices trickled into the room through the limp fabric, punctuated by high-pitched, lifeless laughter. Mr. Hon reached for the only door in the room and pulled it open.

A man, stooped-over and gray, looked up from behind a table covered with scattered papers. "My old friend, welcome." Surprise flickered across his face when I came through the door, and a flash of fear when Neil followed. "I'll get the tea. One of the girls just brought a fresh pot." He shuffled to the corner of the room, where a teapot rested next to cups in a basket. As he poured the steaming tea, his elbows poked at the worn spots on his faded robe. He held the cup out to Mr. Hon, who did not move.

"Mr. Lo, there was a problem," Mr. Hon said, his voice calm and steady.

Mr. Lo raised his head. "A problem? With the Americans? You

said she would be off that island today," he stammered, his friendly tones pulled tight.

"She arrived this afternoon as promised. She is here in Chinatown."

"Fine. Then bring her here."

Mr. Hon cleared his throat, but continued in a strained voice. "We do not have her to bring to you."

Mr. Lo dropped the cup, letting it clatter and spill. Tea pooled on the table, steam rising from it. "You sold her to someone else after promising her to me!"

"No, of course not, my friend. She was arrested."

"Impossible! She arrived today. She did not have time to get arrested!"

"It is not a problem. I can deal with the police. Though perhaps you don't want her. She was too thin and brown. She would have brought shame to your establishment."

"She would have brought *money* to my establishment. Now I have to wait months for another girl — *years*, with all the rules the Americans are making." He put his face in his hands.

"We will make this right," Mr. Hon said. The strain of the night made his face heavy with emotion it was not used to holding.

"You have had many chances to make this right," Mr. Lo said.

"I am sure we can come to an agreement."

Mr. Lo shook his head. "There can be no agreement."

Mr. Hon's voice hardened. "Do not say words you will regret."

"I will say whatever I want. The police will close my business. That Donaldson woman will take my girls while you watch through your silk curtains." I glanced toward Neil when I heard the name of the woman he wanted to send me to, but he refused to look at me. "The tongs don't want to protect Chinatown anymore. The young are too busy dying, and the old are counting their coins." He leaned on the table, gripping its sides.

Mr. Hon faced him, his lips pressed tightly together. "What are you saying?"

"Someone has to pay for the trouble this has caused," he said, ringing a bell on his desk.

"You are threatening me. You are wasting your time."

"I don't think so. I am not the only one in Chinatown unhappy with the way you do business. I will complain to the tong. They will decide who is in the wrong." Mr. Hon put up his hands in protest, but Mr. Lo ignored him and continued. "The Sen Suey Ying boys have been offering their help getting girls. If you will excuse me, I have letters to write."

A curtain hung across a door pulled back.

As soon as I turned, a figure filled the door frame, and a familiar pair of eyes locked on mine. They belonged to Sterling Promise.

CHAPTER 31

STERLING PROMISE'S MOUTH started to move. Any word that dropped from it could give me away, but he was still staring, his mind working to link the familiar to the unfamiliar. "You . . . you . . ."

Neil froze.

"What are you doing here?" Sterling Promise finally managed.

My heart battled with the anger lingering inside it. Neil looked at Sterling Promise, clearly weighing the possibility that he knew my secret. But when I saw him ball his fists, I took two hurried steps, pulled back my arm, and punched Sterling Promise myself.

The punch felt good. Sterling Promise staggered.

"What are you doing?" Mr. Lo said.

Mr. Hon looked at me, head tilted with curiosity.

"We have history," I said. And at least Sterling Promise would not have to endure one of Neil's punches.

Mr. Hon smiled coolly, catching the scent of a fight he could win. He turned to Sterling Promise, who was pressing his palm to his face, eyes blinking in surprise. "Fire Horse has been under my protection since he arrived here," Mr. Hon said. "Do you have a complaint against him?"

"Fire Horse." Sterling Promise let out a quick, broken laugh.

Neil moved to my side, but Mr. Hon put his hand out. "Let him handle his own affairs."

Sterling Promise was watching Neil, so it was a little unfair when I punched him again. He was starting to sway despite his efforts not to. I pushed him up against the wall.

"Don't say anything," I hissed in his ear.

Mr. Hon announced, "The tong takes care of its own — something your associate might want to remember. I won't tolerate anything that causes a member to lose face."

Neil strolled over and stood behind me. "I thought you didn't have any more friends here," he said in a low voice.

"I don't know if he would want to be called a friend," I whispered.

"You see how we protect our loyal members, Mr. Lo. You might consider that before you start doing business with the Sen Suey Ying boys," Mr. Hon said.

Sterling Promise groaned. "Who would be foolish enough to teach you to punch?"

"You have to keep your mouth shut," I said.

"What trouble have you found now?" he said.

Neil leaned close to Sterling Promise's ear. "If you don't mind your own bloody business, I'll knock every one of your teeth out and shove them up your arse."

"He agrees," I said.

Sterling Promise stared at me for another second before letting his lids drop and slumping down to the floor.

"We are done here," Mr. Hon said, strolling past me to the door.

I looked back at Sterling Promise, who had tried to abandon me. He had lied to me. Cheated me. He also would have married me and spared me all of this deception. He had loved me, in his own way, and I felt a stab of how different things could have been. My heartbeat throbbed to the tips of my fingers.

It might have been less painful to be slumped in the corner with a sore stomach and black eye. Instead I had to go out into the street and listen to Mr. Hon congratulate me for the way I handled Sterling Promise.

"I enjoyed that more than I thought I would," he said. "How dare Lo threaten me! You remind me of myself at your age." Another wave of nausea hit me. "And that young man, Lo's assistant, he has wronged you, yes?"

"We were on Angel Island together. He cheated me out of something . . . when we were gambling."

"This is exactly what I have been trying to teach Harry. You can't let people cheat you or lie to you. It takes away all your dignity."

How much dignity could I have left after all the lies I had bred and borne?

When we returned to the house, Neil took his paper and stomped out. Mr. Hon locked the door and went to his office. I had never felt so alone.

CHAPTER 32

AFTER A LONG, RESTLESS NIGHT, the memory of Sterling Promise still crawled through my every thought. I replayed the moment I saw him in my head, my memory shifting his expression from sad to angry and back until I was dizzy with emotion.

Still, I found myself pulling his suit on over my bindings that morning. The New Year would begin in two days, and I did not want to start it sharing a house with Mr. Hon and his cruelty. I would leave today, I decided, taking only the things I had brought.

Mr. Hon was on the phone in his office. "What do you mean she is not in the jail? Where did they take her? She couldn't disappear. Someone has her. I bet it's the Sen Suey Ying boys. Dig them out of any holes they crawled into and find out what you can. Let our boys know that I am willing to pay for information."

The house had the hushed feel that often surrounds deep, thick anger. Neil was back in his chair. "You have more enemies than Hon," he said, continuing to read his paper.

"Is Harry back?"

Neil shook his head.

"I need to get out of here," I said.

He lowered the paper. "Ah, maybe you have a little brain in that head of yours after all."

"Hon's just sent soldiers to search for hatchet men from Sen Suey Ying. If you tell him that I'm looking too, I could sneak away."

"They could follow you. If you lead them to the mission home, then disappear, it would raise suspicions. You put the girl at risk."

"I'll be careful."

"Jaysuz. Wouldn't that be grand." Neil gave me directions, and I left the Hon house.

In the bright sun of the morning, I made my way through the city. The mission home was not far in distance, but it felt worlds away. Chin and his men patrolled the streets, but they were not looking for me, so their glances slipped past me as I climbed the street that led to the mission home.

The facade was plainer than much of Chinatown, with flat sides stacked with windows, lacking the flourishes of curved iron balconies or brightly tiled rooftops that decorated the rest of the neighborhood. It reflected the hard reality of the place more than the illusion.

When my hand knocked against the door, a voice behind me commanded, "Stop right there!" in English followed by rough Chinese. A pale-faced woman marched up the street, her heels clicking under her long, dark skirt. She'd gathered her wild hair into a chaotic bun, but strands of it still flew across her cheek. "Go away. I'll call the police," she said in the most polished Chinese I had heard from someone with a pale face.

"I want to see a friend," I tried in my best English, hoping to convince her to trust me.

"And take her back. I can spot a hatchet man a mile away." Her frown heaped accusations on me.

"No, I . . ."

She grabbed my arm and pulled me toward the street. I jerked away and ran toward the door. In two long steps she had my arm again. I was thinking through the moves I could use to escape her grip when I heard a familiar voice.

"Jade Moon!" Spring Blossom threw the door open.

"Stay there!" the woman and I both called. I was terrified she would step into the street and be seen.

Spring Blossom froze in the shadows of the doorway. "Miss Donaldson, this is the girl I was telling you about. The girl who sent me in her place."

The woman's face softened as she studied me curiously. "Extraordinary." She released her grip on my arm and held out her hand. I looked at it suspiciously, but she held it steady, waiting, so I reached to shake it. "I'm Miss Donaldson. I've been looking forward to meeting you." She led me through the front door and shut it behind her.

She turned to Spring Blossom. "I would like to talk to your friend. I will bring her to you shortly," she promised.

Spring Blossom smiled at me. "I'm glad you're here."

Miss Donaldson took me into her office and sat down behind a heavy desk. It never occurred to me that a woman would have a study full of dark furniture, as many ledgers as Mr. Hon, and as many papers as my father. I sat down across from her. Her face was a mix of angles, and everything was just a little too sharp and wild for beauty — her pale skin too fair for her dark eyebrows, her face too thin for her large, bright eyes. But at the same time, those features demanded admiration. She looked like a woman who decided things, who molded the world around her instead of letting it push against her. She had the calm determination of those who feel right, deep in their bones, so they have no need to prove it to anyone.

"You are a brave girl," she said. "Imagine my surprise when another girl who needed rescuing showed up on my doorstep. I should have known you would do something bold like that, considering the pride Neil takes in you."

"I could not bring anything with me. I hope you can give me some clothes."

She waved my words away with a flick of her small hand. "Spring Blossom told me your story. It was wonderful what you did, sending her here in your own place. The girls are all talking about it."

"It was not much," I said, looking down at the jacket I was wearing. I wanted so badly to peel it from my skin, and with it, the past five months.

"Don't diminish its value with your false modesty," she snapped. I jerked my head up. Was she *angry* with me? The steely taste of outrage settled on my tongue.

"If I could just change into something else," I said, the binding around my chest cutting into my skin.

"You know, there are girls all over Chinatown who cannot escape the brothels. I have spent decades trying to rescue these girls from prostitution. Do you know what their lives are like?"

I shook my head.

"I hope you never find out. Some of the tongs are desperate for the power that is slipping from their hands. Thirty years ago they ran these streets. Now we are slowly taking them back. But the more desperate they get to survive, the harder it is to find girls."

"The girls should find you," I said.

"How would they?" she said, her voice rising. "How would Spring Blossom have found me without you?" Flashes of anger gave more of an air of wildness to her features. I watched, waiting for her to yell. But she didn't; her face settled into strength. "Most girls are never allowed on the streets, and if they are, they are told terrifying stories about me and the police to keep them away from those who would help them. I can only rescue girls if I know where they are. And information rarely leaks through the wall of silence that the Chinese have built. I have lost friends to the cause. Community members, the police risk their lives for every favor I ask."

She measured me. "You probably want to stay here, but I have another proposal. I think you might be able to find those girls."

"Me?" I said.

"Yes, you. You are uniquely placed. Mr. Hon must know the addresses of all the brothels in Chinatown. You can find them out for me. Bring the addresses here. I will take care of the rest."

"Why can't Neil do it?" I demanded. Freedom from one cage only seemed to bind me into another.

"Neil's interest in rescuing Chinese girls is recent." Her mouth pressed in a line. "And limited to ones who give him particular trouble."

"You ask too much." I shook my head, feeling her steady stare push at my defenses. "I may not get another chance to escape the Hons' house. I can tell you where they were taking Spring Blossom, but that is all. I can't go back to that prison."

"Then you leave those girls in *their* prisons."

"You are saying that it is my duty," I said, rising to my feet.

"No, it is your choice," Miss Donaldson said, her voice firm.

And with that, all the walls I had imagined dissolved away.

"You can stay here. I would not ask this of any other girl," she said.

I stared at her for a moment, then sank back into the chair. I rubbed my forehead, trying to think.

She rested her hands in her lap. "Spring Blossom said that you liked stories."

"I used to. I don't find them very useful lately."

"Perhaps you just don't know the right stories. Stories are supposed to provide light when we are stumbling around in the darker parts of our lives. But eventually, we must all find our own story. Maybe this could be your story."

Nushi had told me to find my own story when I got to America. My hand went to the pouch where her jade hung around my neck. "If it was, nothing good would happen to you or the girls."

"Why do you say that? You have proven yourself to be clever and bold. You seem fearless."

"I cause destruction everywhere. I am a Fire Horse — very bad luck in China."

She leaned forward with another small smile. "This isn't China."

"I haven't managed to escape my curse yet."

"It's not a curse you are running from. It's yourself. And you will have to run much further to escape that."

"You don't understand," I snapped. I crossed my arms and broke away from her stare.

"You're wrong," Miss Donaldson said gently. "I understand perfectly. It is frightening and dangerous to be so bold. And that is powerful. Very powerful. You let it out and it causes harm to others. You grip onto it and it pounds away at you inside. But if you use it, if you channel it for good, it does the impossible."

She was a strong woman. I could tell because her words battled against the words of my father, my grandfather, Auntie Wu, the rest of the village. Maybe the world didn't mold itself around her. Maybe she faced it, took its blows, and remained standing.

"You won't help, and I understand that too. Few people would. But, Jade Moon, you are not trapped — not like these girls are between walls. You say your spirit is trapped? No one has the key to that. I can't release you from that prison inside you." She stood. "Let's find Spring Blossom. She will show you your room."

Miss Donaldson led me to a large room filled with young girls sewing. She signaled to Spring Blossom, who rose from her seat in the back and stepped past more than one girl staring openly at me. Spring Blossom took me to a small, bright room on the second floor, furnished with three beds and a dresser. Tokens of the girls who lived there lay scattered around the room — ribbons, books, needles stuck into stitchwork. Spring Blossom sat on the edge of her bed.

"I am so glad you are here. I worried all night. Miss Donaldson told me a little about the people who tried to take me. What were you doing with the Hons?"

"It is a long story," I said.

"You know how I love stories," she replied.

I told her about meeting Harry and Chin at the dock. About Harry taking me to the wrong laundry on purpose, letting me think the Yings had left Chinatown. About the Hon house, and the plans Mr. Hon made for me. About running the lottery numbers and learning to fight. About the laundryman and his gun. And finally about going to the docks with Harry and Chin. "I suppose you know the rest," I said.

"How did you manage all that time? In all that danger?"

"Neil would say it was luck."

"Well, you're here now." She smiled. "It is so strange here after so long at Angel Island. The girls don't seem to have a care, even though many came from the most devastating circumstances — slave girls, beaten, half-starved. One of them used to work for Mr. Lo, the man they were taking me to."

"Oh." That was all I could manage. I was home now, I told myself, too exhausted from pretending to return.

"Her sister is still there, and it destroys her. She doesn't know where it was because he never allowed the girls on the street." Spring Blossom wrung her hands. "She cried when I told her that I did not know where it was either."

"I will give the address to Miss Donaldson," I said.

"You are so good! Her sister will be so happy."

I opened my mouth to say, "It was nothing," but I couldn't.

"I am grateful for what you did for me. Think where I would have been, what I would have had to do if you had not saved me."

That was exactly what I was trying *not* to think about. "You seem happy."

"Oh, I am. I am going to learn English, and Miss Donaldson said she would teach me to knit." She paused. "And it isn't just that, Jade Moon." She looked at me. "I feel safe, maybe for the first time. In China, I was a pawn, a daughter that could be married, a daughter-in-law that could be blamed. On Angel Island, I was a prisoner. Here, I think I can just be Spring Blossom."

I hid my face in my hands. It was exactly what I wanted, but I couldn't have it yet.

"You'll be safe now too," she said, smoothing the blanket at the end of the bed.

I shook my head.

"Why not? What could hurt you here? You don't need to pretend anymore."

"I might need to pretend a little longer," I said, standing. "Miss Donaldson asked me to help her find other girls. I have to return to the Hon house."

Spring Blossom stood and faced me. "No. You should not have to go back there. Think what they would have done to me! What they could do to you." She started to run her hands under her sleeves, the familiar shadow settling over her face. "I don't want you to do this."

"I know."

"What if something happens to you?"

"It is the first good thing I will have done," I said, reaching out and lifting one of her hands from her arm. "I can't keep being this person who people are afraid of. I want people to look at me and see something good."

"I see good," Spring Blossom said. "Because there is good. You don't have to prove it."

"I think I do."

"To who?" she said, her voice shaking.

"To myself."

*   *   *

Miss Donaldson sat in the front room, adjusting a bow on the head of a small girl.

"I'll do it," I said before I had time to think of the difficulties.

She clapped her hands together, then tried to dim her excitement. She folded her hands again and rested them in her lap. "Are you sure?"

I nodded. "Neil will be furious. This is the second time he has tried to get rid of me."

Miss Donaldson smiled. "Maybe he's the cursed one."

CHAPTER 33

MISS DONALDSON EXPLAINED what she needed — the locations of as many brothels in Chinatown as I could get Mr. Hon to reveal. When I had a list, I could deliver the addresses to the mission myself, or pass them to Neil a few at a time. He knew how to reach her, she said. I gave her Mr. Lo's address.

"You are doing something good, Jade Moon," she said, patting my shoulder.

I walked back into the street, too lost in my own worries to see who stepped from the alley. "How did you know about this place?" a sharp voice said.

"Harry!" I moved to embrace him, but then stopped, putting my hands behind my back. "I'm so glad you are safe. I was worried when you still weren't home this morning," I said in an extra-low voice, one that I hoped would cover my concern.

"That doesn't explain why you are here."

"What?"

"The mission. How did you know where it was?"

Of course, the mission. Already I was destroying Miss Donaldson's plan.

"I saw that woman take you inside," he said.

"Of course you saw me go inside." My mind raced for an explanation.

"Why were you there?"

Heat dug deep into my cheeks. "I . . . What are you accusing me of?" My breath was shallow and rushed.

"Did you bring the girl here? Help her escape? Is she in there?" His voice grew louder with each word.

"How would I bring her here? I was with you when she was arrested."

"Then what were *you* doing there today?"

I had to think. *What would he want me to do?* And there was Sterling Promise in the background of my head again. "I checked to see if she was here. I thought I could sneak her out."

The edges of his words softened. "Was she there?"

"I would have her with me if she was." The weight of the lies I had told and the ones I would tell returned.

Harry's shoulders slumped and his head dropped. My heart steadied its rhythm, and my fingers relaxed by my sides. "That was a good idea," he said. "No wonder my father is so impressed with you."

"Isn't that why you're here?"

"No, I saw you a couple of blocks away, and I followed you."

We fell into step next to each other. "Where are you staying?" I asked.

"There are plenty of places for an outcast like me." He looked down the street. "The easiest thing to find in Chinatown is a place to hide." We wove our way through another set of alleyways. Harry

dug his hands deep into his pockets. "You are going to keep looking for her, aren't you?"

"Your father thinks Rat Face and his Sen Suey Ying boys took
her," I said.

"Someone took her. But I don't think it was Rat Face."

"Then who?" I said.

"Someone who sells girls," Harry said. "It is getting impossible
to get girls off Angel Island."

An idea formed. "So you think a brothel owner bribed the police
to pretend to arrest her and then bring her to his brothel," I said.
"Do you know where the brothels are?"

Harry nodded. "My father knows every brothel in Chinatown.
He wants to expand the tong's reach beyond gambling. There is a
lot of money for someone who can supply girls. He wanted me to
direct that part of the business, with your protection."

My throat tightened. So *that* was his plan for me. "If you gave
me the addresses of people like Lo, people who might be interested
in purchasing a slave girl, I could go to them and look for this
girl," I said. Or, I could turn around, hand the addresses to Miss
Donaldson, undo these wrappings, and never see Mr. Hon again.
"Are there a lot of people who might have her?"

Harry shook his head. "Bribing a policeman would cost a lot."

"So we check the brothels. Just give me the addresses," I said. I
had forgotten the warmth hope brought with it.

Harry thought for a minute. "I want to help."

The hope collapsed. "I don't think that is a good idea. Maybe
you should stay out of your father's way."

"You don't think I can do this," he said, his words stretched tight.

"It's not that."

"I'm not you. I can't blur the disappointment in people's eyes. It hurts to see it every time my father looks at me." He turned to face me, blocking my path. "I have to do something."

"Harry, these men are your father's friends and business partners. Do you think he wants you confronting them about a missing girl? Does he even want anyone to know about the girl?" Harry crossed his arms. "I will take care of it. We can tell your father that *you* found her," I said.

"I don't need you to protect me!" he shouted.

"That's not it!" I shouted back.

He poked his finger into my chest. It pressed against the bindings, which sent me back a step. "When you look at me, you see the same thing my father sees. I know Father is grooming you to chaperone me."

"Harry . . ."

"I don't need a nursemaid. I need a friend."

The word "friend" broke me. I knew how deep that need buried itself. What would be the harm in Harry looking for the girl? His father might appreciate that he had tried. It might heal some of the damage I had done.

"Fine," I said. Relief spread across his face. "I need your help anyway. You know every corner of Chinatown."

Harry nodded. "It won't be easy. They sometimes sell girls as quickly as they buy them."

"We'll figure something out," I said.

He fell in step beside me again. "Thank you. I know you don't have to help me. You didn't lose the girl. Most men would be trying to carve out their own place rather than helping to save mine."

"Maybe I don't want your place," I said.

"Maybe that's why I trust you."

That sent a sharp pain right into my heart, which I had started to forget I had.

We walked along Stockton, one of the main streets. Lantern shops with giant red paper globes hanging from their awnings sat next to stores selling baseballs and bats from the American game Neil had tried to explain to me one morning. Vegetable men with baskets balanced on long poles resting across their shoulders twisted through clusters of children. Boys leaned against bicycles, English books from the American school they went to during the day stuffed next to papers from the Chinese school they attended at night. You could see the people of Chinatown sweeping the criminal tongs into the corners, like a wife claiming a wider and wider piece of the floor with her broom. Did Harry not see it, or is that another reason he avoided the streets?

While we walked, we planned.

"I can go into the brothels and cause distractions while you search for her," I offered.

"I don't know if we can get away with something so direct," Harry said.

A woman came out of the drugstore we were passing. I pulled him back so he would not crash into her. She glared over her shoulder at both of us. "Let's turn here," Harry said. We veered onto another street and then into one of the alleys he was so fond of. "So we have to look around without seeming to look around."

I thought for a moment. "Neil said that you have to add up your strengths and weaknesses before you start fighting. We have your knowledge of Chinatown."

"Your skill and talent for fighting." He leaned against one of the flat brick walls looming over us.

"What we don't have is time. Especially if you think she might be sold again. We should start now."

"And we don't have a reason to go to these places," Harry said.

"How many places might she be?" I asked.

"A dozen, maybe more."

"You said your father was having you study the business. Is that enough of a reason?"

"The brothel owners are secretive, suspicious men. They feel attacked by the police, the community. Even the tongs. They don't often want to talk about their business."

"So like you said, we need a reason to look around. A way to talk our way in."

"You can talk to people. You convinced that laundry man to help us with the lottery," Harry said.

"I convinced him it would make him money," I said. "That was easy because it was true. But when it comes to favors — people don't trust me. We need someone who could charm the venom from a snake."

"You talked your way into the mission home."

I shrugged. I didn't like the idea that we would be relying on my charm.

"What about your friend? The one you traveled with — Sterling Promise."

"We don't need Sterling Promise," I said, stones settling in my stomach.

"Why not? You said he is good at talking people into things. If you can't talk our way in, maybe he can. Is he here in Chinatown?"

"He will want something in return."

"What will he want?" Harry asked.

"I don't know. He may not even tell us until it is too late."

"I'm sure my father is offering a reward. We will make a clear bargain."

"Sure. Then we will force the tiger to take out his teeth and hand them to us." I shook my head. I did not want Sterling Promise involved for thousands of reasons I couldn't admit to Harry, much less myself. "He doesn't trust me."

"Then *I'll* make the deal with him."

"He will twist this to his own ends." I looked at Harry. "It is who he is."

"He can make whatever he wants from it as long as we get the girl back. I don't see any other way."

"I punched him the last time I saw him," I tried.

Harry raised an eyebrow. "And where was he the last time you saw him?"

I opened my mouth, more protests lining up on my tongue, until I realized that Sterling Promise would want to work with me even less than I wanted to work with him. "He works for Mr. Lo."

"The man who was supposed to buy the girl?" Harry said.

I nodded.

"That is only two blocks from here. Go get him." Harry said, his eyes starting to burn with purpose. I hesitated. "You just have to introduce us. I will handle everything from there. I will wait at the noodle house," he said, pointing across the street. "Try not to punch him this time," he called after me.

CHAPTER 34

I WALKED TOWARD the building we had visited the night before. Washed in light, it blended easily with its neighbors, nothing on the outside hinting at what was on the inside. Going in didn't seem wise, so I waited half a block away in the shadow of a small balcony.

It wasn't long until Sterling Promise stepped out of the doorway and walked toward me. I watched until he was only a few feet away. A bruise was blooming around the corner of his left eye. I almost reached out to touch it. A deep hum of emotion grew in the pit of my heart. I thought I had silenced it long ago.

His face did not register any of the surprise or anger I expected. Instead he reached out and grabbed my hand. "I saw you from upstairs. Let's get you away from here. I know someone —"

I snatched my hand away — half-shocked, half-embarrassed.

"Let me help you," he said.

I tried to cool the warmth that was spreading from his touch. This was just one of his tricks, after all. "I don't need your help. Harry does. Harry Hon."

He turned his face away from me.

"Yes, you will probably not want to get involved. Harry needs to find the girl his father promised your boss."

"That doesn't concern me."

"Exactly. Say no and I'll go away."

It was there, ready to drop off his tongue, the no I needed. Then Sterling Promise closed his mouth and swallowed it. "Why don't you want me to do this?"

"What? No, *you* don't want to do this."

"You aren't telling me something," he said. "Why would Harry Hon want my help?"

"I might have mentioned that you have a talent for getting people to trust you," I said through tight teeth. Then I swallowed. "And I may have used a few of your tricks in the past to get out of trouble."

"I guess they didn't work," he said.

"Just say you won't do it."

"How did you get tangled up with the Hons?"

"I needed a friend. Harry was willing to take me in when I didn't have anyone else. How did you end up in a brothel?"

"The brothel is one of Master Yue's investments."

"I don't see how the company you've chosen is superior to mine," I said.

"It isn't any better, just less dangerous." He narrowed his eyes. "You are very protective of this Harry."

"How would you know?" I barked.

"I can hear it in your voice."

"He is a good person, Sterling Promise. He doesn't lie about who he is like I do. He doesn't break promises like you do. And he doesn't use people like we both do." I sighed. "Still, I'm glad you made it to America."

He shrugged. "They blamed me for what you did at first. I almost didn't get to land, but . . ."

"But you had already paid the bribe, so they had to let you go."

Sterling Promise flinched. He never liked plain truth. "I will tell Harry no myself. I would not want to offend him. His father is a very powerful man." Words that should have rolled smoothly off his tongue were bitter instead, but I ignored it.

"Good. Let's go." I turned and led him through the streets.

I opened the door of the noodle house and walked to the back table where Harry sat. They bowed, eyeing each other warily. I watched for Sterling Promise to mimic Harry's loose stance, but he kept his chest lifted and his arms stiff by his sides.

"I have heard that you can help us," Harry said.

"Unfortunately, he does not think he will be able to," I said.

"Then what will we do now?" Harry said, the panic seeping back into his voice.

I patted his shoulder, trying to ease his disappointment. I wasn't disappointed. This would be simpler without Sterling Promise. "Don't worry."

Harry smiled, his genuine smile, the smile that said he trusted me and we were in this together. It stung deeply.

"I will help," Sterling Promise said.

"What!" I said, my shoulders tightening.

"Wonderful!" Harry said. "Fire Horse says you can talk your way through walls."

"I thought you didn't want to help," I said, glaring at Sterling Promise.

"I would hate to disappoint your friend, Fire Horse." He said the last two words with a little more emphasis than necessary, then turned back to Harry. "You are trying to find the missing girl. You need me to get you into these places so you can look around." I could see him weighing what we had said.

"Yes. We need to know if they have purchased any girls recently or heard of any who are available to purchase."

"What you would like in return?" I asked.

Sterling Promise looked at me. "I don't know if I will be much help."

"My father will surely offer a reward for the return of the girl. And even more for the person who took her." Harry was eager to secure him. "My father could help a new businessman like you."

The thought of Mr. Hon getting hold of Sterling Promise made my stomach turn. I braced myself for his smile and a wave of charm, but he kept his expression blank and nodded.

"Let's start with Lo's. How do we get in?" Harry asked.

"I'll take you there now. He won't be there for another hour."

"No, how would we get in if we did not have a connection there?" Harry asked.

"Oh, how do you *talk* your way in?" Sterling Promise said. "The obvious choice would be to become a customer. Unless there is something preventing that." He looked at me, then at Harry. Both our faces reddened, mine with irritation.

"There is," I said. "Time. We need to work quickly."

"Of course, I understand. Then if you want someone to do something for you, and you don't have a good reason, you have to rely on what *they* want." His gaze flickered to me and then focused on Harry again. "Take Mr. Lo. You go to visit him, and he offers you tea. Accept his offer."

"For tea? We don't want his tea. We want to see his girls," Harry said.

Sterling Promise wore a patient look, like he was speaking to a child. "He will send one of the girls to make it. Then when she comes in with it, you can compliment her fine figure."

"But we will have seen only one girl," I said.

Sterling Promise smiled gently and shook his head. "Mr. Lo is very proud of the girls he offers. It upsets him that only the Americans come to see them. He suffers under the idea that his girls are not good enough, and he is desperate to prove that they are. So if you compliment her figure, he will feel compelled to show you another girl with a far better figure, whose eyes, you might mention, are the loveliest shape."

Harry and I stared. "Would that work?" he asked.

"Probably," Sterling Promise said. "But only with Mr. Lo, because you have asked him to do exactly what he wants to do. He does not want to show you around the building. The walls are dirty and thin. The curtains are threadbare. He does not want to talk about the trouble he has getting the girls, because it worries him day and night. But he does want to show you the beauty of his girls. When you are asking a favor, make sure it has the flavor of something they desire."

"How do we know what they want?"

"You might already know if you think about it. Or you might have to figure it out when you are standing before them, pushing gently against walls to find a door."

Harry stood and bowed politely to Sterling Promise. "I'm going to call my father. I think he will be pleased. We have a lot of work to do."

CHAPTER 35

AFTER HARRY DISAPPEARED into the back, Sterling Promise looked at the pattern of dark wood on the table. His face was sour. "I don't like him."

"Then don't help."

"I thought you hated these tricks."

"This is important," I said quietly.

"Important to you?" he asked, pushing for something.

"Important."

"Jade Moon, the game you are playing is dangerous enough already. Are you sure you want to play it with a fool?"

"Harry is not a fool," I whispered.

"Then you are an even bigger fool for not recognizing it," he said.

"If you aren't willing to help him, then walk away," I hissed.

"Why do you care so much?" he asked, lifting his gaze to meet mine.

"Because Harry doesn't see me as the burden so many others do."

Sterling Promise looked back at the table. "Your suit — is that mine?"

"Yes. You can have it back when we are done with all this. I'll be glad to be rid of it."

"I don't care about the suit anymore." He looked tired, bruised. Under his cheeks, the skin held tightly to the bone, and shadows had appeared under his eyes. He was not the hopeful young man who had showed up at our farm almost a year ago. "Are you happy here in America?" he asked.

"What would I have to be happy about?" I snapped. "Nothing has worked out the way I hoped. I thought I would be staying with the Yings, laughing over bowls of Jell-O."

"But you're not with them," he said. His confusion reminded me how far I was from where I wanted to be.

"No, I'm not. Plans changed."

He studied me, then looked down at the table. "It is harder than I thought." I knew there should be tricks behind his words, but I couldn't find them. "I am looking for more legitimate business opportunities."

"Like fireworks?" I asked.

"Like fireworks. But I have to pay Master Yue back first. I never wanted to use that money, but I had to. Now I am going to be tied to him longer than I'd hoped."

I tilted my head with surprise. It was the first time he acknowledged the bribe. "Harry might help. His father is looking for new businesses for the tong," I said.

"Mr. Hon is one of the most brutal men in Chinatown. A cold, calculating man. Everyone in Chinatown knows it."

My face reddened. "Harry is a good person."

"So you say." Sterling Promise's face hardened. "But Harry cares most about Harry. You always refuse to see that, and it does nothing but get you in trouble."

"Yes, it does." I leaned back and crossed my arms. "It is a good trick — asking someone to do something they already wanted to do, to get what you want." I pushed back from the table and stood. "Like when you offered to marry me."

"That was not something you wanted to do," he said softly.

Harry returned and motioned me to the back.

"Father said to do nothing," Harry said. "He said Chin is handling it. You are supposed to go back to the house."

"Have they found her?"

"No. But this girl has brought nothing but trouble. Maybe I *can't* do anything right."

I couldn't let Harry quit now — I needed those addresses. With a sick feeling in the pit of my stomach, I said, "It is too bad. You had everything worked out."

"I know. We would have found her."

"He would have been so proud when it worked." I swallowed. "You sounded so much like him back there. You'll have to find another way to prove yourself . . . if you can."

Harry thought for a moment. He leaned against the bricks, then came to the decision I was steering him toward. "We're still going to search for the girl."

Back inside the restaurant, he returned to the table. "Let's talk about the first brothel," Harry said, sliding into his chair.

"Fine," Sterling Promise replied with a stiff nod.

Harry pulled out a pencil and a piece of paper, scribbled a list of names, then handed it to Sterling Promise, who scanned it. Eventually, his finger lingered over one.

"What do you know about Mr. Sing?" Harry asked.

"He is a friend of Mr. Lo, so I have met him several times. From what I have heard him say, it seems he used to be one of the most successful businessmen in Chinatown, but he has been declining in influence for the past fifteen years."

"That is true. I think my father has loaned him money several times," Harry said.

Sterling Promise continued, "He refuses to recognize this, and lives his life as if he had the same wealth and influence as he did before."

It was interesting to see Sterling Promise work, peeling back the layers on people. Some of the men he already knew. For others, he would pull scraps of information from Harry and mold them into the necessary key that would open the door. It was free of both the magic and the cruelty I had imagined he must possess in my weaker moments. He just knew people, the way I knew stories, the way Harry knew the streets of Chinatown.

"So how do we get Mr. Sing to show us the slave girls he has?" Harry demanded.

"Flatter his sense of importance. He should lap it up like a dog that hasn't been fed for a month."

Harry looked at him, his face still dark with confusion.

Sterling Promise's voice was weary as he tried to explain. "I will say I have heard that he is having great success, tell him that everyone is talking about how cleverly he manages his businesses."

Harry nodded. "What if he asks why my father doesn't come down himself?"

"Tell him what he wants to hear. Look down at the ground, shift your weight nervously. Say that he does not know of your visit. You wanted your new friend, who would like to set up his own business, to see an excellent example of success."

Harry nodded. He turned to me. "Do *you* think it will work?"

Sterling Promise frowned. "He won't be able to resist. You are offering him the influence and respect that he craves. People don't care if it is only a fragile bubble of success created simply by your words. If you find out what they really want, they will accept even a shadow of it." He dropped his eyes down to the table and said, "Sometimes."

I lifted my chin and looked away.

"Fire Horse, what do you think?" Harry asked again.

"It will work," I said.

CHAPTER 36

AND SO WE BEGAN OUR SEARCH. The brothels were noisy, busy businesses during the day. The girls who spent their nights behind the curtains now sat like disgruntled wives, sewing buttons on jackets and cuffs on pants. Daylight hardened and hollowed their faces. The brutal women charged with controlling them tried to hurry their languid movements with loud slaps. In some brothels, silk hung on the windows, and pillows rested on rich furniture. In other places, the walls were bare, and rats scratched behind the plaster. No curtains could hide the boards nailed across the windows, and even the finest carpets only muffled the hollow sounds of trapdoors beneath our feet. Harry said they were used for hiding girls if the police came.

Miss Donaldson was right — these were prisons.

Harry cast his eyes around each place, looking for the missing girl. If any of the girls lifted their gaze to meet his, he turned away. Sterling Promise smiled and bowed to every owner, his eyes never wandering. I had only ugly looks for the owners and sad looks for the girls, so after pretending for Harry's benefit to search for Spring Blossom, I stared past all of it.

Harry took us through the series of heavy doors and hallways that hid each brothel. I collected a string of street names and buildings in my head to pass to Miss Donaldson, while Sterling Promise doled out the right combinations of words to gain us entry: "I have heard your girls are the finest that come from China. Have you been able to get any new ones?" Or "You've lost none of your girls to the police. You must have clever hiding places." And even "Clearly, you only pay the lowest price for your girls, always getting the best side of a bargain. Tell me about the last clever bargain you struck." He took us faithfully from place to place, covering Harry's and my rough manners with a silky flow of sweet words.

Harry's frustration grew. And, yet, the more we failed, the more convinced he was that someone had taken Spring Blossom from the police. Halfway through the day, he pulled me next to him and muttered, "You were right about Sterling Promise. We can't trust him."

"He is doing exactly what we asked him to do."

"Yes, but like you said, he is tricky," Harry said, waiting for me to agree.

"He has done nothing but help us so far. He had sour Mr. Tou showing us around like honored guests."

Harry shook his head at me and led us to our next brothel, his shoulders hunched over, his fists stuffed deep into his pockets, and his long legs leaving Sterling Promise and me scrambling ten steps behind. Sterling Promise caught up to me, leaned over, and said, "He blames me for the fact that he hasn't found the girl yet."

"He is disappointed. Don't worry."

"I don't think he trusts me."

"He has seen what you can do. People have to keep their guard up when they are around you." I knew. I was exhausted from it.

"I don't care what he thinks," he said, looking hard at me. "But you should know, I'm not trying to trick either of you."

"That is a relief, until I realize that it is exactly what I want you to say. Which I know you are well aware of."

Sterling Promise frowned, but it was the hurt in his eyes that threw me off balance.

"Don't worry," I said. "Harry will look everywhere for the girl. He won't find her, but his father will be proud that he did something."

"He won't find her?" he said.

"What?"

"You said he won't find her. How do you know that?"

"I didn't say that." My breath tightened.

"Yes, you did." Sterling Promise's voice was raised. Harry turned to look at us, so he dropped it to a whisper. "I should have known," he said, bringing his fist to his forehead. "What is it about you? I can't think straight when you are involved." He turned to me. "You are going to get hurt."

"I . . . I didn't do anything," I said.

"You have no idea what you do."

I tried to swallow, squeezing at the guilt lodged in my throat.

"Harry may want his father's respect, but your influence over him is strong too. I don't know how you do it, Jade Moon. I can win influence like a chess game, with carefully calculated moves and strategies. Yours just grows like a seed. You shine your sunlight on someone and he cannot help but stretch toward you."

"I . . ." But Sterling Promise slowed his steps and dropped behind me. By the time I caught up to Harry, Sterling Promise was half a block behind.

"He is making fools of us," Harry whispered.

"What are you saying?"

"I am saying that I think he took the girl or at least knows where she is. Maybe he is opening a brothel of his own. Maybe he is trying to take over Mr. Lo's."

"You think Sterling Promise took her? Why would he do that?" Harry's words sent flashes of fear through me. "Sterling Promise wants to sell fireworks. He has no interest in selling girls. He'd rather have the reward," I said.

"How do you know that?"

"I know."

"Do you? You know everything and nothing about him at the same time. You have seen the way he digs into people, becoming the person they want right at that moment. Do you really think you can know someone like that?"

"If you don't trust him, trust me," I said.

"*You* told me not to trust him. You said he only does favors that will benefit him. I don't think he is helping us at all." The purpose in his eyes had burned away and left only a fearful desperation.

"Harry, let's focus on finding the girl."

"What if that is impossible?"

"Then you will have tried, and your father will respect that."

"There is something he will respect more," Harry said.

"What?"

"Finding the man who took her," he said, looking over his shoulder at Sterling Promise.

This day was making me dizzy. I felt like I was standing on the edge of a cliff, and a single gust of wind could send me tumbling to the rocks below.

We continued our search, but Harry's attitude became increasingly hostile. His back stiffened and his feet marched down streets and around corners. He barked out one-word answers to Sterling Promise's questions. By the time the afternoon had cooled, a thick cloud of disgust and frustration hung around Harry. Sterling Promise had started to tap his leg with his finger two addresses ago.

At the last place, Harry stood like a stone while Sterling Promise listened sympathetically to Mr. Chu's complaints about the police. He was the most paranoid of all the owners, and after Sterling Promise had admired the clever way he avoided police raids, we got a peek at a few of the hidden panels that lined his walls and floors.

"So that is where the girls hide when the police come?" I said.

"Yes. The police think they are so clever, but I know they are spying on me, and I am ready," Mr. Chu said.

Sterling Promise nodded, the same wrinkle between his eyes as Mr. Chu's.

"I am sure I was being followed this morning."

"I would not be surprised," said Sterling Promise.

"So, your father thinks he can do something about the police?" Mr. Chu said to Harry.

"Do you have a new girl or not?" Harry snapped.

"A new girl?" Mr. Chu blinked, trying to recapture the line of the conversation.

"No, you don't, do you?" Sterling Promise and I looked at Harry. "Of course you don't. This has been a waste of time. The girl is far away by now." Harry spun on his heels, threw open the door, and stomped out, leaving Sterling Promise and me staring at his back.

Mr. Chu moved toward a door at the side of the room. "If you are playing some sort of trick on me, I want to know," he said. He knocked, and two men came through. Their rough faces and sleepy eyes made me suspect that they were hatchet men. Their black jackets, loose enough to carry knives and guns, made me sure. I looked around the long, narrow room. It would be hard to avoid three men *and* their guns and knives.

I nudged Sterling Promise, trying to get him to say something, but he stared forward, his finger tapping against his leg.

"What is this?" Mr. Chu said.

If Sterling Promise wasn't going to save us, I would have to. What would this man want to hear?

The two men moved closer and one reached under his coat. The truth? Everyone likes the truth, right? "We are looking for a girl," I stammered. I could hear the shaking in my voice.

"Yes, I heard. One you think I have." One of the men moved behind us, blocking the door.

"We didn't want to worry you, but this girl is dangerous."

"Dangerous?" Mr. Chu said. "What do you mean?"

"We think the girl may be working with that Donaldson woman, informing the police," I said. "That woman has always been trouble."

Mr. Chu spat on the floor and cursed Miss Donaldson's ancestors with a vigor that brought pink to my cheeks.

"The girl poses as a girl for sale. Then she finds out where the brothel is, escapes, and brings Miss Donaldson to its door."

Sterling Promise looked at me. He was nodding his head slowly. "Mr. Hon is worried, but he doesn't want any panic to hurt the business," he said. He looked at the two men. "You understand."

Mr. Chu narrowed his eyes and motioned the men forward. Words left me as the fight started to flood my veins.

"We thought she might be here because of the difficulties the police have had raiding your establishment," Sterling Promise said. He grabbed my arm and moved me behind him. I could feel the trembling of his hand, but he continued with a steady voice. "Of course, we never intended to search your hiding places, but when you offered . . . Who could resist such a treat?"

Mr. Chu paused. I gripped my hands into fists and swept my eyes over the room, calculating. Then a smile spread across Mr. Chu's face. "Ha! I predicted this. I have been telling Hon for years about the spies, but he has ignored my warnings." He waved a hand at the two hatchet men, who slipped back through the door. "Sit, have a drink."

We sat. Sterling Promise rattled off a string of perfect responses to the man's complaints, and by the time we had been served tea, I could barely see the cup shaking in my hand.

Sterling Promise rose and bowed when we had finished. "Let us know if you notice anything suspicious."

Mr. Chu nodded. "I will," he said.

After we left, Sterling Promise stopped in the hallway, leaning against the stained wall between the second and third door.

"Are you all right?" I said.

"I . . . I just need a moment." He covered his face with his hand. "He was going to kill us."

"Not necessarily."

"He was. I saw it."

"You could have gotten out. I would have fought them."

"You should have run."

"I couldn't have left you there."

"Harry left you."

I shook my head. "I'm sorry I got you involved."

We stood next to each other, letting the strain of the danger wane. When I pushed away from the wall, Sterling Promise closed his eyes. "I knew the risk."

I opened the door to the street and took a deep breath of the fresh air.

"Are you coming?" I asked.

"I . . . I just need . . ."

"Don't worry. I'll wait outside," I said.

I had been even surer that he was going to kill us than Sterling Promise was, and my heart was struggling to return to a steady beat. Then Harry stepped from behind the door and said, "I told you we couldn't trust Sterling Promise."

"At least he didn't leave us in there to be killed," I said.

"When are you going to stop defending him?" Harry shouted.

"I shouldn't have to defend him. He is doing what we asked," I said.

Sterling Promise stomped out the door. "You can't leave like that, Harry. You put both of us in danger."

"Don't tell me what I can't do."

Sterling Promise turned to me. "Just remember, I kept *my* promise."

Harry's glare followed Sterling Promise as he walked away. "I am taking care of this," he said.

I held out my hand to block him. "What are you going to do?"

"I don't know yet. Are you with me?"

"No," I said warily. "Not for this. You're wrong about Sterling Promise. This isn't who you are. You aren't your father." I watched Harry's anger get buried in sadness for a moment, then resurface. He pushed past me. "Wait, where are you going?"

"If you won't take care of this, Chin will. We will find the girl. Chin will gladly convince Sterling Promise to talk. My father is going to be very disappointed in you."

"Good," I yelled after him. It was the one good punch before the sickness settled in.

CHAPTER 37

I HAD ALL THE LOCATIONS of the brothels tucked inside my head, along with as many secret panels and trapdoors as the owners had shown us. Miss Donaldson could rescue more girls than the mission could hold. Gathering addresses was all I had agreed to do, so I turned toward the mission home.

As I moved down the streets, I told myself that Sterling Promise would be fine. He would have left me in the same circumstances, right? He could talk his way out of this. But I knew that Chin wasn't much for talk. Then the irritating reality that Sterling Promise had helped us, just as he promised, tunneled itself into my head and refused to leave. And behind it came another shock — I didn't want him hurt. He was not the same Sterling Promise who had tossed aside my dreams and broken my heart.

I was so distracted that about two blocks from the mission home, I almost ran straight into a giant of a man.

"I have been looking for you," Neil said. "When I came to see that you'd made it to Clara's" — he cleared his throat — "Miss Donaldson's, she told me the bloody foolish errand she had sent you on. I should have known better than to put the two of your heads together."

"She didn't make me do it. It was my choice."

"Oh, I blame both of you."

I grabbed Neil's newspaper out of his hand and scribbled a quick map of Chinatown, adding a few landmarks to help orient Miss Donaldson.

"I have to help Sterling Promise," I said, continuing to draw.

"The guy you hit at Lo's."

"Chin and Harry think he is responsible for the missing girl. They are searching for him. I can't let him take the blame for what I did." I marked the spots where the brothels sat, with the street numbers if they had them, and handed the paper back to Neil.

"Like hell you can't. You get back to the mission home."

"Take that to Miss Donaldson. I'll come right back."

He reached for my arm, but I had always been quicker than Neil. He'd taught me that if we ever fought, my only choice would be to run away.

I buried myself in the endless alleys of Chinatown. Without Harry's guidance, I made several wrong turns, but I still caught Mr. Lo just as he was closing the outside door to his building, his shoulders bent. He looked at me, surprised.

"If you have come for money for Hon, there isn't any." He shook his head, his hand pressed to his forehead. "That Donaldson woman came here with the police today and took my girls. I don't know how she found me. I'm ruined."

I pressed my lips together. So Miss Donaldson had already started her raids, with the one address I gave her when I saw Spring Blossom. If I had a moment, I would have enjoyed that news, but I was racing against Harry, Chin, and Mr. Hon's many eyes. As soon as Miss Donaldson raided the other addresses, Sterling Promise would be in even more danger. "I am looking for Sterling Promise, the young man who works for you."

"You're the one who beat him up," he said, turning to go.

"I'm not here to hurt him. He needs my help."

He waved his hand and started walking. "I have lived in Chinatown longer than you have been alive. Some things have changed, but the hatchet men have never been known for helping people."

I put my hand on his arm gently. "I am not a hatchet man." I willed him to see past his assumptions. "Please, I need to find him."

Mr. Lo looked at me for another moment. "He lives in a boarding house two blocks from here," he said, pointing down the street. "I don't know the room, but someone there can tell you. If you find him, you might as well tell him about the raid. Yue cannot complain about the money I send him anymore."

The air inside the boarding house was thick from too many people breathing it. Sleepy-eyed men squeezed past one another down the narrow hall. I knocked on the door that one had pointed to when I asked for Sterling Promise. When it cracked open, I pushed past Sterling Promise and shut the door.

"What are you doing here?" His shirt was open, and he hurried to button it.

"I don't have time to explain." I grabbed at the things scattered around the room and dumped them on the blanket covering his small bed.

"What is all of this about, Jade Moon?"

"I am getting you out of here," I said, tying the blanket into a bundle before holding it out to him.

"I'm not going anywhere until you explain why. Does this have to do with Harry?"

I stared at him, wondering if I could knock him out and drag him away, but I knew that was not the way to help him. What would help him was the truth. I sat on the cot, hugging the bundle filled with his things to my chest.

"What have you done?" he said slowly, standing over me. His eyes were serious, not plotting, just waiting.

"I rescued the girl we've been looking for. Actually, a policeman rescued her, but I might have helped."

"I knew you didn't want to find that girl! Why would you do something so reckless?"

I stood to face him. "You saw what happens to those girls."

"Jade Moon . . ."

I pushed my face closer. "No one should have to survive that way — suffocating inside life. You and I know that." I grabbed his shoulders, using him as an anchor in the chaos I had created. I needed him to believe that I had not destroyed everything for nothing.

"But the risk," he said weakly.

"I know. I am not any different here."

"No, you're not," he said. He hung his head, and I dropped back down onto the bed. He sat next to me, balling his fists on his knees, the muscles across his back tightening under his shirt. While I had spent five moon cycles getting used to the closeness of men, I could feel every inch of Sterling Promise's leg as it pressed against mine.

"We have to get you out of here," I said. "Mr. Lo's girls were taken today. And Harry thinks you're responsible for it. Mr. Hon's hatchet men are looking for you."

His fists gripped tighter.

"I should have never gotten you involved," I stammered.

Sterling Promise raised his head and studied me. "How much danger are we in?"

Tears swelled in my eyes.

He took a slow breath, then he seemed to decide something. "Go to Mrs. Ying."

"You have seen her?"

"Of course. I went straight there when I came."

I stared at him, my mouth open.

"To find you. To make sure you were safe."

I shook my head.

"Forget Harry. Please. He cares for you, but not as much as he should. I would know." He stood up and pocketed a few more items without looking at me.

"Harry lied to me," I said. "He was supposed to bring me to the Yings, but instead he took me to the wrong place on purpose." My chest tightened. "Look at me. The Yings won't want me. I'm a hatchet man now. I am just as stuck as I was the day you saw me in that mud."

He did look at me, and it made my heart jump. "No, you have become yourself. You . . . you are as captivating as the flame that dances in a fire. And just as destructive." He resumed packing. His face had darkened with an anger I had never seen him allow himself. "I'll get myself out of this," he said, his mind far away. He opened a drawer, fumbled for something, then stuffed a piece of paper into my hand. It was a laundry slip with the Yings' name and address on the top. "Dress as a woman again and no one will ever know."

"Let me help you," I said.

"I don't want your help," Sterling Promise said, grabbing my hand.

"Because I'm unlucky?"

"Because you're dangerous." He squeezed my hand and gave me a small smile.

"You can't bribe or talk your way out of this. Chin, Mr. Hon's hatchet man, is going to want to fight. It might help to have someone dangerous on your side."

Sterling Promise shook his head, dropping my hand and lifting his to touch my face before turning toward the door. He picked up the bundle. "No, Jade Moon. I never want to see you again." Then he lowered his voice. "I'm not lucky enough for you."

"You don't mean that," I said, but he slipped away from me into the hallway, leaving me standing among the things he left behind.

I was no longer trapped on Angel Island. I was free from the locked doors and nailed windows of Mr. Hon's house. I had gotten the addresses Miss Donaldson needed. I had earned my place here. I should have felt light without all these chains. But I did not. Even leaving Sterling Promise on the shore of Angel Island had not felt this final. "Never" meant no second chances, no change of heart. And part of me knew that I deserved "never." I had stolen away his dream, and when he helped me anyway, I had taken every-thing else.

After a few seconds, I made my way to the front door and stepped into the street. Chinatown stood in the shadows of the evening. A group of children had gathered in animated conversation at the mouth of an alley, one holding the handle of a bright red wagon. They looked every inch American with the wide sweeps of their gestures and enthusiastic voices.

I crossed the street and looked back at the house Sterling Promise had stayed in. A man leaned against the corner of the building where an alley emptied into the street. His suit was dark enough to hide him at night. His jacket was loose enough for guns, knives, and a little padding. My heart started to beat faster. Was I imagin-ing danger because I had lived with it for so long? I scanned the storefronts and saw another figure in dark suit and a low-set hat stop in front of a grocery facing the same alley. A woman quick-ened her steps as she passed him. He was one of Chin's men. If Chin's men were here, there was a chance that Chin was here. If Chin was here, Sterling Promise was in danger.

I squeezed my eyes shut, trying to erase the men, and started to walk toward the mission home.

Sterling Promise doesn't want my help. He never wants to see me again.

Then my feet stopped.

When had I ever done anything he wanted?

CHAPTER 38

I SWUNG AROUND and walked down the alley to the back of Sterling Promise's boarding house, strategies crowding my head. When I turned the last corner, I saw Chin holding Sterling Promise in front of Harry.

Harry pulled back his fist. It was past time for strategies; it was time to fight. I ran at them. No one saw me until it was too late. I lowered my shoulder the way Neil had taught me and rammed it into Harry. His fist was already in motion, but it only grazed the side of my face.

"What are you doing? He helped us," I shouted.

"I am not listening to his lies," Harry said, glaring at Sterling Promise.

"I told you to stay out of this," Sterling Promise said to me, his teeth gripped tight.

"Get out of the way, Fire Horse," Chin said, shoving me into a wall of bricks. "This doesn't concern you," he challenged. "Does it?"

All Sterling Promise had to do was tell them who I was, and their anger would switch over to me. "Tell them the truth," I begged him.

"I don't tell the truth," he said, staring at me.

"Please, Harry," I said. "You made a deal with him."

"You can't make deals with cheaters," Harry said. His eyes burned with the fire I knew so well.

"Don't do this. You are too angry."

"Get out of my way," he growled. Harry pulled back his fist. I tried to grab his arm, but one of Chin's men seized me. I struggled as Harry punched Sterling Promise in the mouth. Sterling Promise turned his face and spit out a mix of saliva and blood.

"I am going to kill you for what you did to my brothers of the tong, to my father," Harry shouted. I saw fear flash across Sterling Promise's face, but he did not open his mouth. Harry pulled back and let loose another punch to his stomach.

"Stop it," I cried, wrestling myself free.

But Harry heard only the furious pounding of his own anger. "You tried to take away any chance I had of winning my father's respect. He will respect me after I rid Chinatown of you." He punched Sterling Promise again, this one landing on his jaw, knocking his head to the side. Sterling Promise was slumped over now in Chin's arms, his breath coming heavily through his nose. Harry's fist reared back again. Chin had a satisfied smile on his face.

"He did not do any of that to you, Harry."

"Stay out of this," Sterling Promise said.

"*I* sent the girl to the mission home," I announced.

Every face turned toward me.

"You're lying," Chin growled. "You're just protecting him."

"You know," I said to Harry. "You caught me there the first time."

"But you were checking for the missing girl," Harry said.

"I was checking *on* the missing girl," I said.

The anger broke from his face and a deep hurt filled the cracks it left. "You . . . you . . . ," Harry stuttered.

"You know it is true, Harry," I said. "I did this to you."

Harry looked at his feet.

"I knew we couldn't trust you," Chin said. He let go of Sterling Promise, who collapsed to his hands and knees. "So it is you we should kill." He stepped closer, reaching inside his jacket.

My body tensed, and my feet found the stance Neil had made me practice thousands of times. Harry made a small automatic motion to stop him, but he didn't finish it.

Sterling Promise rose to his feet and leaned against the building. "You can kill her, but it would be a cowardly thing to do," he said, loud exhales between each word. "You will be the laughingstock of Chinatown. People will think you didn't know."

"Her?" said Chin. The smile fell from his face.

"Her?" repeated Harry. His eyes searched mine.

My heart trembled, and I started to feel cold.

"Of course you knew. I would have told you sooner, but I knew it was impossible that she was fooling you." Only Sterling Promise could find the single thread to pull in this wreckage. "I am simply concerned for your reputations," he said.

"A girl?" Harry's face was all confusion and shock. "Impossible!"

"It's just another of his lies," Chin said. He grabbed at the shirt I wore under Sterling Promise's suit and ripped at the button. It gave way, and he pulled his hand back. In it was a fistful of my wrappings, wearing thin after months of use.

Chin dropped the strip of material like it was a snake. I pulled my shirt closed again and held it there.

"My name is Jade Moon," I said, letting my voice return to the octave where it belonged. The fighter in me pushed off its final mask, and I felt the pressure in my chest release.

Chin shook his head. "This doesn't change anything. We should still kill him . . . her." His voice was a little unsure. "Women have been killed before."

Harry's face was drawn tight. I had never seen him look so much like his father. "I . . . I'm not . . ."

But Harry's hesitation only fueled Chin's old anger with me. "I'm in charge of protecting the tong, and she is a threat." He reached his hand into the inside pocket of his jacket. I started to choke on the air around me.

"Harry, this isn't who you are," I tried.

Harry pressed his lips together. "I swore I wouldn't let my father get cheated again." He nodded at Chin.

Sterling Promise lifted his head. The curtain over his eyes that I had seen many times was dropped yet again, hiding all his emotions. "Wait." He pulled himself up. His shoulders relaxed. "I'm not saying you can't kill her. Of course you can. I'm saying you shouldn't. There is another solution."

Harry turned to Sterling Promise. "What do you mean?"

"You lost one girl. Now you've found another."

Harry stared at him, weighing each word.

"Maybe you can earn your father's respect after all."

I looked at Sterling Promise. "What . . . ? No." The world had shifted so quickly; it seemed to be spinning. He didn't look at me.

"She has no family here," Sterling Promise continued. "She's alone, belongs to no one." He wiped a trickle of blood from the corner of his lip. "It is certainly a more complete revenge. You could hold your head up as you walk the streets."

Chin smiled. He called to the two men guarding the alley. They were there before I had a chance to run.

"You can't," I shouted, struggling against the hands that suddenly gripped me.

"You can go tell your boss that we have a new girl for him," Harry said to Sterling Promise. He was forcing every word past his lips, like they stung.

"Harry, no! You can't do this to me."

"You stole from my father," he said. "I have to."

"I didn't steal anything," I said. "The girl was never his! You hate this life as much as I do. You know it's wrong. You said —"

Harry shook off my words. "Don't tell me what I hate." He looked at Sterling Promise again. "She lied to you too, didn't she?"

Sterling Promise looked away and stuck his hands in his pockets, mimicking Harry's easy stance perfectly. "She's a Fire Horse. She will destroy all of us to survive."

His words were like a punch in the stomach; they pushed all the breath out and left me scrambling for air. "I know you must hate me, but this?"

He took a step closer. "I warned you to stay away," Sterling Promise said. "But you didn't. And now you leave me no choice." He looked at me as if I was supposed to understand something. "I am tricky, remember."

For a second the curtain rose and I glimpsed a deep sadness in his eyes, but I didn't know anymore what was real and what was pretend.

Chin's laughter broke his gaze, and Sterling Promise's face hardened. "You *are* tricky, my friend," Chin said. "The tong has work for people like you."

"I do find myself looking for work," Sterling Promise said.

CHAPTER 39

HARRY AND STERLING PROMISE stood shoulder to shoulder. "Take her to Lo's and lock her up. I'll talk to my father." Harry's mouth was stiff.

Chin nodded, grinning, and tightened his grip on me. "Your father will be very pleased with you."

"I don't want to hear another word from you," Harry shouted at him, his cheeks red with fury

Chin's face darkened, but his mouth stayed shut. He and his men forced me down the street. Sterling Promise followed behind. I tried to add up my advantages and disadvantages like Neil had taught me. I had some training, a talent for getting involved in things that were none of my business, three people who I had betrayed, and a ball of outrage deep in my stomach. But Chin was stronger than me, and Sterling Promise was cleverer. Harry was just desperate.

Chin marched me to Lo's place and up the stairs to his second-floor office.

"Behind the curtain," Sterling Promise said, pointing to one wall.

Chin pulled back the curtain to reveal what looked like a paneled wall. Sterling Promise slid back two of the boards to reveal a slice of a room. I stumbled back into one of Chin's men. Chin grabbed my arm and yanked me toward the opening. I jerked my arm back and jammed an elbow into his belly. A hatchet man grabbed my arm from behind, and Chin pushed me across the threshold, slamming me against the back wall. I dropped to my knees. By the time I scrambled up, Chin was sliding the last board into place. He didn't hide the satisfied smile on his face.

The room was dark. I waited for my eyes to adjust, but even when they did, there wasn't enough light to see anything. The stale air smelled of sweat and tears, sour and sweet, the perfume of lies and broken promises — just like my father said.

"I told you that one was trouble," Chin said to the other guys.

I slammed my fist against the wall. The solid wood hummed back.

"Mr. Hon will give you to the ugliest man in Chinatown," Chin called back to me, his voice fading down the hall.

"Perhaps a drink while we wait for Harry?" I heard Sterling Promise say. Out of this mess, he would build a fireworks business.

I ran my hands over the walls. The panels were firmly in place. The other three walls were solid wood.

"This is impossible," I said to the air. "I can't just wait for them to come get me."

After making myself dizzy with pacing, I slumped to the floor, leaning against the wall. One hour passed, then another and another. The emotions tossed inside of me. If I could hurl them at someone, I might feel some release.

This was Harry's fault. He had me locked up. He was probably basking in his father's chilly pride now. But Harry did not force me to get the addresses for Miss Donaldson.

It was definitely Miss Donaldson's fault. She had sent me back to the tong. Except that I could be safe in the mission home now if I had not gone back to help Sterling Promise.

It was Sterling Promise's fault. I seethed, pulling my knees to my chest. He had betrayed me again. Except that he had told me to stay out of it.

It was my fault. The reason I found myself constantly in traps and prisons is because I went running into them. I banged my fists against the floor by my feet.

Something rattled.

I hit the floor again. The rattle came from where my feet sat. My fingers ran along the rough wood until I found it. A latch.

Most of the floor of the small room was a trapdoor. Sterling Promise had not locked me in a prison. He had given me an escape. I scrambled to my knees and put my ear against the boards below. Nothing.

I had to balance myself on the strip of floor where the hinge was attached, one hand on the door, one pushing against the opposite wall. Then I lifted the latch and pulled back the trapdoor. It opened onto the main hallway below, a few feet from the front door. I couldn't see anyone down there. I took a breath and jumped.

I scrambled to my feet and reached for the front door, but not before the knob turned and the door started to inch open. My heartbeat roared in my chest, pulsing into my head and hands. I lifted my fists to my face and took my stand. I would have to get in the first good punch if I wanted to get out fast. One punch was probably not my best strategy, but it was all I had.

I swung with all my force. My fist made good contact with the dark figure standing in the doorway, and his jaw snapped to the side, but his feet didn't move. Then when the face came into focus, I saw why.

"Good hit, Fire Horse."

"Neil!" I wrapped my arms around his waist. He unraveled them gently. "I know you are mad at me, but Chin and Harry locked me in here. They're going to sell me. They could be back any minute with more people. You have to help me."

"Sure, now you want my help." A crooked smile spread over his face.

"What are *you* doing here?"

"Chin called Mr. Hon to tell him what happened. It would have been good news if Chin hadn't been drunk."

"Drunk?"

"That is what happens when you unlock another man's liquor cabinet. Too bad I'll have to tell them that by the time I got here, you already escaped. It's like a ghost, you are," he said, ushering me into the alley.

I hesitated. "What if we run into someone?"

"I'll knock them unconscious and blame it on you."

That seemed like a good plan, so I stepped into the night.

"Apparently, you've got a bit of a curse on you," Neil said as we threaded our way through the narrow streets.

"I told you!"

"When Mr. Hon found out he was keeping a Fire Horse *girl* . . ." Neil smiled. "I've never seen a Chinaman with such a white face.

He was blathering into the phone for hours trying to get rid of you. And he would have too — if everyone in Chinatown wasn't talking about you already."

"Why are they talking about me?"

"Someone has been telling stories about all the bad luck you bring."

"Who would do that?"

"I don't know. One of your dozens of acquaintances. I think it was the guy you knocked out the other night."

"Sterling Promise?"

"That's him."

My stomach twisted. "But . . . He . . . Why would he do that?"

"I don't know, but it sure saved your arse." Neil looked at me. "Maybe he is your friend after all."

"He couldn't be, after what I have done."

"Hmmm . . . then it is a bit of a mystery."

Only a few windows beamed their light onto the street below.

"I was so scared," I said.

Neil glanced at me before focusing his gaze back on the street in front of us. "Ah, maybe you *are* a fighter, girly," he said.

"What do you mean?"

"There are two types of people who fight — fighters, who learn from their mistakes, and troublemakers, who get themselves killed. I was half sure you would be the second."

When we got to the mission home, Miss Donaldson stood like a paper cutout against the light of the front door. She hugged me close. "I could never have forgiven myself if something had happened to you."

"I told you, I'm destructive."

"A Fire Horse."

I nodded.

"That's what all the men are talking about. Everyone has heard what a danger you are, that your father and your village sent you all the way to America to be rid of your bad luck, that you stole another man's papers." She smiled. "I'm afraid you have no choice but to stay here now. No one else will take you. You're probably the only girl I can send through the streets without worrying about you being stolen."

"She shouldn't be wandering the streets," Neil grumbled.

"I wish I had six or seven more of you. Those tongs would walk a mile around this place."

"You best wait and see if you can handle this one first," Neil said. "I'll be back, and I expect her to be here, not in some opium den."

"Where are the opium dens?" I asked, just to watch his face redden.

"This will be her home as long as she likes," Miss Donaldson said, putting her arm around my shoulders.

CHAPTER 40

THE GIRLS WERE SCATTERED around me on the floor, their skirts tucked under their knees. "What happened next?" our newest girl asked. She had come to the door this morning, wide-eyed and scared, and was the reason I was treating the other girls to the story they begged for.

"I stayed here, with Miss Donaldson and Spring Blossom," I said. "Neil still comes by to make sure I haven't joined the army or run off with the circus."

The little girl next to me stopped twisting the braid that trailed over her shoulder and announced, "He brought me ice cream."

I smiled and pulled her into my lap. "Yes, he did. He is very taken with you, isn't he?"

"I could never do what you did. I would never be bold enough," the new girl said. It was the most words she had strung together since she arrived.

"Of course you could. Did you think that girl who fell in the mud eavesdropping on Auntie Wu would do anything brave?"

The girl giggled and shook her head.

"One more story," one of the older girls begged.

"That's enough for now."

"But Cowherd and Weaver Girl meet tonight. You have to tell their story."

"The one where she throws things," said another girl, clutching her hands to her chest. "Please, Jade Moon."

"Why don't you tell it to the others?" I said, smiling at her. "You know it by heart."

The young girl blushed.

Spring Blossom walked through the doorway. "Are you ready to go?"

"Yes," I said, lifting the girl from my lap.

She twisted around to look up at me. "Are you going to see Mrs. Ying?"

"We are." I cupped her chin with my hand.

"She said she could find a husband for me. A nice man, like Mr. Ying," one of the older girls said.

"That would be lucky, wouldn't it?"

"Last time we had a wedding here, the whole house smelled like flowers," a girl explained to our new arrival.

"And cake!" said the little girl with the braid. She turned her excited eyes on me. "Who will you marry?"

"Whoever suits me best."

"Me too," she said, smiling. "I'll marry Neil."

"Good choice. I guess I will have to keep looking." I rose, brushed my skirt with my hands, and followed Spring Blossom out of the room.

We stepped out into the evening. The night was a gray one, but the lights on the street bounced off the mist, giving the darkness a sort of glow. A figure pushed from the shadows across the street and walked toward us. The brim of a hat pulled low over his brow hid his face.

I put my arm on Spring Blossom's to pull her inside. The tongs had left us alone after Sterling Promise's stories of the bad luck I brought tore through Chinatown. Truthfully, they were leaving everyone alone, too busy trying to destroy each other. Had Mr. Hon escaped that cycle of retaliation long enough to get his revenge on me?

"What's wrong, Jade Moon?" Spring Blossom asked. The smell of a summer rain lingered in the air. The figure lifted his head a little, and I could see his chin and the bottom of his mouth.

"I think it's . . . It can't be." I watched the movements of his walk. He took one hand out of his pocket and started to tap his fingers nervously against the side of his leg. "Sterling Promise."

I dropped Spring Blossom's arm and turned to escape inside. When I was halfway through the door, her small hand grabbed my wrist.

"I can't," I said, my wild eyes pleading with her calm ones. "He doesn't want to see me."

"Then why would he be here?" she asked.

"Good evening," Sterling Promise said, walking up the steps to us.

His presence had hung in my heart for months. I watched the fireworks light the sky for the New Year, thinking he might also be looking up at the explosions and remembering that first night when he had shown us his fireworks. I would hear notes of his voice on the street, then turn to find a stranger. For a week, a month, four, five, I thought he would come to the mission home. Then I remembered how much trouble I was and knew he needed to stay away.

He was smiling nervously at Spring Blossom but stealing quick side glances at me. "I am Sterling Promise, a friend of Jade Moon's from China."

"I know who you are," Spring Blossom said. "I am Spring Blossom, Jade Moon's friend here."

"Are you going out? Could I walk with you?"

I felt my head shaking back and forth, but Spring Blossom said, "Certainly." She looked at me and then back at Sterling Promise. "Well, we better go." She turned and headed down the street, leaving me on the porch, avoiding Sterling Promise's stare. I followed her, and he matched his steps to mine.

"You . . . You . . . ," I started, shaking my head.

"Tried to sell you?" He looked down at the ground. "Jade Moon, I would have never let that happen. I went all over Chinatown trying to make a sale impossible. They wanted to kill you. I had to do something."

"No. You never wanted to see me again."

"Oh. Yes." The back of his hand brushed mine. "Of all the lies I have told you, that was the biggest."

Spring Blossom stopped at a corner and turned to glance back at us before continuing down the street.

"Where did you go?" I asked.

"I had to leave for a little while. Chin and Harry would have made life very difficult for me here. Not to mention, I didn't have a job with Mr. Lo anymore. I took a position on a steamship that travels between San Francisco and Hawaii, just to stay out of sight."

"And now you're back. Is it safe?"

"Safe enough. The tongs have bigger worries than me. I wanted to make sure that you were all right."

"I am fine. Mrs. Donaldson guards us girls like a tigress." I was trying to keep the desperation that had shadowed my heart for the past six months out of every word. "What do you want from me?"

Sterling Promise swallowed and struggled to find the words. "Nothing . . . Everything . . . I want a fresh start, as ourselves. It is why we both came here."

"It isn't that easy," I said, shaking my head.

He looked at me, and I slipped a little into the darkness of his brown eyes. "No, it is almost impossible."

I nodded.

"Jade Moon. I was blind. The whole time I was using your father, I really needed you. You show me all the best and worst parts of myself."

"You want to know the worst parts?"

"I want to know the truth. Do you remember what you said to me on Angel Island, when I refused to take you to America?"

"I said a lot of things." My face warmed with the memory of it.

"You said I was nothing but smoke and shadows."

"I am sorry. I shouldn't have been so cruel."

"It was cruel, but when the sting faded, I realized it was also true. I was only what others wanted me to be. I had lost myself. Maybe that is why I could not hold anything as my own."

"I . . . I had no right . . . I am always too bold."

"You hold tightly to things. Sometimes the wrong things, but at least you hold on. It is very brave."

"I thought you were one of the thousands of traps that I fall into." I looked up, the words huddled in my throat. I didn't want to ruin whatever this was.

"I was, but now I want to hold on to something. Something that is mine."

My heart sputtered. "That is always what you wanted. To own something."

"Not own, hold." He stopped and stared into my eyes. "I know the difference now."

Drops of rain started to wet my cheeks. Sterling Promise held his hand out to me, palm up. This is what I told Spring Blossom love should be — offered with an open hand. I set my hand gently in his. We walked silently for a few blocks. I opened my mouth a dozen times, but then the old fractures in my heart would start to ache again. I put my other hand to my forehead to protect it from the thickening rain. "We'll be soaked by the time we get there," I said.

"It's just a few lovesick tears. I can survive those."

"A day early. Cowherd and Weaver Girl aren't supposed to cry until tomorrow."

"It's their beginning. And that can cause as many tears as an ending."

I smiled. "I suppose you still say exactly the right thing."

"I suppose you are still a Fire Horse." He grinned.

"Neither one of us is likely to change."

"At least you aren't still punching everything that moves," Sterling Promise said.

"Spring Blossom rarely lets me punch anyone anymore."

"I'll have to thank her."

"I wouldn't. She may make an exception for you," I said.

"She thinks I tried to sell you?" Sterling Promise asked.

"No, she knows how much it hurts when you love someone and they don't love you back," I said, struggling to keep the pain from my voice.

Sterling Promise stopped. He turned me gently to face him, lifting my chin until my eyes met his. "It is a crippling, blinding pain."

"You know it too," I said, my voice choked with tears.

He nodded.

I raised my face to the sky, trying to keep the tears inside. Spring Blossom stood on the steps of the Yings' home, waiting. "It is a horrible match," I said. "A snake and a horse. We will do nothing but fight."

Sterling Promise squeezed my hand and took a step closer. "No one will approve."

"I'll never know what you are thinking," I said.

"I'll always know what you are thinking," he said, wincing.

I looked up at him. "Only fools would try."

He brushed his thumb against my cheek. "It will bring bad luck."

"The worst," I said.

"I can't promise you anything, Jade Moon, except that I love you. I have always loved you."

"That is a good start."

The windows above the Yings' laundry glowed yellow in front of us. When Mrs. Ying opened a side door for Spring Blossom, a beam of light poured onto the pavement, turning Weaver Girl's tears into gold.

I took a deep breath, and I could feel it, the beginning of a story.

AUTHOR'S NOTE

THE FIRST PIECE OF THIS STORY that found me was Angel Island. In 2009, Angel Island was reopening after millions of dollars of renovation, and there was a story about it on the radio. I had been thinking a lot about immigration — our naïveté about its hardships, the immigration stories buried in many Americans' pasts. The reality of immigrating through Angel Island, particularly for Chinese immigrants, ran counter to the myth of coming to America that I had been taught, that I believed. That contrast was what first drew me to this story.

I had been thinking even more about China. I was getting ready to go through the immigration process for my son, our first child, who we were adopting from an orphanage in Shenzhen. Because of this, the center of my whole world had shifted: Our family was suddenly spread across two continents, and a piece of me and my husband now resided in China.

While we went through the final steps of the adoption, I took Chinese language classes and discovered the beauty of Chinese — its specific tones, its exactness and economy. I read translated

Chinese poetry, reveling in its elegance. I studied the history of the early twentieth century in China. And, finally, I traveled to the country to get my son, Jack. The gracefulness that is in China's language and poetry is also in its land and its people. When I was there, I fell in love with the way the Chinese hold on to what is good and true even through the chaos that change and progress can cause. They cherish their family, culture, history, and community, not with grand gestures, but in thousands of small, daily acts — singing groups meeting in the parks, families gathered for New Year's, the young giving subway seats to the old, or a stranger smiling at someone visiting from far away. My visit deepened my respect for the Chinese people — their sincerity and their kind and generous spirits.

Throughout the adoption process, I was also taking writing classes. That is when the second piece of the story arrived — the character Jade Moon. She came to the first draft as curious and strong-willed, adventurous and idealistic as she is today. The facets of who she was never fit perfectly with who people wanted her to be. She was too bold for China, too Chinese for America. She didn't think things through enough according to Nushi, while she probably thought far too much for Mr. Hon. Jade Moon had to decide who she was, outside of what everyone told her she must be. That journey of settling into who you are was familiar to me, as it's been familiar to many young women across all cultures throughout history.

I believe in the value of history. It can show us truths about our present attitudes and give us perspective. It is important to me to know the history of Chinese-American immigration, because I want that history to influence how I think and feel about immigration today.

I also believe in the power of stories to reveal our humanity, our connections, our mistakes, and our triumphs. I hope I have honored this story of Jade Moon, China, and immigration the way I wanted to. It was an honor to try to write it — one I definitely didn't deserve. But the things we treasure most, we rarely deserve. The very day I am typing this, at the end of my journey through this story, my husband and I have been approved to adopt a second child from China. It is true what Jade Moon said about stories: Sometimes one ends so another can begin.

I am indebted to many authors and their work for giving me a glimpse into this world I love. I found *China: Empire of Living Symbols* by Cecilia Lindqvist particularly enlightening. It offers a unique look into the history and culture of China through its written characters. The stories that Nushi, Jade Moon, and Spring Blossom tell were adapted from versions in *Cloud Weavers: Ancient Chinese Legends* by Rena Krasno and Yeng-Fong Chiang, and *Chinese Folktales* by Howard Giskin. *Island: Poetry and History of Chinese Immigrants on Angel Island, 1910–1940,* by Him Mark Lai, Genny Lim, and Judy Yung provided the translations of the poems, which give voice to the feelings and frustration of the Chinese immigrants. *Angel Island: Immigrant Gateway to America* by Erika Lee and Judy Yung, and *Miwoks to Missiles: A History of Angel Island* by John Soennichsen were both excellent resources. I also enjoyed many wonderful hours on the Angel Island Immigration Foundation's website at www.aiisf.org.

San Francisco's Chinatown by Charles Caldwell Dobie, written in 1936 and complete with charming sketches, allowed me to travel back in time. *Good Life in Hard Times: San Francisco's '20s and '30s* by Jerry Flamm also offered valuable details. *Unbound Feet: A Social History of Women in San Francisco* by Judy Yung told the story of women in Chinatown. *Hatchet Men: The Story of the Tong Wars in San Francisco's Chinatown* by Richard H. Dillon explained much of the tong activity of the late 1800s and early 1900s. The Virtual Museum of the City of San Francisco provided additional information about tongs and the police in the 1920s. You can visit them at www.sfmuseum.org. Any mistakes that remain are my own.

Many people have put their tremendous talents into the creation of this book. I am thankful for Suzanne Frank and Dan Hale with the Southern Methodist University Creative Writing Program. They are talented writers in their own right, and yet they choose to share their wisdom with those of us who come to class with not much more than a laptop and a dream.

I am so grateful to my agent, Rosemary Stimola, who can always be relied on for encouragement, sound advice, and kindness. She gave early recommendations that made this book whole. And she didn't just find my book a publishing house, she found it a home.

That home is with the wonderful people at Arthur A. Levine Books/Scholastic. Special thanks to Cheryl Klein, my editor. She gave the book depth. Her thoughtful comments and her devoted reading nursed this story into its potential.

Thank you to my mom and dad, Ted and Nancy Hankamer, who raised me with such a steadfast love. That love makes anything possible in my life. And thanks to my sister, Sarah Hankamer, who is honest, intelligent, and kind. I have had to rely on those traits countless times.

Most important, I am grateful to my husband, Jeb Honeyman, who was the first to believe in Jade Moon, and the first to tell me I could whenever I was sure that I couldn't.

I hope this book will inspire people to learn more about the real-life people, places, and history mentioned in it.

Chinese Animal Signs

In the Western calendar, your zodiac sign is determined by the day and month of your birth, but in many Asian countries, especially China, each year is assigned one of twelve animal signs (rat, ox, tiger, rabbit, dragon, snake, horse, ram, monkey, rooster, dog, and boar) and an element (earth, wood, fire, metal, or water). A combination like horse and fire will only appear once every sixty years. The last year of the Fire Horse was 1966, and while women in China seemed to shake off the stigma, birthrates in some Asian communities still dropped unexpectedly. The next Fire Horse girls will be born in 2026.

Chinese Exclusion Laws and Paper Sons

In 1882, the Chinese Exclusion Act was passed by Congress, blocking the entry of Chinese into America. Never before had American immigration policy been directed against one specific ethnic group. Other laws restricted the Chinese from owning property, testifying in court against white citizens, or gaining citizenship. The Chinese reacted by finding loopholes in American laws. The 1906 San Francisco earthquake and the citywide fire that Sterling Promise describes offered an opportunity to add new names to the records of American citizens. This created a thriving black market in the false identities known as "paper sons," through which thousands of Chinese men and boys applied to enter the United States. In 1943, the Chinese Exclusion Act was repealed and replaced with a quota allowing one hundred and five Chinese immigrants into America annually, while also making the Chinese eligible for citizenship. It wasn't until the Immigration Act of 1965 that the quota system based on country of origin ended, and immigrants from China were put on equal footing with immigrants from other nations.

Angel Island
Angel Island was called "the Ellis Island of the West," but the immigrants who landed there, many from China and Japan, had a very different experience than the Europeans who arrived in New York. While immigrants on Ellis Island were processed in three to five hours, the average stay for a Chinese immigrant on Angel Island was two to three weeks. Records show some immigrants detained for as long as two years. The narratives of detainees tell of the unsanitary and overcrowded living conditions they had to endure: The food was terrible, the bathrooms were filthy, and the officials and guards treated them like criminals instead of immigrants. There were suicides in both the men and women's barracks.

When Angel Island opened in 1910, it was declared a first-class immigration station, but enthusiasm soon cooled, and Chinese-Americans and politicians raised concerns over the safety of the island. Those concerns proved valid when a fire began in the Administration Building, burning it to the ground in August 1940. Immigrants were then moved to the mainland, and the Angel

Island facilities were used for other purposes, such as housing prisoners of war during World War II. After the war, the buildings were abandoned until 1963, when Angel Island became a state park. The barracks where immigrants stayed were scheduled for destruction in 1970, when Alexander Weiss, a park ranger, discovered the *tibishi* poems written on and carved into the walls of the men's barracks. Today, people can visit the restored barracks on Angel Island and see some of the poems for themselves. (A little artistic license was taken in putting all the poems Jade Moon reads into the same room.)

Tongs

The term *tong* means "hall" or "meeting place" and can be used as a label for any Chinese society. When Chinese immigrants first journeyed to America, they often came without their families, and these associations provided support, security, and even legal services. The tongs of San Francisco's Chinatown ranged from orderly groups of men who worked in similar occupations to gangs devoted to illegal activities such as drug trafficking and prostitution. These latter kinds of tongs clashed in infamous "tong wars" that plagued Chinatown in the late nineteenth century. By 1923, violence between the tongs was still present but dwindling, as community and police pressure had robbed the tongs of much of their power. Chinatown was changing from a community of first-generation immigrants who planned to make a fortune and return to China to a neighborhood of Chinese-American families with children, as it remains today.

While it may seem unlikely that Mr. Hon would be protected by an Irishman like Neil, a tong boss known as Little Pete started the trend of having a white bodyguard during the tong wars. His thinking was that his enemies would not want to risk killing a white man and possibly facing a lynch mob. It became a popular form of protection.

Donaldina Cameron

Miss Donaldson is based on the real-life figure of Donaldina Cameron, who served the Presbyterian Mission Home in San Francisco for almost forty years, from 1895 to 1934. Miss Cameron devoted her life to helping the Asian women brought to California as slaves and prostitutes. The women she rescued referred to her as "Lo Ma" or Beloved Mother. Miss Cameron would often go on rescue missions herself, accompanied by a police officer. Some stories even have her jumping across rooftops to rescue girls hidden up there by their owners. Today, the mission home Donaldina Cameron ran is known as the Cameron House and is dedicated to helping immigrants in San Francisco. For more information, you can visit the house's website at www.cameronhouse.org.

This book was edited by Cheryl Klein and designed by Natalie Sousa. The text was set in Garamond, with display type set in Tongyin. This book was printed and bound by R. R. Donnelley in Crawfordsville, Indiana. The production was supervised by Starr Baer. The manufacturing was supervised by Irene Huang.